A Simple Taste of Miss Kitty

Ameka J Burton

A Simple Taste of Ms. Kitty

Prologue

MY NAME IS Katrina Marshalle Richards, better known as Ms. Kitty. I inherited that name when I was a little because of my grey cat like eyes and my fear of cats. I've always been terrified of them. I think the reason is because I witnessed a cat giving birth to kittens and they sounded just like real babies and the whole experience was just horrific but Mama said the real reason I'm so terrified of them is because I act just like a one; sneaky!

I never met my father. He walked out two months before I was born. I've heard all kind of sad stories about single parents raising children in the hood'. I don't know how my mother did it but we always had the best get up. I always wore the flyiest kicks, hottest clothes and rocked the latest hairstyles. Now we did have our share of some hard times, but I wouldn't say it was all bad. In fact, it was fun growing up in my neighborhood. Everybody stuck together like glue. We had fish fry's, yard sales and block parties all the time. As kids, we played outside until the street lights came on and you better not be late getting home. I remember never wanting to grow up, wishing things would be this way forever.

As I got older I thought I was the shit'. Nobody could touch me with a ten foot pole.

All I had to do was flash a quick smile, throw my petite, hourglass body around, blink my gray eyes and at the snap of a finger, guys were at my feet.

I was always the Queen of something; Beauty pageants, Homecoming, Prom and cheerleading captain. I had it all but would've traded that title, Queen, years ago if I knew it was going to bring me pain the rest of my life. I'm only seventeen years old, not quite legal, and I've had so much drama in my life I could start my own talk show. I would probably call it Drama Queen. Each day would be a different topic based on one of my life experiences; baby mama drama, baby daddy drama, homosexual drama, crazy people drama, and just plain, damn, drama! The way I see it, everybody goes through something rough in their life. Without hard times, you wouldn't get strong. If every thing was all peaches and cream you or somebody else would start making up stuff to worry about. Sometimes I sit and meditate, wishing I could start my life over. Maybe I could be a cute little white girl with curly, blond hair and a rich father who owns a huge corporation that I'll inherit some day. Laugh at that thought..Nah, I doubt that I could ever be white. Maybe I could win the lottery and buy a good looking man that's deaf and mute and only knows how to make....

Aww hell, that will probably never happen either but maybe, just maybe I could be me again. I wouldn't repeat the same stupid mistakes in my new life. I would live out all my dreams and fantasies to the fullest. Oh well folks, that's life and unless you're a buddhist, reincarnation is out. That's why I'm here now; to tell you my story.....

Pain

"Ms. Richards', are you awake?" I felt a shove in my arm and excruciating pain in my abdomen. "Ms. Richards, please give us a signal if you can hear me…. She's not responding Doctor. Should we notify her next of kin?"

"No! She is a minor and I'll be held liable if anyone knows I performed this procedure without parental consent."

"But sir, she has lost a lot of blood. She could even Die!"

Wait; say what? Back the hell up one minute. Where am I?

"I can see motion. If you give her time, she will come around. I see this type of thing all the time."

See what? Hell I want to see too. Let me wake up out this dream.

I awoke to what appeared to be a white man in a white lab coat and a white female with white hair wearing a white lab coat also. All this damn white must mean Im dead…. Wow, I'm in heaven.

"Ms. Richards, the procedure is complete but I have some disturbing news. You lost too much blood and it appears to be a lot of damage done to your uterus lining. I'm sorry but you may never be able to have children."

Well, I guess that's what I deserve. I don't believe in luck or fate and I'm starting to question God, but I do know one thing; in this game it's three strikes and You're Out!

I've had two abortions in the past two years before this one. Each time I vowed never to do it again. I loved children. I even wanted a whole baseball team of kids but now was not the right time. I had plans, a future. These sorry, half assed, men were not going to keep me down. I really hate to see some ghetto looking woman all dressed up in some hoochie outfit that she bought from the beauty supply store, wearing pleather shoes on ashy feet demanding money from a guy for some lil snotty nose kids. I always wondered why? Why in the world would a woman keep having babies with a broke, down, no-good man and repeating the same scenerio? Now I know that love is blind. That mess will sneak up on you and boom, bam, you're in love with some smooth talking guy that's only out for sex. Each time you think he's the one. Just because your panties get wet each time you hear his name is not a sign of true love. It's only lust. I've never been loved or in love. Let me make a mental note. Today is the day I ask myself "What's love got to do with it?" From this day forward it's all about Ms. Kitty; my needs, my wants. Men have been selfish for years so why is it wrong in society for a woman to act the same?

"Ms. Richards, we need you to sign some more forms and you'll be on your way. I have prescribed some pain medicine for you and please get plenty of rest once you get home. No sexual intercourse for 6 weeks."

Wow. So, Is that it? What a cold hearted man. First he damn near kills me, then he tells me I will never have children and now I'm supposed to just walk out of here and try to forget it? I wish I could sue his ass but it won't do any good. I already signed liability forms and the bottom line is this is his world. I learned from my ancestors to keep silent and just deal with it.

When I arrived home, my Mom was in the kitchen frying fish. It was torture enough for me to ride that hot, over crowded bus home in pain, smelling the stench of alcoholics and now I had to smell this crap. I hate fish. I hate the way it smells and I hate any food that you have to pick through before you can eat it. I rushed to the bathroom to change my supersized pad. Who's bright idea was it to make a miniature diaper for a pad? Why did I ask myself that; a man obviously.

I unexpectedly threw up in the sink. That smell just added fuel to the fire. I will be so glad when August comes next month. I will be out of this hellhole and away in college. Whoohoo! Party time! Freedom; because a mind is a terrible thing to waste.

"Ms. Kitty. Is that you?"

Well who else would it be? If I was a burglar she wouldn't have a thing left by now.

"Yeah," I answered.

"Yeah? That's yes maam to you!" she hollered back.

Wait…What? Now you want to get all proper. All my life I've answered yeah and no and now that I'm going off to college it's yes ma'am this and no sir that. Well those college professors can kiss my ass. If it weren't for my brains and my money they wouldn't have a job. I'm the first person in my family to go to college. Now that's a lot of pressure on one person. I should feel happy and excited instead of stressed. All my home girls have flipped on me because I'm going away. They always said I thought I was better than them. I never really hung around them because they would act so stupid when we were out. I mean I can't help it if a group of guys walk up to us and they all want my number. I didn't ask to have long silky hair, a pretty face and the number one killer, my gray eyes. I also work hard to have a body like this. I do at least 100 sit ups and squats each night and Richard Simmons is as close as I'll get to a personal trainer.

I clean up the mess in the sink and head to my room. I feel like I'm about to faint so I lie down on my bed. I wish I could cry but I've gotten too tough for that. My eyes won't even form a tear. Besides, it won't change the fact that I already killed three children and now will never have another chance. I wonder what they all looked like. I know they would've definantly been smart and beautiful and outgoing. If they were boys I'm sure they would've been athletic. I guess it's good to dream since reality is so painful.

I notice that my radio is on. My mom is always snooping around in my room when I'm not here. She always forgets to put things back in place when she leaves. It takes a lot of nerve for someone to listen to the radio while going through other people personal belongings. I wish one of my skeletons would jump out the closet one day while she's in here and curse her out. Then she wouldn't have to look so hard to find them.

My thoughts were interrupted by my mom. I saw her standing in my door way wearing this old ugly, worn out housecoat and a greasy spatula in her hand. "Ms. Kitty, you need to make a list of school items you'll need so I can take it to Moe. Time will be here soon and I'm not runnin' round' here like a chicken with the head cut off trying to get the stuff you need."

"Okay Ma." My head was pounding in tune with my heartbeat. *Please let her leave, PLEASE.*

I don't need this drama right now.

"What's wrong with you? You act like you up to no good." She raised that one eyebrow and tightened her lips. *Fasten your seat belt because here we go!*

"I just have a headache. Could you turn on that fan? It's really hot in here." I laid down on my bed.

"Oh my Lord Jesus! You pregnant! I knew that little nappy head boy you call yourself sneaking round' with was no good."

"Ma, please! I am not pregnant. I'm just hot. It's 98 degrees outside and you're in here frying fish with no air condition."

If looks could kill, I would be dead. She asked," If you aint pregnant, then why did you just throw up in the bathroom?"

"Damn Mama. You know how much I hate fish and I already told you I'm hot because its summer and it's hotter in here than it is outside." I tried to sound convincible.

"Well I didn't want to turn on the air because the power bill is so high and I'm about to leave to go get my hair done anyway. Since you so hot, try paying the bill and then complain but until then don't touch my air!"

I wanted to say, Bitch, but I knew better. She started to leave but she stopped to add one last comment.

"I'm going by Moe's house to take him some fish after I leave the hairdresser. When you have a good man like Moe, you need to feed him and do all you can to keep him; especially after all the trouble you caused."

Trouble? Me? I dont start trouble. I finish it. Is it my fault that his horny self wanted me and not her? While I hated the ground he walked on, she worshiped it. That man would stare at me like I was a piece of meat and if you saw him eat a steak, you would be scared too. When my Mom wasn't looking he would lick his tongue out and roll it around his lips. He used to tell me how pretty I was and how he wished my mom had a body like mine.

I was thirteen when I met first him. I woke up one Saturday morning and went in the living room to watch television. He walked in the room with a robe on, sat on the couch, got the remote and started changing the channels. He didn't even acknowledge that I was in the room but I know he saw me. I stood up, walked over to the TV and changed the channels back. Do you know this man had the nerve to ask me what I was doing? I didn't even reply. Instead I walked to my mom's bedroom to ask her who was this man and what was he doing in our house. When I walked in and saw the used condoms on the floor and her half naked, lying there on the bed, I knew exactly who he was; another Friday night fantasy, only this time the tables got turned. His little Friday night sleepovers turned into all weekend parties and then the weekend got stretched into week nights until eventually his name was on the lease. She treated him like he was a piece of gold. She bragged to all her friends about all the wonderful things he had bought for our apartment. After our first uninformal meeting, I came home one day from school to find a brand new color television in my bedroom. I guess you could call me unappreciative but I didn't want anything that man had to offer. That's the least he could do for me since he had made himself so at home. I quickly realized that his little gifts weren't for us but actually for him.

One month after he bought all that stuff, I caught him and another guy taking everything out our apartment. See, I had sneaked home from school with this guy I was crushing on. We were in my bedroom about to hit it off when I heard voices outside my door. Now I'm thinking, Who in the world is in my house at this time of day? I cracked my door and peeked out. That's when I saw them. They were taking everything. Everything that he ever bought and some things he didn't as well. I quickly closed the door and tried to think about what I should do but before I had a chance to come up with an idea, my door swung open. Moe looked startled to see me. He started cursing and yelling asking me what was I doing here and not at school. Now I'm thinking to myself the same thing about him but apparently my thoughts came out through my mouth. Before I knew it, he slapped me! The room was dead silent. So dead, I had to look back at my little boyfriend to see if he was still breathing. Moe's friend came in the room to see what the commotion was all about. He looked at me then at Moe then at my friend guy and all he could do was go sit on the bed next to him. It was a real awkward situation. Moe spoke first. He told me that he wouldn't tell my mom I skipped school if I didn't say anything. His reason for taking everything out was to have them fixed. He said they were old models and tearing up and he was sick of looking at that old furniture. He and I knew it was a bunch of bull but I had no choice but to play along. I made it clear that he was never to come in my room and touch anything; not even a lint ball off my floor! We all left the apartment peacefully but Moe and I had only one thing on our minds; revenge.

I came home later that evening to find the police at my house. Moe had made up this huge lie that somebody broke in and stole everything. My mom fell for it. He told her she shouldn't have bragged so much about all her new stuff because people would get jealous. She lost a lot of friends after that because she starting accusing everyone she ever talked to for stealing her things. She even accused me because the thieves didn't touch my stuff. She never realized that the guilty party was right in her face.

After that incident, things went downhill. Moe didn't know when I would break the silence and let our little secret out so he started rumors about me. He told my mom that he saw me out during the day while he was doing a construction job. He said he saw me getting in and out of cars with older men and going in bars by his job site. He told her he saw me smoking a joint with some boys behind an abandon building. Now that he had transformed my mom against me he decided to make his ultimate move. My mom put me on punishment for months. She basically entrusted me into his care night and day. He was to take me and pick me up from school. This was to ensure that I didn't leave. After school and on weekends he stayed at home with me until she got off work. He was so kind as to rearrange his hours to 'baby-sit' me. The first week of our new arrangement, he fondled my breasts. He said he knew I wasn't a virgin anymore because my tities were so big. One day he told me they reminded him of big juicy plums and how he loved to suck plums. Then he threw me against the wall, pulled up my shirt and started sucking my nipples. I heard him unzip his pants and eventually heard the belt buckle hit the hardwood floor. He turned my body around and shoved me in my back until I was completely bent over. He snatched my panties pushing them aside until I felt a hard, painful, thrust inside me. My knees went numb and I collapsed, not remembering anything from that moment on. I guess he thought I was turned on by all of this because he continued week after week without my protest. I didn't protest it because I knew it wouldn't do any good. My mom would never believe me because she believed all the other lies he told. I was fed up with his antics but didn't know what to do to make him stop. One afternoon, we came home from school and he went in the bathroom to take a shower. He came out dripping wet and naked. It was the worst site I had ever seen. He looked like a big, greasy nasty pig. He stood there with the towel around his neck, rubbing his penis. He said, "I know you ain't never seen one this big." I laughed and said, "No, I'd never seen a stomach that big before." Well now I had pissed him off. He charged toward me and grabbed me by my hair. He threw me on the floor and tried to push my face towards his penis. He said he was gonna teach me about talking back. He stuck his penis in my mouth and I started to gag. He was pulling my hair so hard, I just knew I would have a bald spot and I couldn't scream out in pain because his manhood mixed with pubic hair was stuck down my throat so I did the only thing my natural instincts would allow. I bit it! He let out a wail and punched me in the face, temporarily knocking me out. When I came to, he was rolling around on the floor in pain. I jumped on top of him and fought him with all my might. Flashbacks of all the lies and years of abuse popped in my mind until all I could see was red. I wanted him dead. The strength came from rage and anger as I stretched my hands around his fat neck. He couldn't breathe and he started trying to pry my hands away when when my mom walked in. All she saw was me on top him so she grabbed a broom and began beating me. I ran to my room and slammed the door. I could hear him trying to explain. He said I came in on him while he was taking a shower and made a pass at him. He told her I offered to suck his dick and when he rejected me, I got mad and tried to have sex with him. He moved out the next day. It was too 'painful' for him to stay there and he didn't know when I would try to pull that stunt again. Yeah, right. I guess he didn't trust himself anymore. It was too painful for him to look me in the eyes knowing he ruined my teenage years.

I always knew my mom had a weakness for men. She depended on them like the air we breathe. I never thought she would love men more than her own flesh and blood; her only daughter.

Freedom

HALLELUJAH! THIS DAY has finally arrived. August 16,1997; a day I will never forget. I finally had my shot at a better life. College life. I brought everything I own because I didn't plan on ever going back home. My mom and Moe were so eager to pack up my things and load them on the rented U- haul. Moe was driving so fast that he got a ticket on the way. I was glad too. What normally would be a four hour drive was done in two. If it weren't for all my junk, I would have taken the bus. Nothing was said during the whole trip. It was the first time in months since I've seen Moe. I guess now that I was out of the house, he could come over anytime he pleased. Hell, he could move in for all I care because like I said before, I didn't plan on going back. He kept staring at me through the rear view mirror with this smirk on his face. A scary thought flashed in my head. What if this pervert tried to sneak on campus and rape me? I decided to shoot him my middle finger and roll my eyes to let him know I wasn't scared. He just smiled and shook his head.

He drove onto the curve in front of my dorm and threw my bags out on the ground. My mom didn't even get out of the car to tell me goodbye. I couldn't tell if she was sad and was going to miss me or if she was anxious to hurry home and screw Moe. I was her competition and now she had won. I took one last look at her face and saw a very familiar expression.

I remember, when I was little, I came in the house crying demanding to know why the other girls don't like me. She asked what made me think that they didn't like me. I told her that they wouldn't talk to me or play with me at recess. They just stared at me. When I got up enough nerve to ask them to play with me they sucked their teeth and walked off like I wasn't even there. She told me that there is such a thing called jealousy and whenever somebody looks at you like they're jealous, roll your eyes and walk off. Today was the first time I valued her advice. I rolled my eyes at her and walked into my dorm, ready to start my new life.

I noticed a sign with an arrow pointing to the dorm manager's room. She was sitting there watching TV when I opened her door.

"Hi, I'm Kitty, I mean Katrina Richards and I need my key to my room."

"Well, Kitty or Katrina whatever, here are your keys. Oh, by the way, next time knock first before you enter my room."

Bitch!

I took the elevator to the fourth floor and saw my room number, 428. As I turned the doorknob I felt a rush of relief. I am finally free. Free to a whole new world. Free to a new me. Free to, to ...... What in the world is this? Why does my room look like the bubblegum scene from Willy Wonka's Chocolate Factory ? I don't believe it.

Everything in this room is pink; the bedspread, the curtains, the pillows, even the damn picture frames. I walk over to get a better look at one of the pictures and everybody in it was white. In fact all the pictures had white people in them. Now this was a major culture shock! I am so use to my own room that I totally forgot I would have to share a dorm room. On top of that I must be the only person on campus to have a white roommate. I mean, am I at the right school? I thought it was an HBCU.

I turned around to find a white girl with long blond hair standing next to a black male; no wait female. Now I'm really confused.

"Hi roomie. My name is April Showers and this is my best friend in the world, Olandis."

This heifer was tripping. What kind of name is April Showers? Is she serious?

And Mr/Mrs. Olandis needs to take off those black bell bottom pants and that see through, neon midriff shirt! Somebody pinch me, quick, I must be dreaming.

"Oh my goodness, girlfriend. Where in the name of Jesus did you find those contacts?" says the Outlandish Olandis.

"What? These aren't contacts. These are my real eyes."

"Hmm...Yeah right, honey like this is my real ass. And just wait until my money comes from this man I had to sue. Sista girl will have some real tata's too!"

"Olandis you so silly. She doesn't care to hear about all your plastic surgeries. So any way, whats your name?", says the blond hippie.

"Katrina but people call me Ms. Kitty"

"Child, I likes that. I need me a stage name but nothing rhymes with Olandis. Now if I had a name like Ms. Kitty, I couldn't keep the men off me." He let out this cat howl that was supposed to sound like 'meow' but it sounded more like a wailing chicken. I'm still trying to process this; a white roommate with a gay black friend. It could only happen to me.

"So, Ms. Kitty, is this your first year here?"

"Yeah."

I didn't feel up to small talk but I needed to be nice because my things were still sitting on the curb outside and I was going to need some help getting them up to my room.

"I can tell," she replied.

Now what the hell is she talking about? This girl just met me and now she thinks she knows me.

"So April, what is it that you're so sure you can tell about me?"

"Well for one, you don't have any luggage or items in this room so those must be your things that everyone outside is going through and taking!"

"See, that's why I'm so ashamed of my colored people. You did know that this was an all black college, Ms. Kitty?"

Olandis strutted over to my window, raised it and started shouting at some of the looters.

"Hey! Leave that shit alone! Okay I know where you stay. Remember last year when you called me at 3:00 in the morning. Well it won't be any more booty calls if you don't leave."

I heard all kinds laughter, mostly from males, outside my window. I had to admit it was kind of funny but then I realized they were taking my stuff.

"Please you guys. Come and help me get what's left. I.O.U."

I was begging. I never begged anybody in my entire life. I had been on this campus less than 30 minutes and I had stooped to this. I tried to look sad and stretch my eyes. That usually worked.

"Sorry sista girl." Olandis didn't buy it. He had been putting on for years so my performance must've been dreadful. "I just got my nails done and my man would be upset if I broke one." Just then his pager went off. Talk about perfect timing.

"Well, speak of the devil. That's De Wayne now. Lord that man can sense me talking about him. Don't you sweat my pet, I'll get the rest of your stuff back."

He went to the medicine cabinet mirror to check his face then he pulled out a black streaked with blond wig from the back of the mirror!

"I just remembered that I left my favorite hair over here. Well, I'm off. Check you later April Showers and remember to bring those May flowers. I just crack myself up. Nice meeting you Kitty, darling."

Like the cat in the hat, he was gone like that.

"Don't pay Olandis any mind. His bark is stronger than his bite. We better hurry and get what's left of your things ."

I couldn't complain. I was stuck here for the next four years. Maybe April could teach me a few things. She was the only white girl on campus and the only one brave enough to hang around with Olandis. It might not be all that bad. One thing's for sure; there will never be a dull moment .

The elevator had a big out of order sign stuck to it. What else could go wrong?

That dumb dorm manager downstairs probably put it there for revenge. April informed me that there were some stairs on the back hall and to get use to them because the elevator was always broken. When we passed by the dorm manager's room, she was laughing with some of her little preppy friends and when she saw us she stopped. I knew they were talking about me. I had just about had enough out of her but I could not afford to get kicked out of school over some idiot. I would deal with her some other way. I just have to give myself some time to scheme.

April and I were able to save most of my clothes and some personal hygiene items but the TV was history along with my jam box, towels, and sheets.

By the time we finished carrying everything up four flights of steps I was soaked with sweat. April let me use one of her towels to take a bath. When I came out the bathroom she was on the phone talking about a frat party. There was this loud, agonizing, noise coming from her stereo. I started changing into my nightshirt when April motioned for me to stop. I hope she's not gay like her little friend. I continued to put on my nightclothes and let that gesture slide but she started waving her arms around and mouthing the word 'no'. Okay, now I know she's tripping. We need to have a talk right now, mainly about this music if that's what you want to call it. She finally hung up the phone.

"April, what is that noise you're listening to?"

"It's my meditation music. It's a Japanese tape that a close, spiritual friend gave to me and I fell in love with it. It clears the passages to my mind and I usually have complete silence but my friend called to tell me about the back to school party at the frat house. You wanna go?"

"No thanks. I'm real tired after all that moving. I think I'll just go to bed."

"Oh come on. You'll have the rest of the weekend to sleep. This is college. This is what we do, girlie, we Partay!"

I could see that this girl was not going to leave me alone so I decided to go with her and dis' her time I got there. Besides, there may be some cute pre-med guys there. I doubt

I'll be able to dance because I really am tired but I'm a flirt at heart and I can't pass this opportunity up to pick up some new skills. Now the next question was what do I wear? I've only been to house parties in the 'hood' with thugs. I don't know how people college dress.

April told me I could wear something out of her closet but when I looked at what she had to offer, I declined. Her closet looked like something from Woodstock. I guess she could tell my distaste by the horrific look on my face so she said we could go over to Olandis's place and pick out something. It was on the way. I oblidged because I was dying to see what Olandis actually had in his closet for me. I took an extra outfit just in case.

We got outside to this parking lot in the back of our dorm and April turned the alarm off her red B.M.W. Now I'm thinking, Wow, things are starting to pay up.

"Damn April, is this you?" I asked.

"Yeah, It was a graduation gift from my parents."

"Oh, ya'll must be rich. My mom can't afford a pinto or the gas to put in it."

"We don't measure our richness by money."

"Well how else can you measure ' richness' if it's not about the Benjamins?"

"You must have love and honesty. A good heart. Umm, communication ."

We got in and pulled off. After a lot of jerking, screeching and possibly whiplash, we finally made it across campus to Olandis's dorm. Then it hit me. How were we supposed to get in his room if he wasn't here?

"Now where did I put that key? Oh, here it is. I guess you noticed that Idont know how to drive a 5 speed. Olandis has been giving me lessons for a year and I can't seem to get it right. He says its because I'm still a virgin and If I learned how to ride a real stick, driving would be a piece of cake."

Did she just say she's a virgin? That must be a white girl thing. I don't know anyone that hasn't tried the 'wild thing'! We went inside and up to his room. April did not warn me about what was behind his door. This man had a huge life size poster of RuPaul, a bed shaped like a hand, purple, crushed velvet curtains and comforter to match. His desk and dresser was spray painted with tons of neon colors and there was a wall of wigs hanging in a neat fashion, arranged by colors and styles. April turned on the lights and flashes of blue and red raced across the room.

Yes, he had stolen police car lights rigged up to his ceiling. I had to sit down so I figured out how to climb on his 'hand' bed and I eased back. When I looked up, there were lifelike sized pictures of Prince on the ceiling. He had pictures of Prince that I doubt Prince even knew about! He had put Prince's head on the bodies of other men, some were even naked.

"Okay April, tell me what kind of freak is Olandis?"

"He's perfectly harmless. Just because he chooses to dress and act different doesn't make him a criminal. It's the ones who are in the closet that scare me.

Besides, who made up the rules that you are supposed to act a certain way. The way you act is all up to you."

"I guess your right. I mean who says that I have to dress like everybody else and walk with two feet? I could save money by shopping at Goodwill and walk around on my hands. It's not a crime."

"Yeah, but you will have some messed up hands. And your face will be all scratched up until you learn how to do a handstand."

April started looking through Olandis's closet and she pulled out this slamming bell bottom denim outfit.

"Awe, I think this will look good on you." She held the suit up to my body.

"I know this will look good on me. Girl, hand that over, let me work it. I want to know why Olandis has so many clothes in here?"

"Well, he's a fashion, marketing major so he has to play the part." She continued," And he does drama so he needs different outfits for his auditions."

"So does he have a job or are his parents rich too because some of these clothes have price tags still on them."

"No. Dewayne buys most of them for him. As for his parents, they cut him off about 4 years ago when he came out and told them he was gay."

"Damn, that's cold."

"No, Ms. Kitty. That's life."

When April and I stepped in the party, all eyes were on us. I didn't feel uncomfortable because I was use to being stared at. April didn't seem to be disturbed by it either. The frat house was packed. Never in my life had I seen so many fine men in one place. I am so glad that I decided to come. We were swamped with guys asking us to dance and I immediately forgot how tired I was. I did every dance I knew. A couple of times I looked over and saw April shaking her tail too. She could really dance to be a white girl.

She made her way over to me and asked me did I want a drink. I told her that I didn't drink because I don't want a beer gut. I couldn't help but think about Moe once I said it. I'll probably never get that picture out my mind of him standing there naked, wet with soap suds all over him. He looked like a big greasy pig.

I walked with April to the homemade bar. She told the guy to make her some crazy sounding drink and then she started telling me about one guy she danced with that had bad breath. I could barely hear what she was saying because my attention was on something or rather someone.

He was tall, sexy and fine as wine. He had a body that made you want to go over and yank his clothes off to get a better view. His skin was so beautiful. He could do a Oil of Olay commercial for men. His teeth were so white and perfect and his hair was silky and neatly trimmed. He was slow dancing with her, the diva from my dorm. He caught me staring at him and he quickly pushed her off him. She gave him this puzzled look then she walked off, leaving him standing on the dance floor alone. Oh well I thought, her loss, my gain.

The D.J started playing the electric slide and everyone rushed to the dance floor. I lost him. I scanned the room like a security camera looking for him. He was gone. I wanted to slap the shit out that corny D.J. for making me lose sight of him and for playing the slide' 5 times! He finally announced that he was gonna take it back to the old school. I thought that's what he had been playing all night. He started playing my favorite slow jam, *Being In Love Ain't Easy*. I was moving to the beat in a world all my own when a male voice behind me asked me to dance with him and not the wall. I turned around and there he was. I almost fainted so I don't know how I made it to the dance floor. He put my arms around his waist and started grinding his pelvis.

"What's your name?" His voice was smooth like velvet.

"Ms. Kitty," I whispered softly in his ear.

"Ms. Kitty, huh? Is that your real name or your made up name so I won't be able to call you after tonight? It's cool though, I will cherish this one night forever."

"My real name is Katrina but all my life I've been called Ms. Kitty."

"So, are you new? Wait. Never mind that. I know you're new because I would remember your beautiful face anywhere."

Oh my God. He said I was beautiful. I already knew that much but it sounds so sweet coming from him. What should I say next? I don't want to make any mistakes and sound like I'm stupid. Just then a guy came over and whispered something in his ear.

"Look beautiful, I'm sorry but I have to go check out the new pledges. Can I call you?"

"Sure. My number is ….is… I don't know. See, I just moved in today and I didn't,"

"I understand if you don't want me to have it. I'm just happy to have been able to hold you 2 minutes tonight."

He walked off. Why didn't I stop him and make him listen to me? I went to look for April and tell her I was leaving. There was not another guy in this place who could measure up to...umm... Shoot! I don't even know his name.

The next morning, I awoke to feel water dripping on my face. When I opened my eyes, there was Olandis standing over me splashing water wearing a hot pink, spandex cat suit and a hot pink wig to match.

"Well hello, Sleeping Beauty. You need to get out more. If you can't hang with the big dogs then stay on the porch."

"Olandis, what are you doing here?"

"News flash; I'm always here. To my agenda is trying to wake your lazy ass up. It's 1:00 in the afternoon. April called me to check on you because you wouldn't answer the phone so I had to get out the registration line, walk all the way over here in my good high heel shoes to find you asleep?"

"Where is April?" I asked.

"She's down at the library helping with registration which is where you need to be.

You did come here for a higher learning didn't you? Or did you just think that you could get your degree in partying 101?"

"No Olandis. I just over slept and I forgot that today is registration day. I don't even know what day of the week this is."

My head was banging in pain.

"Sunday. Now get up and do something with your hair. You know how you women are. It's gonna take all day for you to get ready."

He started going through my clothes which by the way were still in bags.

"Not me. This is natural beauty. I just have to shower and throw on some clothes and I'm out."

"No, No, No, see you don't understand sista girl. You are hanging with me today and Olandis doesn't step out with any old looking thang'. You got to dress to impress and your hair must have flair."

With that he did a two step twirl and snapped his fingers. I didn't know how to break the news to him that I did not want to hang with him all day. He had some nerve to tell me how to dress when he was wearing a hot pink catsuit and spandex at that. I was dying to know where he stuffed his penis in that suit because there was no print in site. He sat on my bed and crossed his legs and started reading a Cosmopolitan magazine.

"Are you serious? You're gonna watch me get dressed?"

"Watch you? Ha, ha, ha, Sugar pie, I've seen plenty of women before and trust me when I say I was not impressed."

Olandis is the man or should I say woman on campus. He is the main attraction. We were stopped every five seconds by someone wanting to speak to him or just shake his hand. The only thing missing was the red carpet.

I guess you can't help but stop and stare at him considering what he had on but these people acted truly genuine. They were serious, not jokingly, wanting to be his friend. I should have known he would be the most popular student on campus, well next to April, but I didn't want this much attention drawn to me so soon.

We finally arrived at the library. Olandis said that this was probably the only time I would see so many people here. During school, the best place to hang out was the student union building across the street. The lines were so long that they came out the library and around the corner. I guess Olandis didn't see the lines of people because he just shuffled his way past a few and walked right in, pulling me behind him. I heard a couple of threats and name calling but he didn't pay it any mind. Once inside, he continued walking past the lines like he was looking for someone then he stopped.

"Ms. Kitty, dear, what is your major?" he asked.

"My what? Oh, um... . I'm undecided."

"Well honey, you better decide now because I'm not standing in these lines all day waiting on you to make up your mind."

"Well, tell me what's good. I mean what is your major?"

"No Charlotte, I won't get tangled in your little web. You have to make that decision on your own."

It may seem crazy but I never thought about what I wanted to be. I just wanted to be happy. When I was little my teachers would make the class write and draw about what they wanted to do when they were old. Of course everyone said they wanted to be a doctor or lawyer but no one truly knew what they did. We just heard our parents talk about it and we knew they made lots of money. No one ever said policeman because in my neighborhood, police were bad people that took mamas and daddies to jail. Now that I'm grown I feel free to decide on anything but I'm scared that I want be able to reach my goal. I thought about things I'm good at. Things I enjoy doing. Sex. Dancing. Sex again. I could be a model but I don't think you have to hold a degree in that. Just then I overheard someone saying something about physical therapy. That's it! It sounds like a new, revised word for sex. I can't wait for the final exams.

Olandis helped me fill out the necessary forms for my classes. I could tell he knew that I didn't know what I was doing. I found out later after all the papers were signed and stamped that my first class started in the morning at 8:00. It was too late to change and Olandis was getting very impatient. We stopped by April's desk to tell her we were leaving.

"Can you guy's give me a few more minutes? I'm almost done here and then we can go grab a bite to eat."

"Only if you're treating?" Olandis replied.

"No way, Landis. I treated the last time."

"If you call buying me a hot dog from Danny's Dogs a treat, then I must be the next Madonna. Silly girl, Tricks are for kids."

"Okay, Okay. But this is the last time."

"Honey, don't think I'm begging you to do this because my man buys and supplies all my needs. Plus, you're the one that wants us to wait for you."

He walked over and started talking to a group of girls about his new hair. April finished typing her paper work and kissed this tall, Rasta looking man with dreadlocks goodbye. She motioned for me to come on and then yelled over to Olandis.

"This train is about to leave, Olandis. Are you coming or what?"

"Don't rush me girlfriend. And what's all this about trains and cumming' and shit. You might give people the wrong idea about me."

When we got to the car, Olandis stopped at the driver's side. April knew what he was trying to say but she wouldn't bulge. They just stood there at the door looking at each other like they were in a western movie about to have a gunfight.

"April, I don't have time to get whiplash. The last time you drove, I ended up in the emergency room and that wig I was wearing will never be the same. I had to throw it away."

Finally, April handed him the keys and we were off.

"I do not drive that bad."

April needs to hush. This is one argument that she won't win especially if they ask me my opinion.

"Tell that to my chiropractor. Oh, Oh, Lord have mercy."

"Olandis, what's wrong? Are you hurting?" I had to ask. Hell, now he was scaring me behind the wheel.

"Oh, girl. I just had a flash back of that fine ass man massaging my neck and back. His hands were so big and you know what they say about men with big hands. Maybe I need to call him and make another appointment. I've been feeling kind of tense lately."

I fell out laughing. I can see why everyone loves Olandis.

Olandis took us to his favorite restaurant, Le Chateu. Our waitress knew him on a first name basis and she was talking so much that April had to clear her throat in order for her to take our order. I didn't recognize any thing on the menu so I whispered in his ear for him to order something for me. I don't know what he ordered but he had the same so I figured I would let him eat his first and see if he lived. I looked over to my right and saw two women at the bar kissing. They were right there in a public place kissing and holding hands. I looked over to my left and saw two guys sitting at a table close together. One of them had his arm around the other one and he was resting his head on the other ones shoulder. I tried not to look concern since no one else did but I didn't try hard enough.

"Ms. Kitty, it's alright. I remember the first time I brought April in here. She knew I was involved with a man but she had never seen us show affection towards each other. I brought her here first to break the ice incase she saw us kiss or something and I didn't want her to mess up my groove."

"Is it that obvious? I just have never seen two people of the same sex carry on like that.

Give me time to process all this."

"Why is that?" April wanted to know. "Why is it fine for a man and woman to kiss and hug in public but if a man and man do it, they are frowned upon.?"

"I guess its just not common to see that. You know there have been gay people walking around for years and it's just now coming out with all these gay rights and stuff. What are gay rights anyway? I mean you don't hear about straight rights." I guess I sounded rude saying that but I wanted to know.

"Girl, where have you been all your life? Black people have been fighting for rights for years and women have been fighting for equal rights also. Now gays want a piece of the action too. We are treated the worst, I feel, because some are women and some are black. That's already 2 strikes against us."

I never really thought of it that way. Now that it had been explained to me, I understood it, plain and simple. This world sucks. The waitress brought our food out and I couldn't make out what it was but since I wasn't paying for it, I decided to try it. To my surprise, it was really good or I was just hungry. We finished up our meals and went back to the dorm.

Olandis left to go meet Dewayne and I decided to take a quick nap but April spoiled all that.

"Ms. Kitty, what does sex feel like?"

Oh my God! Is she serious? I was not in the mood to have a sex education class.

She needs to have that talk with her Mama, not me. She looked so desperate for me to tell her so, I guess it wouldn't hurt since she has helped me get through these first two days of college but where do I begin. Oh well, here goes nothing.

"April, sex is what you make of it. I mean if you're in love with that person then it feels good but if you're just doing it to have something to do, then it feels like crap."

"Why would you have sex if you don't love that person?"

"Sometimes once you've done it, you start fiending for it. It's like if you see someone and they look somewhat okay and you haven't done it in a while then anything can happen."

"I think I'm ready. Rakeem and I have been together for a while and although he has never pressured me about it, I feel that I may loose him to some other girl. Like you say, anything can happen since he has already done it and he gets a hard time because he dates a white girl. I know he loves me because we have been through a lot."

So that's his name. Rakeem; the guy with the dreads. He doesn't seem like the type to date a white person. I hope he doesn't dog her out because she'll think all black men are like that but he has to see how naïve she is. Maybe I need to really school her.

"Look, I don't know Rakeem but I do know men. They will make you feel special like you're the only one when in reality they're screwing every Tom, Dick and Harry. Just watch your back and don't fall too deep in love because first loves are hard to get over."

"Rakeem's not like that. Listen to me. I sound like I've already fallen too deep. I will take your advice but I still need to learn for myself I guess." With that, she laid on her bed and fell fast sleep. I guess she was dreaming about Rakeem because she was snoring and breathing so loud.

This eight o'clock class was going to kill me. I almost didn't make it because the Professor locks his door at 5 minutes till and he will not, under any circumstances, open it for any one. There were girls in the class with hair rollers in their hair and the guys had on old tee shirts and raggedy shorts. One guy even had on a terry cloth robe and bedroom shoes. I figured it was a protest against the class early morning time. My next class wasn't until 11:45. I wish now that I had changed my schedule because these people were rude in the morning, even the Professor. He finally ended his lecture an hour later and I haven't heard a word he said. I expected him to be a black man but he was good looking to be white. He looked like a Steven Segal or Superman. His body had it going on too. I was walking out the door when he stopped me.

"Ms. Richards, thankyou." He said.

"Thanks, for what?" I asked.

"For pretending to be interested. You were the only one who didn't fall asleep. I guess your dress depends a lot on that because those wearing bed clothes thought they were still in bed."

"Well Sir, You're welcome." I was impressed that he noticed my effort. I started walking off when I heard another voice. A sweet sounding, familiar voice.

"Hello beautiful."

This must be my lucky day. Thank God I didn't change my class after all.

"So did you finish doing your little thing from the other night?" I asked.

"So, did you remember your number from the other night?" he replied.

"Who says I wanted you to have it?" I was playing hard to get when I knew that I wanted him.

"Oh, so it's like that now. I'm not gonna beg unless you want me too." With that he got down on his knees and started begging like a dog.

"Get up. You are causing a scene."

"So can I get the digits or what?"

"0428."

"Cool. See you around." He left again without me asking his name. Damn.

The rest of the day went by like a breeze. I was on cloud nine after talking to my Romeo. I couldn't wait until Wednesday morning to see him again that is if he didn't call first. I told April I would meet her in the cafeteria for lunch. The place was packed and I was almost scarred to walk in but I decided to make my grand entrance.

It wasn't hard to spot April. She was sitting with Rakeem. They looked like the odd couple. She introduced us and I noticed his accent when he said nice to meet you. He told her he would meet her later and then he left.

"Oh April, I didn't mean to scare him off."

"Oh no, he has a class to go to. I told him all about you and he was here only to meet you."

"I feel like a celebrity now."

I couldn't believe what I saw when I went to the salad bar. My Romeo was sitting at a table with Ms. Dorm Diva. He looked like he was begging her for something and she had her eyes in the sky like he was getting on her nerves. I rushed back over to April so he wouldn't see me. I just had to know what was going on.

"April, who is that guy over there? Wait! Don't turn around so fast. He's with our dorm manager."

She looked over and looked back at me with a frown on her face.

"That's Quinton and Denise. They are like the campus couple. It was so much drama in their relationship last year that the audio visual class asked if they could follow them around and make a reality show?"

"You mean to tell me that he is involved with her?"

"Yeah why? Oh wait a minute. You don't like him do you? No way. He is like totally bad news and everyone knows that Denise is his main squeeze."

If I remember correctly, I was the one who had to tell her about men, black men, and now she wants to tell me about my dream man. Denise better check herself because Ms. Kitty will move in and take over. His main squeeze, huh. I will be the next orange juice then.

I was awakened by the telephone the next day. I waited for April to answer it but after the 5th ring I realized she was already gone. It must be important so after the seventh ring, I decided to answer it.

"Good morning. May I speak with Ms. Kitty?"

"Speaking."

"Did I wake you?

What a way to start my day. He has the sweetest voice but then I thought back to what April had said.

"So you decided to call after you get a break away from Denise?"

"Man, Denise is history. I was asking her if I could buy one of her old term papers. Everybody was in our business last year and it caused a lot of drama so we decided to go our separate ways this year."

"Is that so?"

I couldn't help but believe him since Denise was such a bitch. I definately don't see them as a couple.

"Look, the reason I called was to see if we could hook up later. Maybe check out a movie or something?"

"That's fine. What time are we talking?"

"Is 7:00 too late? Remember we both have the early bird class and I hate to have you out too late."

He doesn't understand. He could have me out as late as he wanted. I wouldn't mind waking up next to him then walking to our class together.

"Okay. Do you know where I live?"

"I knew that the first day you arrived."

Well, Mr. Romeo had been spying on me. If I had known I would've gave him a peep show.

I prayed that my classes wouldn't take long today because I needed all day to prepare for my date. By2:30 I was rushing back to my dorm to bathe and pick out the perfect outfit. I needed total silence and time to myself to prepare for this special evening; our first date. I needed to think about what I would say and do if he tried to make a pass at me. I didn't want to seem like a slut but I know he would be hard to resist. I learned early that you have to make a man wait. Then he will appreciate it more. My silence was broken when I opened my door to find April, Olandis and Rakeem there. Rakeem was trying to install a computer in our room and I guess

Olandis was the expert supervisor.

"Hey Ms. Kitty. I'snt this great? Dewayne bought Olandis a computer and he's putting it in our room." April said.

I didn't want Olandis in our room 24/7 using his computer as an excuse.

"Well, if Dewayne bought it for Olandis why is it in our room?"

"Ooh, Did the jealous bug bite you? If you must know, I'm putting it here because I thought you two could use it more than me. I don't know nothing about no damn computer!"

"Yeah but don't you think Dewayne will be upset if he found out you gave it away?"

"No, Ms. Ma'am. This is only a makeup gift. See, we had a fight the other day and he's just trying to get in good. He knows he doesn't want to loose his Mrs. Goodbar!"

I didn't feel like having a confrontation with him so I shut my mouth. Besides it would only slow Rakeem down because he stopped working to shake his head every time Olandis started talking. They finally finished but it looked like they were never going to leave. After another hour of 'Did man come from man or monkeys' debate between April and Rakeem, I asked could I have a little privacy to get dressed. Olandis was supposedly sleep but, funny, he sure heard me. He jumped up off the bed and started right in.

"Sounds serious ya'll. When the cats away the mice will play."

"Olandis," I asked," do you ever stop picking on people?"

"No. It's good for the soul. It makes you stronger. So any way, who is this mystery man?"

"Who says I have a mystery man."

"I knew time you walked through that door. You had this 'I'm in love' look on your face."

"Okay. You got me. It's Quintin." I blushed.

"QUINTIN !" they all shouted.

The first one to comment was Rakeem. "Yo, Kitty, I'm not one to dis my man but he's bad news." Next comment, Olandis, "Bad news. Hmmp, he's more like daybreaking news! I thought he was involved with what's her face?" April's turn. "Denise? Yeah he is or was. Look Ms. Kitty, I'm not gonna tell you who to date but Quintin is not the man for you."

I had just about had enough. They were talking about him like a dog. He did explain to me the deal with him and Denise and he didn't have to do it. This was just a harmless little date.

"Look I appreciate the concern but Ms. Kitty is a grown woman. I'll be careful, though."

They all shook their heads and left. Finally, I had peace and quiet. I rushed around the room cleaning up and getting dressed. I got ready just in time. He was knocking on my door once I applied my lipgloss and finally got a chance to sit down.

"Girl, you know you are too beautiful for words." He made me blush. I promised myself I wasn't going to act silly.

"I know." Gosh, that was a dumb reply. Okay, get it together, breath and count to ten.

He extended his hand and we walked out the room. The whole time I wished my hand would stop sweating. I didn't notice we went out the dorm a different way, more like the back doorway. We continued walking until I finally asked where were we going. His reply, the movies.

"I know that but where is your car?"

"Oh, so you one of those materialistic girls? That's cool if you don't want to walk all the way to the movies."

Now of course by now I was ready to go off. I went through hell to get ready for him and he expects me to walk and then he gets an attitude. But then again, he is so fine.

Maybe I shouldn't be so mean. He is in college and probably has no money to throw away on a car like April's rich parents. In fact, he probably had to scrape up his last dime to take me out tonight.

"I'm not materialistic. If I was you wouldn't be standing here talking to me. So anyway, I hope you have on your walking shoes."

He had the cutest smile, one dimple on his left cheek. During the movie he put his arm around me. God, it was getting hot up in here. We started laughing at something, which I don't remember, when he rested his hand on my knee. Now it felt like fire in here. My knees started shaking out of control like I had Parkinsons Disease. Now I'm not a spiritual person but my ass started praying to help me get it under control. It must be a God because the movie finally ended. We stood up to walk out the theatre but I stopped suddenly. My panties were wet. I don't believe this. They weren't wet from being hot, they were wet from my period. I must have mis -calculated the dates from my abortion. I had to get back to my room before my panties turned into the Red Sea. Quintin noticed my distressed look and asked me if I was alright. I made up a lie about having a stomach ache and told him I wanted to go back to my room and lie down. He got a taxi and took me to his dorm.

"What are you doing?" I asked.

"You said you wanted to lie down."

"I know and I also said in My room."

"Well the taxi is here now and I don't have anymore money for him to take you back across campus."

I don't believe this. What a jerkoff. He really doesn't understand that my period is on.

"Fine. I'll walk."

"Suit yourself."

I'm glad that I'm not a violent person because I would have murder charges by now. The stomach cramps were hitting full force by the time I walked back to my dorm. April was asleep when I came in. There was a note on the mirror that read,

Ms. Kitty,

I'm sorry for the way I acted this afternoon. Quintin deserves a chance and all that bull happened last semester. I hope you guys had a great time tonight. Please forgive me.

Your roomie,

April Showers

That April. She's always making things so perfect. I can't let them find out that tonight was a disaster.

The next morning, it was obvious several people had dropped Professor Phillips' class. That early bird gets the worm motto just doesn't cut it in this case. Quintin must have dropped out too because he was nowhere in site. I wonder why he didn't mention it last night.

Towards the end of class, the professor gave out his syllabus and I notice a typing error.

"Um, Professor Phillips."

"Yes Ms. Richards?"

"Your syllabus states that there is a test and paper due in less than a week."

"Yes it states that but what are you saying?"

Oh, I wanted to kill this smart mouth man.

"I guess nothing."

He shrugged his shoulders and continued lecturing. I felt like crying but once again, no tears would form. After class he called me to his office. I didn't want to go but I was curious to find out what he had to say.

"Ms. Richards. I see a lot of potential in you so don't let this easy work scare you. If you need anything, here's my card but don't call too often. I wouldn't want the other students to call you teachers pet."

I couldn't tell if he was flirting with me or just being concerned but I took the card any way. I mean, he was my instructor and I didn't want to seem disobedient. I could handle whatever came up. I was use to older men by now.

I was resting on my bed when I heard the keys in the door knob. I shut my eyes and pretended to be sleep. The last thing I needed was to talk to April about my date last night and it sounded like Olandis was with her.

"Shhh, she's sleep. Let me grab my sociology book and get out so she can rest. She came in pretty late last night."

"The hell with that. I got to find out about this date. Wake up Miss Thang! He must've whipped the good shit out on you. I know you aint sleep because you would've heard me and woke up by now." Olandis hit me with a pillow.

I let a grin sneak out. Then it turned into giggles.

"Oh my Lord Jesus! He got her high. Don't worry, it will be out your system in about a week." Olandis said.

"I am not high. The way you act I would say you're high all the time."

"What you talking bout'? I am high all the time, off love baby. What the world needs now is love, sweet love."

"Please Olandis," April screamed, "spare us the singing. So how did it go?"

"It was magical. He is such a gentleman. So sweet and kind." I felt guilty lying to them but I for them to say I told you so.

"Wait. Holdup. Rewind that. You did go out with Quintin, right?" I was two feet away from slapping Olandis.

"Yes I did and he was everything I thought he would be."

"I'm so happy for you Ms. Kitty." April's eyes lit up when she said it.

There she goes again with that mess, making me feel so bad about lying to her.

She grabbed her book and left but she had to come back in the room to pull Olandis out. He was still in a state of shock to learn about the new and improved, Quintin.

The telephone rung just then and startled me. When I went to answer it, it wasn't on the base. I started throwing clothes and underwear all over the place trying to find that damn phone. I knew it had to be Quintin calling me to apologize for being so rude last night.

I could sense that it was him. I had completely messed up the room when I finally found the phone hiding under April's pillow. I was shaking so bad that I had to stop and check myself. I answered in the sexiest voice I could imitate.

"Hello."

"Hello, is April there?"

What the hell is going on? This isn't Quintin. It sounds more like Rakeem with this Jamaican accent. Now I'm pissed!

"No she isn't."

"Well you're the one I wanted to talk to."

"About what and who are you?"

I already knew the answer to that question but I was annoyed and tried to drop a hint to show it.

"I apologize for not introducing myself over the phone. This is Rakeem. I wanted to talk to you about helping me plan a surprise birthday party for April. Her birthday is next month and I wanted to do something special. Olandis already agreed to do the decorating and be in charge of the food."

"Well it looks like you have everything covered."

"Not exactly. That's where your part comes in. All I want you to do is get her to the party without her finding out about it."

I agreed to go along with his scheme even though, deep down, I was a little jealous.

Besides, I needed something to take my mind off rude boy Quintin.

I busted my ass the next couple of weeks to turn in all my assignments for Professor Phillips' class. He kept giving me courage that I could do it. My only hang up was if he knew his class was a brainwrecker, why did he strive to make it so hard? One day after class he asked me if I lost his card because I haven't attempted to call. I told him that I still have it and I was trying to see if I could do his work on my own. He made me promise to him that I would give him a call if anything came up that I didn't understand. He was starting to give me the creeps. I mean he didn't treat the other students like he treated me. They had to either sink or float. I didn't want another Moe episode so I decided to keep my distance from him. I had come too far for him to flunk me. My grades would prove him wrong and then the Deans' and President of the school would see that he tried to hit on me. I better start keeping documentations on every time he calls me in his office and practically begs me to call him. I may need to watch my back and see if he's following me back to my room after class or does he have another class after this one? I am really tripping out. This man may be perfectly harmless but I can't be too sure just yet.

Another week passed by and I still haven't heard from Quintin. It has been exactly 4 weeks, 2 days and 13 hours since our date. It's like he just fell off the face of this earth. I hope he landed straight in hell.

Everything was all set for April's surprise party tonight. I told her that I was going to treat her to this new restaurant about a block away. We were to meet Olandis there. She never suspected a thing. There was something heavy on her mind, I could tell, because she was acting strange.

"Ms. Kitty, tonight is the night."

I almost blew my cover because I thought she was talking about the surprise party. I tried to act normal. "Tonight is the night for what, April?"

"Me to loose my virginity."

Where the hell is Olandis when you need him? I can't talk her out of it, it sounds like her mind is already made up.

"Are you sure, I mean does Rakeem know about this?"

"I was hoping you could give me some ideas, you know, some pointers on how to get him in the mood."

Now that I can do. I am the master at suduction.

"First you need some sexy lingerie and plenty of condoms. I know he doesn't have any since you all haven't been active. Then you suggest that you go back to his place. After that the rest is history."

"I got condoms but no lingerie. It's too late to go out and buy some and I promised to meet him after I went out with you guys."

"Ok, Well skip the lingerie. He'll be happy just to see your bra strap." I said with a laugh. I couldn't help thinking about my girl April, about to do the wild thing. I vaguely remember my first time. I think it was a dare or something. Any way I do remember the sting every time I went to the bathroom. I should tell her to rub plenty of Vasaline up in there because she was gonna be sore for a few days, especially with Rakeem. He was a Mandingo type of man!

We arrived at the restaurant at 7:15 just like Rakeem instructed. Olandis was waiting outside in the lounge chairs sipping a Blue Martini with the little umbrella and cherry sticking out the glass. He must've thought he was a movie star or something because he was wearing his Marilyn Monroe wig and dark sunglasses even though it was nightime.

"Well, it's about time you arrived. I was starting to put out an a.p.b. on you!"

I knew he was acting. He knew exactly what time the guest of honor was scheduled to arrive but I must admit he is good. He sometimes goes overboard into his acting.

"Follow me. I went ahead and reserved us a table."

I almost choked when he stood up and wrapped his flowered scarf around his neck.

To top it off, he had on a long, white flair dress to match his wig, of course. We followed him to the ballroom in the back of the restaurant and he swung the double doors wide open for us to see the extravaganza.

I heard all kinds of versions of the Happy Birthday song, then screams and laughter.

April was shocked. I was too but not in the same way. Olandis had really outdone himself this time. I couldn't believe my eyes. He had turned this entire room into a minature Hawaii. There was a pig being roasted in one corner and big tropical trees everywhere. The buffet table was packed full of fruit dressed up like faces and small sandwiches cut into the shape of fishes. The male servers were walking around wearing grass skirts and no tops carrying trays of horderves. I don't think they had on anything under the skirts, either. In the middle of the room was a swimming pool with live fish and real sand around it. People had begun to take off their clothes and jump in. This was too wild for me. I saw Olandis hugged up in the corner with some guy. It must be Dewayne. He wasn't bad looking. At least we know Olandis has taste. They started heading toward me.

"Ms. Kitty, I want you to meet Dewayne. He's my inspiration behind all this."

"Is that so?" I asked.

"Yeah. I've been dying to go to Hawaii and since he won't take me there, I decided to bring Hawaii here."

That damn Olandis is a trip. Dewayne must be use to his remarks by now because he didn't say a word. He was dressed as sharp as a tack. His black suit must've been tailored to custom fit his body. He was wearing a skin tight black, shiny, tee shirt underneath. He had so many waves in his hair that I got sea sick. I couldn't tell if his long pony tail was real or fake since Olandis was good with the weaves and wigs. He was also a little shorter than Olandis but he stuck to his side like glue, never letting him out of his site. When Olandis did get a chance to get away from him, he rushed over to me. I guess he noticed that I wasn't really in the partying mood because I was still in the same spot that I started in.

"Ms. Kitty, You all right?" he asked. "You look like you're bored and Olandis doesn't throw boring parties."

"I'm alright. Ive just never been to a party like this before."

"Well, you may never go to another party like this again so get on out there and shake your ass, girlfriend. Why don't you take a dip in the pool, it will cool you off."

"Excuse me but I didn't bring any swimming clothes. I must pass." I waved my hands, trying to brush him off.

"Hey, look around. Your eyes must not see what I see. You don't need any clothes to skinny dip ." He was staring one of the male servers down as he walked by with a tray.

"Oh excuse me, can I get a sample. Of the horderves of course." he said. "Now that was a fine young gentleman. Go ahead Ms. Kitty, make your move."

"He's not my type."

He really wasn't my type because I didn't want a man that would not walk around like that, half naked. I needed Quintin. I would give anything to see him again and redo our first date. I was having mirages now because every guy in here looked just like him. I could see his nice physique taunting me to come take a taste. I could see his tiny dimple in his left cheek and those perfectly shaped teeth that would take years of dentistry and braces to fullfil. No. Wait a minute. I'm not seeing things. I saw Quintin holding a girl over his shoulder about to throw her in the water. Who put his name on the guest list because non of my friends liked him? He jumped out the pool dripping wet where everyone could see his silk boxers. My God! This man has the biggest ....

"Ms. Kitty, I cant believe you knew about this the whole time ." It was April again to spoil my groove.

"And I can't believe I kept it from you all this time."

"Well I'm glad you did. I don't think I can make up a surprised face. Olandis, maybe but me, no."

"So are you still gonna go through with it?" I asked.

"Yes and I'm so nervous. We are gonna leave and go back to his room in about 30 minutes.

I think he knows what I'm planning to do because he was ready to leave an hour ago and this is our party."

"Well wouldn't you? I mean you made him wait forever and he's probably afraid that you might change your mind. Just remember what I said about falling too deep and I'll see you tomorrow. Have fun, okay."

She gave me a hug and told me thankyou. Then she scooted back over to Rakeem's side and I watched them as they held hands. I couldn't help but feel envious. Everybody had a man except me. I have never felt this way before because I was never without someone. I want someone to call my own. I know eventually that they will be all lovey, dovey and wont have time for me. I heard a loud scream come from a group of girls near the pool. I looked over to see my man, Quintin, and some other guy holding a girl outside the pool by her hands and feet. They were swinging her back and forth until they finally threw her in the pool. She cursed them out when she came up for air because her hair was a mess. Quintin went over to her and shoved her head back under the water. He and the other guy gave each other a secret hand shake and called her a stupid bitch. Some girl walked over and slapped Quintin in the face. Just then the room grew quiet. The other girl that was thrown in the pool was crying loudly. Quintin had his victim by the arms and was about to shove her in the pool when Olandis stepped in.

"Wait just a minute pretty boy! This is not the ghetto so get out, you got to go! And take your little do boy with you. Coming up in here like acting like wild animals and shit. I got a good mind to call not the cops but the zookeeper! Hurry up and take your little dingy clothes too."

He tossed his shirt and pants to him with one finger, like they were poison or something. Quintin knew not to step to Olandis. Everyone in the room started clapping as they walked out. I kind of felt sorry for him. He was just having fun. After that disaster, I was ready to leave. One part of me felt compassion for Quintin and I don't understand why but the other part of me felt happy. It was sort of like my own personal revenge. Besides, if he had been with me tonight that episode would have never happened.

The music came back on and the party started again. I guess the dejay had a drink because he was putting on tracks with a lot of flavor. He was mixing old school jams with new school hits. Before I knew it I was on the dance floor with a guy I had never seen. It didn't matter that he wasn't cute as long as I was having fun. We exchanged numbers and I immediately dissed him in time to dance with another guy.

Now he was sort of fly until he opened his mouth. Damn! This man had teeth running every where. His lips looked like they were stretched out of shape for trying to hold back all his teeth. Somebody needs to smack his mama for not getting him braces, or in his case a damn gate! I was relieved when he saw someone he knew. He actually thought I was going to walk over with him and meet them. I assured him that I was following right behind him but actually I hid behind one of the tropical trees while he wasn't looking. I could see his confused expression when he went to introduce me and I wasn't there. I felt a poke in my back. When I turned around there was another guy standing there asking for me a dance. Since I'm here I might as well. We started moving and grooving and things were going well until I put my arms around his neck.

What the hell is going on back here? I started running my hands up the back of his head. He started moaning and telling me I was touching his hot spot. I was trying to figure out what in the world was on the back of his head. Then it hit me. Razor bumps. Not just any old ordinary razor bumps but the infected kind. I rested my head on his shoulder just to get a better view and those things punched me in the eye. It looked like some Freddy Kruger shit! Puss was leaking out so bad that the back of his shirt was wet and he had the audacity to wear white. It was too out of control for a dermatologist to treat. He needed a whole new neck. I know his barber has to cut his hair after hours because he would loose all his clientele. He started blowing in my ear, whispering that I had turned him on. I whispered back that blowing in my ear turns me off. I left him standing there on the dance floor. I didn't care, all I cared about was the nearest bathroom to wash my hands. One of the servers told me where the rest room was and I made a beeline straight to it. I was scrubbing my hands when Olandis walked in. "Olandis, this is the ladies rest room!" I squealed.

"No, for real?" he said in a sarcastic way.

He started pulling and straightening his wig. Then he pulled out some lip gloss from his stuffed bra and applied it evenly on his lips. He smacked and puckered his lips then applied some more.

"Child, this is the best lip gloss money can buy and men just love the fruity scent. Damn Ms.

Kitty, you been washing your hands for twenty minutes."

"Long story. Just remember to look at the back of the head instead of the face when you dance with someone." I got a chill just thinking about those bumps.

"Oh snap. You must've danced with Head. His neck look like the crack of somebody's ass.

Don't worry, after a little alcohol and Clorox your hands will be good as new."

"I hope so. I think I'll head on back to my room."

"Okay, girl. Do you need a ride?"

"Nah, I'm cool. See ya' tomorrow."

"Chow."

The air was brisk as I walked back to the dorm. I could tell it was time for fall. This kind of weather always makes me sad. Sad because I would love to cuddle up with someone to keep me warm. Sad because love was in the air and I had no one to love me. Out of 150 men tonight, not one could compare to Quintin. I can't understand why I'm so crazy about him.

I turned on the radio when I got in my room. They were playing the quiet jam, more depression for me. I didn't bother to turn on the lights. To add to my torture, it started raining outside. It was only midnight. I know how Cinderella must have felt the night of the ball. I kept expecting to wake up out of this long, dark, dream. Maybe if I try a little harder I can fall asleep. I felt myself drifting away when I heard a soft, tap at the door. Who could this be? April was with Rakeem and Olandis was with Dewayne.

This better be good because I don't feel up to any bull tonight. I stomped my toe on the way to open the door and the pain was severe. It was throbbing so I bent down to take look at it as I opened the door. I saw a pair of brand new pair of Air Jordan tennis shoes. I stood up to put a face with the feet. He stood there with the saddest puppy dog eyes I've ever seen. His shirt was wet from the rain. He ran his fingers through his curly hair and smiled, showing his dimple.

"May I come in?" he asked.

I wonder if that is a trick question? Anyway, I decided to let him in.

"What happened? Did y'all forget to pay the power bill?"

I turned on the lights and stood at the door with my arms folded across my chest. I was speechless but he took it as being mad so he started explaining.

He pulled out my desk chair and sat down. I don't recall telling him he could stay.

"I know you're mad at me but I was trying to give you time to cool off. I was wrong for not bringing my princess back to her room but at the time I was upset with you. I mean, I wanted to make our date special and take you out to eat or something after the movie but then you started complaining about your stomach. I didn't believe you, I thought you were making it all up because you didn't like me and you needed an excuse to get the hell away from me. Baby, when I saw you around campus, I wanted to come over and talk to you but I was afraid of rejection. I fought with myself all night on whether I should come over here and then I decided that I couldn't bear another waking moment without hearing the sound of your voice. Come here, Boo."

I walked over to the chair and he sat me in his lap. He started massaging my neck and continued talking.

"Girl, I don't know what you did to me but I cant get you off my mind. I missed you.

Please give me another chance. I'll never fuck up like that again. I promise."

Call it an omen but at that moment the radio started playing *Being In Love Aint Easy*.

His hand slid down my back and began unsnapping my bra. "They're playing our song, baby."

He turned me around to face him and gently put my legs around his waist. He held my face gently in his hands and kissed me on the forehead, then the very tip of my nose, then my lips. He parted them with his tongue and we kissed forever. I felt his hands undoing the button on my jeans and the traction sound of my zipper coming undone. He put his hands inside my underwear like he was trying to keep them warm.

I felt a tingle as he rubbed my clitoris and kissed my neck. He used his other hand to take off his shirt exposing a muscular chest. He was so warm and desirable. I could smell my favorite cologne on his chest, Obsession. He lifted me in the air and pulled down my jeans in one second. I was straddled across his lap with my panties still on.

We started kissing again, this time harder. Our passion for each other was well over due. We continued kissing, our tongues wrestling to over power the other, as he ripped my shirt off. He grabbed my breasts and put them in his mouth. The hot moisture from his tongue made me demand more from him. I wanted it all, the total package. I reached inside his pants and pulled out his penis. I knew I had to have it once I saw him at the party in his boxers. It was firm as it kept growing in my hand. I rubbed it and squeezed it until I knew it couldn't get any bigger. He was moaning and calling out my name as I played with it some more. Then he just couldn't take it anymore, he slid my panties to the side of my vagina and crammed his jewels inside of me. I grabbed the back of the chair for support while he grabbed my butt. He lowered me up then back down again on him with slow movements at first. He picked up the pace when I threw my head back and screamed out his name. The chair rolled around until it was subdued by one of my shoes. He let one hand free in order to place it behind my head He raised his body up slightly and I could see his muscles flex as he supported me in mid air. He was trying to get his whole body inside of me.

Sweat dripped down his forehead unto his chest and he pushed my head into it. I started licking the salty substance enjoying the flavor every minute. Our bodies danced to a rhythmic tune together until we couldn't hear the invisible music anymore. We reached our orgasims' together, breathing wildly out of control. We collapsed back in the chair making it push off a little. I felt his magical tool shrink inside of me as we held each other, listening to the rain beat against my window and the radio play *Adore* by Prince. Now I understood why Olandis was such a Prince fan.

Truth

APRIL CALLED EARLY in the morning to see if I was okay. I was more than okay. I was splendid, like a child on Christmas. I didn't know how or when we made it to the bed but I didn't care. I was enjoying the oral sexual pleasure Quintin was giving me this morning. I tried to act normal, like no one was here as I talked to April. She said something about being in Olandis's room and helping him get into role, whatever that meant. I didn't want to be rude but she was spoiling my fun so I told her that I would call her back after while. Quintin lifted his head up from under the sheets. I laughed at him because he looked like he was trying to play Casper the Friendly Ghost. He pounced on top of me and flipped me around on top of him.

"So 'I'm amusing to you, huh? Well was I amusing last night?"

"No baby, you were the bomb' last night. Maybe we could try it again to see if you still got it going on."

My body was hot and ready, wanting another sample of last night. I started sucking on his neck to try and tempt him but he resisted me by pushing my face away. He crawled out from beneath me and stood up, exposing his better half standing at attention. He started rummaging through the clothes on the floor and found his underwear and pants. He hurridly shoved them on. I was wondering what happened, what did I do wrong? I asked for an explanation, that's the least he could do.

"Where are you rushing off to?"

"Huh, oh I um promised one of my frat brothers that I would help some little kids out with a car wash this morning. You understand don't you?"

He walked over to the side of my bed and stood there. His shirt was still off and when I saw those muscles, taunting me, I wanted to tie him up and keep him locked in my room forever. I knew it was impossible but at least he was leaving me for a good cause. He is such a good man. I mean what man would spend their entire Saturday helping out someone else's kid? He bent down to give me a goodbye kiss. I turned my head and pretended to be mad by pouting. He gave me a devilish grin.

"Okay, you win. I cant stand to see you upset so I may have time to squeeze in a quickie'."

Now I was the one with the grin on my face as he took off his pants and climbed back in bed with me. Our quickie' lasted longer than it was supposed to and an hour later I had dozed back off to sleep. I was dreaming about our wedding, me in a beautiful, white, gown and Quintin standing there wearing a white tuxedo with flower petals blowing all around us, until April called again. This time she was in a panic.

"Ms. Kitty please! I need you to come over here, now!"

"Where are you?" I asked.

"I'm in Olandis's room, hurry!"

"Calm down, I'm on my way."

I rushed around the room trying to find some clean clothes to put on. After searching with no results, I threw on an old tee shirt, some faded denim shorts and mismatched bedroom shoes. I hope I don't run into anyone I know while I look like this. I wondered what is wrong. I hope Rakeem didn't do anything to hurt April. I ran all the way to Olandis's dorm. By the time I got there, I was sweating and out of breath. I didn't know what to expect when I knocked on his door. April came and let me walk in. She didn't look hurt or beat up, just serious and concerned. I saw Olandis standing in the middle of the floor wearing a long, silk robe with feathers around the collar and sleeves. He paced the floor with a fierce look on his face.

"Ms. Kitty, I'm so glad you came. We have a slight problem." April said.

"We! Who is the we? I thought I was the one with the problem here. Damn! I cant even get my own sympathy." Olandis stated.

"I wish someone would tell me what's going on."

Olandis opened his robe to show me the 'slight' problem. Once again, I was not prepared for this. He had silver duck tape stuck to his, well you know.

He was packed, stomach like a six pack and his downtown friend was packing a lot, too.

"This little white heifer tried to rip my penis out! I may be gay but I'm still a man and I value my family jewels."

"But I don't know what to do. Why did you…." I was scared of what he wanted me to do.

"Look Ms. Kitty, I don't have time for an explanation. I have a job assignment from my agent and I'm gonna be late if you don't hurry and do something. I can't mess this job up after she finally started finding me work since the last job screw up."

"Okay, Okay. Give me a minute to think."

No matter what I tried, getting that duck tape off was going to hurt. I spotted a bottle of baby oil on his dresser. I grabbed the bottle and began pouring it all over him. He looked at me like I was crazy. I told him not to move, counted to three and yanked the tape off. April winched and Olandis screamed! We rode in silence to the mall where he was supposed to report. He had stuffed his pants with a washcloth to ease the pain.

When he stepped out the car, I noticed the big bulge in his pants. I tried to stop him to warn him but he continued walking.

April and I decided to do a much needed thing, wash our clothes and clean up our room.

"April," I asked, "why does Olandis torture himself like that? I mean, he is a good looking guy and he has a body that is enviable."

"He cant help it. That's who he is. If it takes torture to get his point across, then he'll do it. No pain, no gain."

"Yeah but he had pain and no gain."

She stopped sweeping and fell back in the chair laughing.

"It was kind of funny to see you and him with that baby oil. He had my car smelling like a newborn baby and youre right. He didn't gain anything last night because he couldn't get the tape off."

"Speaking of last night," I said," how did things go with you and Rakeem?"

"We didn't do it. After a couple of tries, we gave up."

"Oh, I know he is pissed by now!"

"No not really. He said it was a sign that maybe we shouldn't go through with it. He said our relationship is fine the way the way it is so why complicate it. We just held each other the whole night and listened to the rain."

"So youre trying to tell me that you all held each other all night and he was okie dokie with it? Girl, he must be getting laid by someone else."

"Well, I doubt it but if he is, he doesn't love her."

"And how do you know that?"

"Because he keeps coming back to me."

I guess she had a point. Why would he put up with her if he didn't care deeply about her? He would be just using some other girl for sex not love. Besides, once you know who you want to spend the rest of your life with, sex shouldn't matter. That's how things are going to be between me and Quintin. April left to wash another load of clothes so I decided to give my baby a call. The telephone rang several times before the answering machine picked up.

"Yo, this is Quintin A.K.A. The Big Pleaser. I'm probably out with your girl right now so leave a message after the beep." Beepppppppppppp.

I hung up without leaving a message. What did he mean by Im probably out with your girl? Oh well, it's just an answering machine. People put ridiculous stuff on them all the time. Back home, my mom had the nerve to put may God bless you on our machine. She never blessed anything, not even her food before she gobbled it down. I thought about her, how she was doing. She had never bothered to call. I sort of miss her in a mother/ daughter kind of way. Maybe I should give her a call. Nah, she didn't want to hear from me. Moe would probably answer the phone and ruin everything. I certainly did not want to talk to him. He might lie and say I called to ask him to come see me. Bastard!

"I HATE YOU !" I screamed.

"Hate who?" April had walked back in the room.

"Oh nobody."

She started folding the clothes and putting them in the drawers. I watched her and thought how did her life become so perfect? Was she born into society this way or does she hold the key to good fortune secret? The phone interrupted my thoughts. It was Olandis.

"I need April to come and pick me up." He sounded hot as fire.

I looked at the clock and realized he had only been at work for 45 minutes. I told him I would relay the message to her. She was upset but she grabbed her keys and went to get him anyway. I didn't want to miss out on this action so I ran behind her and jumped in the car. We arrived at the mall to find Olandis waiting outside smoking a cigarette. April informed me that it must be bad since he only smokes when he's mad.

He saw us pull up and he put the cigarette out, thanked the man standing there with him for the lighter and got in the back seat of the car. April started in on him as soon as he closed the door.

"What did you do this time, Olandis?" she asked.

"Why does it have to be my fault?" he questioned.

"Because it usually is."

"Well you're wrong Little Miss no it all! When I get home I'm gonna call my agent and curse her out before I fire her. Do you know what she had me doing?"

"No. I've been waiting for you to tell me."

"Don't rush me. I have been through enough already. This bitch had me selling mops in the center of the mall while a fashion show was going on. I mean, who do I look like, Harriet Tubman? Any way I decided to try it because I needed the money. After doing three demonstrations with no one buying the stupid thing a pair of wrinkled, old bats walked up and asked me to do another demo. I dipped the mop in the water and bent over to show them the easy squeezy handle when one of them grabbed my butt. Well at first I tried to play it off but then they told me if I gave them my number, they would buy three mops. I thought, oh what the hell, they cant call me if I give a fake number. I turned my back for one second to get a pen and 'Thelma and Louise' ran off with the mops. I started chasing their little geriatric asses across the runway where the fashion show was going on and when I got close enough to one of em', I tripped her with my mop handle. She nose dived right on the mall security's feet. He helped her up and she started crying, saying that I was a very rude, disrespectful young man and she had a good mind to sue the mall. He grabbed me by the collar and literally threw me out the door. Now I'm band from the mall."

April and I burst out laughing.

"Oh you think it's funny? I have been tramatized and now have no place to buy my clothes and you cows are sitting here laughing!"

He made us laugh even harder when he said that. Then April stopped and started slowing down. We didn't notice the police car following us with it's lights on. April pulled over and put the car in neutral. Two white, male, police officers walked up on each side of the car with their guns pointed at us.

"Shit April. What kind of tickets do you owe them cause you need to pay up?" Olandis said.

"None. I wasn't even speeding. I dont know why they stopped me."

The officer on the left said, "Put your hands up and slowly exit the car."

"Now how the hell are we supposed to open the door with our hands up?" Olandis stated.

I tried it anyway because I knew what the police where capable of. Everybody followed suit. One of the officers came over to April and asked her was she okay and did we hurt her. He told her she was free to leave and he made us put our hands on the car so we could be searched." What is going on? These are my friends."

The officer started explaining, "We have a call about a bank robbery that took place about two blocks from here. He fit the description of one of the robbers, a black male."

I was hoping Olandis would leave it alone but of course he did not. He was already upset about the mall incident so this made matters worse.

"Well, I'll be damned. You and Barney Fife here think all Black people look alike so what are you gonna do, stop every black person on the street?"

"Listen to the little sissy black kid. Aint he cute? Now shut up and we'll let you go but if you don't, I'm taking you down to the station. Those prisoners could use some fresh meat."

I started praying to God, Allah, and whoever would listen up there, to please, please, make him shut up.

Olandis started again, "Excuse me Mr. Police Man, but what charges do you have on me. I'm sorry, I didn't hear that. It sounded like you said none. Now if you don't mind, I would like to go home and call my lawyer on your racist's ass." The cop must've gotten scared when he mentioned a lawyer because he let us go.

April was crying so hard that her tears blocked her vision and she couldn't see how to drive. This day has been a nightmare. It started off great and then went downhill. I should've stayed in bed and made Quintin stay with me. Olandis told April to pull over in this fast food restaurant's parking lot. He couldn't stand her driving any longer. As she pulled over, I noticed a bunch of little kids washing cars. Maybe things are going to start picking up. I can't wait to see him, my future husband. When April and Olandis jumped out to exchange seats, I jumped out too and rushed over to the car wash. April started shouting for me to come on but I held my hand up for her to give me one more minute. I can't find him. I asked one of the kids where was their supervisor. "You mean Big Brother All Mighty?" he said proudly.

"Yeah, Yeah, I guess. Where is he?"

He pointed to a guy washing the inside of a van. I walked over to him and asked him where was Quintin.

"Good question. He was supposed to meet me this morning but he never showed up."

I was confused. I started walking off but he stopped me.

"Hey, if you see him, tell him to report to me immediately! He hasn't done any community services this semester."

I called him as soon as I got in. No answer. I called again; still no answer. Olandis and April were asleep on her bed. How could they sleep after a day like today? I called one more time and promised myself that this would be the last. I'm in luck because he picked up on the second ring only it wasn't him. It was a female. She kept saying hello over and over again. I was speechless. The more she said hello, the more I recognized her voice. It was Denise. What was she doing answering my man's phone? I was livid. I slammed the phone down on the receiver and prepared myself for battle. I decided to go over there and let her know who was in charge. He probably didn't even know she was there. She may have broken in his room to snoop around. I pinned up my hair, greased my face with Vaseline, took off my earrings and walked out the door. I walked straight up to his room with the dorm supervisor chasing behind me. He said I couldn't go up without permission and I told him I didn't need permission, this is an emergency! I banged on his door until finally it opened. Just as I thought, it was her.

"May I help you?" she asked while rolling her eyes.

"Oh, don't trip, bitch! You know damn well why I'm here. Where is Quintin?"

"Hold up, don't come at me like that. And who the hell are you calling a bitch, bitch!"

She did it. She pushed the last nerve in my body. Before I knew it, I had punched her in the jaw. She slapped me across the face and the guys in the other rooms came out to see the fight. All I heard was someone say, Lets get ready to RUMBLE and we were rolling around on the floor. I got up and grabbed Quintin's lamp and threw it at her. It shattered into one hundred tiny pieces. She picked up one of the pieces and charged at me. I met her head on with my foot. I think I knocked out one of her teeth because she started bleeding. No, I think it was her nose. Anyway, she wouldn't give up. She bit me on the arm while I had her in a headlock. It was hurting like hell but I wouldn't let her head go. I tried to break her neck but with her thick head, it would never break. I decided to pull a wrestling move on her. I jumped down on my butt never letting her head go. I may not have broken her neck but I know I did some damage to her spine. The dorm supervisor pulled me off her while another guy pulled Denise away. One hour and twenty five minutes later, we were released from the supervisor's office. He told us he could report it to the dean but then he would get in trouble for letting two girls up to a room without the occupant's consent. Besides, it was the best fight he had seen up here in a while. He also said we were not allowed near the dorm again and he took Denise's position away from her stating that she was not to fight in the dorms or on school grounds. He gave her until Monday afternoon to move out her supervisor apartment and into one of the regular dorm rooms. As we walked out the dorm she looked at me and said, "You will pay for this you ghetto slut!" After the fight, I felt great. So great that I decided to take a jog, something I haven't done in a while. I jogged an hour before I realized it. I had so much energy still inside me. Where is Quintin. He could help me release some of this energy right about now. I ran back to my dorm to take a shower in case he came by to see me. I was too late. I ran into him leaving my dorm. I hated him to see me like this but I don't care at this point. I hope Olandis and April have left. He walked up to me and kissed my forehead.

"Baby are you all right? I heard about what happened and I rushed over here to see you but you weren't here. You had me worried."

"I'm okay but what was Denise doing in your room?"

"I don't know. I guess she still has a key from last year and she let herself in. I will get her told as soon as I see her. She can't keep hurting my baby. I won't allow it."

"I thought you two had broke up. Why is she still coming in your room?"

"Look, beautiful, don't worry about Denise. I told you she is history. It's all about you now. Go get some rest and I'll call and check on you later."

He quickly ran off towards his dorm without giving me a chance to invite him up. I must smell really bad the way he ran away. I guess he was going to give me a chance to wash up and then call later for us to get together. I better hurry and get started. When I approached my room, I noticed some writing on my door. As I got closer I could make out what it said. Here lives the biggest slut on campus. For a free nut call 0428. It was written in permanent, black marker. I opened the door and April was on the computer. Olandis was still asleep.

"April did you see who did this to our door?"

"No what is it?" She got up to look at the door and was shocked. "Who would do this to our door? They must have our room mixed up with someone else's."

"Denise did it." I said

"Why would Denise do something like that? Oh no, does Quintin have anything to do with this?"

"No. Denise and I got in a fight. He was nowhere around when it happened."

"A fight! Are you serious?" Just then Olandis woke up.

"Fight, where?" he asked.

"Ms. Kitty got in a fight."

"Shit! A kitty cat fight and you didn't wake me up? Well, who won?"

"Olandis, I know you didn't ask who won. I kicked her ass." He gave me a high five.

"So who was it, details honey?"

I started to tell him about the brawl but April cut in.

"She was fighting with Denise and now look at our door."

He walked over to the door and read it.

"I say you go kick her ass again for this. She must not know who she is messing with. I am the master at practical jokes and revenge is my middle name."

"Your middle name is Reginald and don't go starting trouble, please you guys. I'll get us a new door."

"Were not starting trouble. Unh, Unh, Olandis ends trouble. I nip it, dip it and stick it in the mud."

"She's not finished, April." I said. "She warned me that she would get me back for getting her kicked out her apartment."

"Well what should we do? Do we need to call the campus security?" she asked.

"What! Okay you tripping now, girl." I said. I thought back to my old neighborhood. Police always showed up after the problem was solved and still took someone to jail just to make their trip worthwhile. Olandis and I were laughing until we realized she was serious. This girl has no clue. Sometimes I forget that she is white and her world is different from ours.

"April, honey," Olandis said, "campus security is not real. They are police academy rejects with a stick instead of a gun. We don't run to them with our little problems, we handle them ourselves." April's face had the look of defeat on it. She knew it was two against one and we meant business. She stood up, walked over to us and held out her fist.

"I never liked the bitch anyway. Let's get her!" she screamed.

The entire campus was hype because we were less than a week away from Homecoming and our football team was undefeated. There were rumors going around that L.L. Cool J. was scheduled to attend the festivities and perform free one of the nights. Quintin was busy screening new pledges for his fraternity that he barely had time left for me. I helped him or rather did his paper on What America Owe's African Decents. I barely had time to research my paper for Proffesor Phillips's class. It was for a good cause so I didn't mind doing it for him. I would just have to ask the Proffesor for an extention. He would do it for me. After all he did tell me to call him if I ran into any problems. He answered the telephone on the first ring.

"Hello, Professor Phillips speaking."

"Hello Professor. This is Katrina Richards and I need to ask you a big favor."

"Ah yes, Ms. Richards. What is it that you need?"

"Well, I haven't had much time to do research on my paper so I was wondering if I could turn it in a week late?" Bad news; he was taking too long to answer.

"You say a week, huh? No. But I will be more than happy to give you some vital information on the subject you are researching."

"Okay, when?"

"How about now? If you're not to busy that is." I knew it was a catch. He was trying to get me over to his house and he knew I was desperate. I had to go or else flunk his class and I had come so far. Maybe April can go with me. Then he can't make any passes at me. He gave me the directions to his place and I told him I would be there in about an hour. When April came out the shower, I asked her if she would come with me to his house.

"Sorry Ms. Kitty, but I promised Rakeem that I would meet him in the library to help him with his research paper. I can give you a lift, though."

I started changing my clothes and we headed out. I was so nervous. What would I do if he tried to rape me? There would be no one around to hear my cries for help. I guess the men win again. We followed the directions he gave me to a beautiful house sitting on a steep hill. There was a black Land Rover parked outside in the front. I was starting to think it might be good if he did rape me. At least I would get paid. April pulled up behind the jeep and locked the doors with the power lock.

"April, what are you doing. Let me out." I said.

"Look, Professor Phillips is one of the meanest men I know. He has never invited a student over to his place or offered to help them. Now I don't know what you two have planned but you better watch out. Here's Olandis's pager number. Call him if anything goes wrong."

I took the tiny piece of paper and unlocked my door. She sped off before I had a chance to go to the door and make sure he was here. I climbed up the large steps, taking a deep breath with each step and rang the doorbell. He answered it with a huge smile across his face then motioned for me to come in. His house was beautiful. It looked like something out of Better Homes and Gardens. We walked down a large corridor to the den. It had hundreds of books lining the walls. There was a big screen television in the corner and a dark brown, leather sofa and matching loveseat. I decided to sit on the corner of the sofa so that he would have plenty of room where ever he chose to sit. I jumped up when I looked at the rug. There was a bear staring at me like he was about to attack. The Proffesor laughed at my stupidity.

"Ms. Richard's, he wont bite. He's been dead for 26 years now."

"I know. He just looks so mean, like he wants to wake up and eat me."

"Well, he tried to eat me and that's why he's a rug now."

"You mean you killed him? This bear that I'm looking at right now? Wow, you must be strong."

"I wouldn't say strong. All I had to do was pull the trigger. That doesn't require a lot of strength. I was out hunting deer one day and he just came up behind me out of nowhere. Scared me half to death. I aimed my rifle at him and shot. He didn't go down just yet, oh no, he was determined to get me, so I kept shooting until he fell; four feet in front of me. Since then I haven't been hunting."

"I've never done anything like that before in my life. I've never known any-one to hunt before. That's amazing!" I looked around his den and noticed the moose and deer heads over the fireplace. He had a picture of a beautiful lady sit-ting on the mantle. I walked over to it to get a better look. She was so pretty. She had long black hair like me and grey eyes. Her nose even pointed up at the tip like mine. She could almost pass for my twin but she was much older and white. I started to get scared. He must've noticed our resemblance and wanted me to take her place but what place is that. She had to be his wife or girlfriend. He saw me staring at the picture and started to talk.

"That's my sister. Wasn't she beautiful?"

"Why did you say wasn't?"

"She's deceased. Breast cancer. She died last year but I believe she died of a broken heart."

"Who was she in love with?"

"She didn't know." I could tell he didn't want me to ask anymore questions so I changed the subject.

"This is what I have so far. I know once I type it won't be half as long." I handed him the papers.

"You know you amaze me." he said.

"How so?"

"Well, you are making a B+ right now in my class and no student has ever earned higher than a C, and you are actually doing your own paper. Most of the students buy their papers from my previous students. It's only so many ways you can recycle a paper year after year and I get tired of reading the same thing over and over with a new word here and a coma there. Then they wonder why they receive a D+. When you called, I was worried that you haven't found someone to buy your paper from and you needed more time to look. I didn't want to give you a D+ so that's why I invited you here. Now I learned that you are not like the others, you have spunk. I knew the first day in class that you were smart and a very respectable young, lady. Your mother must be proud."

That last comment jarred my soul. My mother hated me. I was about to break down and tell him off but decided against it. He was too generous to take my personal problems out on and he didn't know her. It wasn't his fault that she was jealous of me and had a deep passion for men and money. I told him thankyou for the praise but we have a paper to finish.

I stayed over the Proffesor's house six hours before I realized it. He had cooked dinner and everything for me. We talked about April and Olandis, whom he said was a real character, and he told me about himself. He had been in love several times but never married. He just didn't find the right person to wear his last name. His hobbies included hunting, of course, swimming, fishing, and watching football. When it turned dark outside he demanded that he give me a ride back to the campus. He didn't want me catching the bus this late, especially as pretty as I was. I picked up my notes and followed him to his jeep. I was hoping no one saw me riding in the car with him. It could result in major trouble. He pulled up to my dorm and let me out. Thank God no one was out there.

"Ms. Richards I want to give you a proposition. I need a lab tech and I was wondering if you would do it? The pay is Okay, it would be considered work study. Don't give me an answer just yet, think about it."

"I'll do it. I could use the extra income."

He smiled and told me goodbye. He's not some mean old freak after all, just misunderstood.

When I walked up the hall I noticed that we had a new door. That April was good at getting the job done fast. I had to knock because my old key didn't fit. Olandis came to the door. I tried to contain my laughter but he looked like a black Dolly Parton with his curly blond wig. He shut the door back and started talking through it from the other side.

"I wonder if I should let you in. We peasants don't get to meet royalty every day and our poor little home is a mess."

"Olandis quit playing and open the door." I shouted.

"What's the magic word?" he said.

I don't believe this. I am too tired to play games. He really needs to grow up, this is my room.

"The magic word is I'm gonna kick yo' ass if you don't open this door."

The doorknob turned and finally, he opened it.

"No darling, there wont be any ass kicking here. I'm not Denise."

"So, how did it go?" April asked.

"He's great. He is a really nice man and he offered me a job."

"See I told you, April. Proffesor Pill' is not gonna invite you over for nothing. So what does he want you do Ms. Kitt, be his personal prostitute?"

"Now see you don't know a thing about him. He wants me to be his lab assistant."

"Hey, that sounds like fun and he needs one. I wonder why he never had an assistant before?" April said.

"Probably because he hasn't seen a girl like Ms. Kitty before. Can I get your autograph because you about to blow up!" He waved his hands over his head like he was making a rainbow. "Well people, I'm off. Chow." He grabbed his shoulder bag and left. I decided to type my paper since it was finished. April called Rakeem to tell him goodnight and went to bed. I'm not that good with a computer so it took me all night to finish. I had one hour to sleep before my early bird class with Proffesor Phillips.

He was glad to see me when I walked in. He began his lecture and told us since it was homecoming week, he would dismiss class early. The other students started whispering among each other with confusion. They were shocked because he never dismisses class early. It was like a tradition of his but traditions can be broken. He noticed that the whispering had gotten out of control so he told the class to settle down. After the room grew quiet he said, "Class Dismissed!" Nobody moved. They were dazed and afraid that it was a joke but when they saw him close his briefcase and head toward his office, they jumped up and ran out. I went to his office to see him.

"Hi, what was that all about?" I asked.

"It's Homecoming week. They should be out partying or what ever it is you all do these days."

"I wish I had known you were gonna dismiss class early. I could've caught some more zzz's."

"Well I'm glad you came. Remember, the early bird gets the worm."

"Yeah but I learned that the early bird goes to sleep early so he can get up to catch the worm. I stayed up until 5:30 this morning typing my paper." I let out a yawn.

"I hope you saved it on a disk."

"No. I didn't know how. I'm new with computers."

"Well I'll have to teach you. You have to know a little bit about computers in order to assist me."

"Speaking of which, when do I start?"

"When ever you're ready; although, I could use you tomorrow around one."

"One is good. My last class is at 12:00 tomorrow so I'll see you then."

He nodded his head for approval and I left. April and Olandis were walking out when I got to my room.

"What you doing back so soon?" Olandis asked.

"Oh, the Proffesor let us out early."

"What you say? Girl friend, you got to tell me your secret because you got that man going crazy. Come on and tell me, I can keep a secret."

"There is no secret. He's a really nice man. Don't believe the rumors, Olandis."

"Tell her the good news, Olandis." April said.

"I have just been nominated for Homecoming Queen! Were on our way now to the meeting." he said.

I thought that homecoming queens were women, full blooded women. There was no way on earth the President would allow this but I congratulated him any way and ran and jumped in my bed. I was fast asleep

in no time. I thought I was dreaming when I heard the fire alarm. Girls were screaming and running down the hall when I opened my door. I rushed outside with the rest of the crowd. After waiting outside for twenty minutes, they let us go back in. It was a false alarm. I forgot to lock my door during all the ruckus. It was wide open when I came back but nothing was missing out the room. Since it looked like I wasn't going to get any sleep around here I decided to edit my paper one more time and print it. I went through all the hand written steps April left by the computer for me and still I was doing something wrong. I couldn't find my paper. I know I saved it on here but its not here. I shut the computer down and tried again. Nothing? It was gone, deleted, wiped out; but how? Olandis never uses it and April hasn't had a chance to use it between now and last night. DENISE! She was the only suspect. The whole fire alarm was a scam! That's why my door was open because I know I slammed it shut when I ran out. I'll kill her. I don't want to type the whole thing over and part of my notes were in the trash. I rushed to retrieve them but someone had emptied the trash can. Oh she is good. Olandis needs to hurry and give me some payback material. My patience is wearing out again. I need to get some rest but I cant sleep. All I could do was think about how I would get her ass back. I couldn't beat her up again because I would get kicked out of school this time. It was lunch and I knew Olandis and April were in the cafeteria. I raced to the cafeteria hoping that they haven't left. They were sitting at a table with Rakeem , 'Head', and some other guys. The cafeteria was unusually packed today. April spotted me and waved for me to hurry up and sit with them. I walked through the crowded room to get to her. "I saved you a seat." she said.

"Whats up? Why are all these people here?" I asked.

"They are introducing the new pledges today. Shh, here they come."

A group of guys walked in wearing jeans and tee shirts with greek letters on them. I spotted Quintin in the bunch. Damn he looks good. He had his sleeves ripped off his shirt and his muscles were popping out. He looks so sexy like that. The guy from the carwash started to speak.

"I am Big Brother Almighty and when I speak, you listen. We have a group of chickens loose and I need your help. Bring them in Big Brother Shake and Bake."

One of the brothers went to the cafeteria door and opened it. In walked ten guys chained together wearing cut off jeans and shirts with feathers glued to them. They had beeks made out of toilet paper rolls on their nose. They lined up and stood at attention.

"We are here to serve you Big Brother Almighty!" one of the pledges said. Almighty told them to introduce the fraternity. They started stomping their boots in time with each other and the chains clanked to make an instrument sound. The audience clapped to the beat and they began to chant.

"Blurr, it's cold in here. It must be some Mu Si's in the atmosphere. I said blurr, it's cold in here. It must be some Mu Si's in the atmosphere. Why must you hate on us? Were just too fine and don't give a fuck I said why is your girl sweating me? Probably because you got a little wee, wee! She said, Whomp, where is, Whomp where is, Whomp, were is, Where is it?"

They turned around and started marching out singing to the army boot camp tune.

"I don't know but I been told. Mu Si fraternity heals the soul. I don't know what you have heard. But we don't take pussies and nerds. Sound off. One, two. Sound off. Three four. Sound off, one, two, three, four. "

Everybody in the room clapped and cheered. They put on a good show. Now it was time to get down to business. I turned to ask Olandis for help but he started talking first.

"Okay, people. What have we got?"

"I say we start a petition." Rakeem answered.

"Yeah. It was the student body that voted for you in the first place so it will be easy to get a thousand signatures." April agreed.

"Wait a minute," I said, "What's going on?" Olandis started telling me about the homecoming meeting.

"That bitch, Denise knows I'll beat her in Homecoming so she's protesting it. She sent a letter to the Dean saying that men can't run for Homecoming

Queen. I don't know how she got nominated anyway. No one can stand her but her little sorority witches. They need to get on their brooms and fly away."

I knew that Olandis would really kill her if he knew what she did to my paper. We would scheme together later when he was calm. Rakeem said he would get started on the petition today. We didn't have long since Homecoming was Saturday, five days away. We all left with a mission, to get revenge on Miss Denise.

I reported to the Professor's office promptly at one o'clock. He was waiting for me to get there.

"Ms. Richards, the first thing I need for you to do is make 100 copies of this. The copier is across the hall. Then I need you to move the glass bottles off the science tables and place them back on the shelf. Lock up when you finish. I have to go to a meeting so I won't be back."

I was sort of disappointed that he was leaving but I would be finished in no time. I didn't want to stay here by myself. I thought he had something important for me to do. I copied the papers and put the bottles up in less than an hour. I decided to wipe the tables off, too, since I had time. The skeleton in the corner looked like he was staring at me. I walked over to it and gave it a shove. "You want a piece of me? Huh? I didn't think so. Ill bring you back to life just to beat you up!" It continued to stare at me. Just then a male voice said hey. I thought I was loosing my mind until I turned around to see Quintin standing there.

"Hey, boo." I walked over to him and gave him a kiss.

"What are you doing?" he asked.

"Oh, I'm doing some work for the professor. He hired me as his assistant." Quintin went to sit on one of the tables. He was trying to process what I said. "You work for the professor? He never lets anyone in here when its not class time."

"Well now he does." I walked by him and he grabbed my arm, bringing me closer to him. He looked in my eyes like he was trying to see if I was telling the truth then he kissed me. He picked me up and threw me on the cold table. He jumped on top of it with me and unbuttoned my shirt. He bent down and kissed my breast. I felt his hand lift up my skirt and slide off my panties. He pulled down his zipper and immediately we were on a roller coaster ride to Pleasure Island. When we finished, he jumped off the table, zipped his pants and left. My back was hurt because the table was so hard and every time I tried to move, the pain would increase. I thought the pain would never ease up and I would hate for someone to walk by and see me like this, so I wrapped my panties in my hand and slowly walked home. I love the freaky side of him, even if it is painful.

Denise and one of her friends were sitting in the lounge of our dorm. I tried to sneak by her without her noticing me. I was not in the mood for games and she probably would win this time because my back was still sore. Her little friend noticed me and pointed her finger toward me. Denise turned around in her chair and rolled her eyes. Then I noticed she was wearing one of my shirts! The nerve of this girl to break in my room and boldly wear my clothes. I looked around to see if the dorm supervisor was in her office. Since she wasn't there, I took it upon myself to say something.

"Um, Denise. You should've told me that you didn't have money to buy your own clothes."

"I don't have to worry about buying my clothes. My man buys them for me." She said.

"Well whoever your monster, oops I mean man is, tell him not to shop in my closet." I gave my best strut away from her, despite the back pain. I could feel the warmth and softness of my bed before I reached the door. I limped inside and went to my bed. It felt like heaven. I must have pulled a muscle or found one I didn't know I had because the pain was still there.

"What's wrong?" April asked.

"I don't know. My back hurts like hell."

She began rumbling through the cabinet and put a coffee mug in the microwave. When the bell sounded, she opened the microwave door and dropped two tea bags in the mug.

"Here, drink this." She said handing me the hot cup of tea.

"What is it?"

"Something for your back."

Now I grew up in the baddest neighborhood there is. I've seen all kinds of fights, stabbings, and gun shot wounds. I have had three abortions. Not one time did the doctor give tea for pain. I mean, what is so special about this tea? I took a small sip of the hot drink. It was awful! She told me to hold my nose and gulp it down. I would do anything at this point to ease the pain. I felt real dreary after I drank it all and before I knew it I was asleep.

"Cold beans and collard greens! Cold beans and collard greens! Cold beans and collard greens!"

What is going on? What time is it? I looked over at my clock. It was 5:45 p.m. The noise was coming from my window. I opened the blind and saw Olandis and Rakeem standing on the steps with about 300 other students. There was an older bald head man standing with them. He told the crowd to go home. They started shouting, Hell no we wont go! Hell no we wont go! Rakeem raised his hands to simmer them down then he began to speak.

"We want to thank all of you for your support and encouragement but please don't get your self in trouble over a stupid college tradition. I thought Homecoming was for the students, not the Dean and the President, but now I see that it's all about making money. Since Homecoming is not for us to pick the student of our choice then we won't be in attendance! Dr. Kendall, you will not use the student body of this college this time. We will not walk around and smile for the cameras or greet all the guests that you are so afraid of. You will have to make your money some other way." The crowd started cheering. Dr. Kendall was about to speak when April pushed through the crowd. She had a manila folder in her hands.

"Dr. Kendall, I have the bylaws for this school's homecoming procedures. I have read this book from front to back and nowhere does it state that a man can't be on the homecoming court. Since you don't have time to change it and get the approval of the board, you have to let Olandis run for homecoming queen, I mean king." Every body waited for his decision. The tension was high. Dr. Kendall wiped his bald head with a handkerchief and said, "You win." He walked off the steps and got into his Cadillac. Olandis waved to the crowd and shouted, "Dinner on Rakeem. Meet at the Pizza House!" Rakeem gave him a slight punch on the arm. I felt a rush of excitement overwhelm me as I ran out my room to find Olandis. He had won more than just being a part of the homecoming ceremonies. He won the power of exceptance from society. He had won the freedom to be who he is and not have to change or walk around in silence and fear. Everyone loves him for him, for his personality. Denise is one person but she represents a multitude of people who are prejudice in this world. I wish we could wipe out all the haters who can't adjust to change or different lifestyles. I mean there is not a prejudice bone in his body. His best friend is white, he doesn't hate heterosexual people no matter how bad they mistreat him and he would give his heart and soul to anyone that asked. I met him walking up the hall and I ran and jumped in his arms. He swung me around and shouted, "It's hard to keep good man down, especially one in heels!"

April grabbed her purse and keys from the room and we headed to the Pizza House.

"So, I have won this battle but Denise is not gonna get off this easy." Olandis confirmed. Now was the right time to break the news to him. "Well, we almost had another confrontation today."

"Today? When did this happen? You've been sleep all day," said April.

"It was before I went to sleep. Can you believe she was wearing one of my shirts!"

"Your shirt! Ah, can you believe that today is Thursday?" Olandis asked. Damn, talk about an eye opener. What was in that tea April gave me?

"Oh, It looks like Ms. Kitty cant hold her tea. I warned April never to give me that mess again. Dewayne thought I was dead. He made funeral arrangements and everything."

"I need to call Proffesor Phillips. He might think I didn't show up on purpose." I said.

"He already called around one. I told him you were sick but you would be in tomorrow. He asked if there was anything he should bring over and he sounded worried but I told him that it was just a stomach virus. He said he hopes you feel better." April replied.

"Thanks for covering for me."

"My, my, my. The professor calling a student? He must be cookoo for cocoa puffs!"

I hurried to change the subject because Olandis could get pretty bold.

"Anyway let's get back to the main subject. What are we gonna do to Denise?"

Everyone thought for a minute then suddenly Olandis snapped his fingers and said , "I got it! Why don't we send her a good luck basket only it won't be from us, it will be from the student body counsel."

"Olandis why would we send her a good luck basket? We don't won't her to win."

"No April, damn. You don't get it. We can fix up a basket with laxitives in the cookies and peroxide in the shampoo." April looked worried. I thought she wasn't going to agree until she said, "You're gonna kill her, lets do it!"

When we arrived at the Pizza House, everyone rushed to the car to shake Olandis's hand. They were hugging him and wishing him good luck. He didn't need luck. His popularity had already beat Denise's. Someone put a dollar in the disk changer and the crowd started dancing. When they ran out of room on the floor, they climbed the tables and counter and began dancing on them. The owner came out finally after two tables were broken and made everyone leave before he called the cops. A middle aged couple with two small kids got stuck with the bill.

The next day, Olandis walked in our room wearing an apron that read, Kiss The Cook. He had on big oven mitts and was carrying a tray full of chocolate chip cookies. I was tempted to eat one but I knew they were laced with X' Lax. I started laughing uncontrollably.

"Ms. Kitty, you aint nothing but the devil," he said.

"No you're the one. Maybe we should hide all the toilet tissue in the supply room." I informed.

"Y'all are mean." replied April. She poured peroxide in a shampoo bottle and shook it up. Then she pulled a beautiful, white basket out of a shopping bag. She began stuffing it with pink tissue paper. I helped Olandis wrap the cookies in clear cellophane paper and placed them neatly in the basket. April took some grapes and bananas out the mini refridgerator and put them in the basket, too. Then she placed the contaminated shampoo and conditioner beside the fruit arrangement. Olandis began to hum a tune. He sounded outstanding.

"I didn't know you could sing, Olandis." I said.

April replied, "He use to direct his church choir and the school's gospel choir."

April stopped working and looked up at Olandis. "Im sorry." she said with sadness in her voice.

"No, girl. It's not your fault. Those wanna be Christians will not make it in the Pearly Gates with all that hatred in their hearts. They may have kicked me out their choirs but I'll be the one on the other side of the fence waving bye to them as Satan pulls them away."

"I take you got kicked off because of your homosexuality?"

"Yeah, but who are they to judge. Only God can judge me! The very ones so against me were the same ones that partied and drank all Saturday night and didn't bother to change their clothes for Sunday service. They would just leave the club and walk right into church. You couldn't tell if they had the Holy Ghost or got confused and thought they were still on the club's dance floor."

"That's deep. You have a great voice and that shouldn't stop you from singing." I said.

"Oh, I still sing. Just not in public."

We added the finishing touches to our basket and put pink, curly ribbons on the handle. April signed, Best wishes from your Student Counsel, on a card and taped it on top. We sat back and admired our work. Olandis began to sing his favorite gospel song.

"They said I wouldn't make it. They said I wouldn't be here today. They said I would never amount to anything. But I'm glad to say, that I'm on my way. I ain't going nowhere I'm here to stay. Now there were many that started out with me, but now they've gone astray. But I'm still holding on, Lord I'm still holding on to his.. ha…." We embraced him while he cried. "Okay, enough with the mushy stuff, we have a delivery to make."

I told them I would do the honor since I had to leave for work study. I grabbed the fabulous basket and walked out the door. Olandis stopped me and shouted, "May the force be with you!"

I tiptoed on Denise's hall and stood near her door. I could hear music and laughter coming from her room. She said something about Olandis and a float. I better be sure to warn him that she's up to something. I dropped the basket and ran around the corner. I waited to see if someone would open her door. I wanted to make sure she got that basket. I started to walk back to her door and knock on it but then I heard it open. One of her friends called her and picked it up. I heard Denise say, "This is so sweet. They know who the better Homecoming Queen is!" I smiled and thought better at what, toilet training?

"Hello, Ms. Richards. I hope you're feeling better today." Proffesor Phillips said when I arrived for work, if that's what you want to call it.

"Yes sir. I feel one hundred percent better."

"Well, I don't have much for you to do today. I forgot to tell your roommate that I didn't need your service but then I realized that you had to come in."

"Why did I have to come in?"

"Because today is payday. Don't spend it all in one place."

He handed me a crisp, one hundred dollar bill. I felt kind of bad taking it because I really haven't done much work. Infact, I had only worked three days.

"Um, Professor, why am I getting paid now? I mean I just started." I asked.

"Well, I know that this is Homecoming Week and you unselfishly gave up your time for me. I don't wont you to not enjoy this weekend because of financial situations."

"Well the least you could do is come to the game with me. My treat." I don't know what possesed me to say that. I just feel bad taking his money. I use to love to take money from men but now it feels different, dishonest.

"I would be delighted to go with you. I have never been to a football game here. Um, tell me what should I wear?" I must be losing my mind because one minute I'm in his office and the next minute, I'm riding to the mall with him. I feel secure when I'm around him. I don't feel pressured to impress or tempt him like I usually feel when I'm with a man. I found a hip hop store and drug him inside. Everything I picked out for him to try on looked funny. We finally settled on some baggy jeans and an army green, lambs wool turtleneck. He thought he was so fly. I told him his outfit wouldn't be complete without the right shoes. His taste improved because he picked out some nice leather boots. We stopped in the food court and ate. I almost forgot that I was supposed to meet April for the step show tonight so we hurried and finished eating. He dropped me off back at the dorm and told me he would meet me tomorrow at the main gate before kickoff. This time I didn't care who saw us, they could kiss my ass.

The step show was held in the gym. It was so hot that Olandis took off his short cut wig and started fanning himself. April motioned for him to stop but he rolled his eyes and continued fanning. He was having a serious conversation with a guy I've never seen before. The lights went out and 'Atomic Dog' began to play. Now those brothers are fine. I wonder where they've been hiding all this time? April informed me that they were from another school. They were last year's winners for the show. I can see why. I need to get at least one of their numbers. It's always good to have outside contacts. They made a hard act to follow but when I spotted my boo, I knew nobody could beat him. Just watching him stomp and glide across the floor made me horny. Then I realized he hasn't called to check on me. He never calls, lately he just shows up whenever he's ready. What about my needs? I must definitely have to get with one of those out of town guys, now. I could use a getaway and Mr. Quintin would never know. They ended their routine and Denise and her sorority were next. If my vision is correct, I could have sworn I saw Quintin kiss her when she walked by. Nah, she kissed him. He would never put his lips on something foul. I wanted to get down there and slap her but I knew my revenge was coming. I pray that she ate those cookies, give them time to digest.

Denise was shaking her tail and slinging her hair like a wild bull at the rodeo. I laughed when I thought about her shampooing her hair. I wonder what color it will be by tomorrow? After the last team competed, they announced the winners. Quintin and his fraternity came in last and he was real upset. I started to run and comfort him until I saw him hugging Denise and another one of her friends. I'm glad they lost. Now I'm determined to meet one of those other guys from out of town. I walked but them with my breast up and butt out. They noticed me because I heard one of them say, "Damn man, she is fine." I turned around to give them my seductive look and I zeroed in on the one I wanted. He was handsome. Tall, built with caramel colored skin. His hair was jet black with silky curls locked on the top of his clean cut head. He had the most gorgeous slanted eyes and lips that looked like they were drawn on his face. He nodded his head at me. I smiled and winked at him. He whispered something to his friend and walked my way. His friend looked jealous and even gave me an evil look, I guess for not picking him.

"Hi," he said.

"Hi," I said back to him.

"So do you go to school here or did you come up to watch us punish the other fraternity?"

"I go to school here. Where are you from?"

"Up north at State. It's about two hours from here." Yes. Hooray. This is perfect, a two hour getaway.

"So you drove all the way down here. I hope I was worth it."

"Oh yeah, you were well worth the trip. I would drive anywhere you are."

"Is that so? Well, why don't you drive back next weekend and show me around State. I may want to change schools next semester if I see something I want."

"You may not get to see much of State if you wear those leather pants next weekend."

"Is that a threat or promise?" I loved flirting.

"I always keep my promises."

"How can you keep that promise if you cant call me?"

He told me to hold on as he walked back to 'jealous man' and retrieved a napkin and pen. "What's the digit's?"

"879- 0428."

"When should I call. I don't want your man to answer the phone."

"Oh, don't worry about him. All this has got him whipped. You can call me anytime." I patted my vagina.

"Hmmm, I want to be whipped, too!"

"I'll be sure to pack my belt!"

"See you then, umm......"

"Ms. Kitty." His smile widened when I said my name. I breathed real heavily between the Ms. and the Kitty. Oh boy was he gonna have a tough ride home after flirting with me. He may need to find a restroom and handle his business.

"Yo, Ms. Kitty, come here!" It was Quintin. He was standing with some of his frat brothers. April told me to come on with her. She knew he was already mad because they lost the Step Off. So what. I had to show him that he doesn't own me. I am not afraid of him or his little posse. I strolled over to him and stood directly in his face, eye to eye. "Yo, who tha' fuck was that nigga you were talking to?"

"That's really none of your business but if you must know, he's from my neighborhood. We grew up together and I haven't seen him in years."

"Oh, so you couldn't introduce me? Girl, you better check yourself before I have to put my foot up your ass!" His what! Did he just threaten me? Well, he must care about me to be this angry. Now he's got me all horny. Maybe I can skip the after party and have a party of my own with him. The best sex is mad sex and right about now he is mad as hell. I decided to persuade him with my idea but he walked off. I called out his name and he kept walking. I guess now I will have to dance some of this energy out of me. April and Rakeem were outside kissing passionately by her car. She gave me the keys and told me to go on to the party. I guess tonight is finally the night!

I have a car, money, and dressed to the max with nowhere to go. I thought about riding up to State but I know I will get lost. I can't go to Quintin's dorm and see him. All the restaurants were closed and I'm tired of going to parties and looking at the same people. I realized how small this town is. I drove around trying to think of something to do when I ran across an old house. It was packed with people, an older crowd. The men were -dressed to impress and you could tell they had money. I decided to check the place out. I need a Sugar Daddy to take of me while I'm here. College guys had it going on in the sex department but financially they were week. If I had a Sugar Daddy, all I had to do was play with him until he fell asleep and take his money. I walked inside the old juke joint and said to myself, "this is going to be easy." All the women looked like worn out whores and immediately gave me evil looks. I knew I was bold to step up in unknown territory with out backup but I didn't care. I was on a mission and they were out for the

same thing, men's money. I heard a lot of noise coming from the back of the house. I peeked in the door to see five men sitting around a table and a woman at the head. They were playing craps at twohundred dollars a game. The way things looked, the woman was winning because she had a stack of money in front of her. Her fingers were covered in diamonds and she wore a black sequined jacket with crepe black pants. She stood up and said, "game" and the men threw their cards down. One of the men said I'm out and pushed his chair back to stand up. The woman leaned back in her chair, lit a cigarette, and said, "Next time, bring more money." The old man put on his hat and walked right pass me. I followed him to the bar. After he ordered a whiskey sour, I went over and sat next to him. He noticed me because he turned around on his barstool and whispered in my ear, "Can I buy you a drink?"

"That depends on if you have any money left," I replied. He ordered me a rum and coke.

"So what's a pretty young thing like you doing in a place like this?" he asked.

"Looking for you. You don't mind do you?"

"No. Do you mind me asking your name?" I took a sip of my drink and it burned my throat. It must have been the original Moonshine! I coughed a little when I started to talk. "Ms. Kitty. And you?"

"John."

"Well John, thanks for the drink. I have to go." I picked up the keys to the Beamer' and

walked out the door. Of course he followed me to the car. I planned it that way. I wanted him to see that I was expensive and it would take a lot of his money to keep me happy. He opened the car door for me but before I got in I gave him the napkin with my number already written on it (I said I was on a mission) and told him to call me. All of a sudden, a big, beat up Lincoln whipped in front of me. A big, burly woman stepped out wearing a housecoat and slippers. She had a butcher knife in her hand and she began walking to us waving it every step of the way. I feared for my life. John told me to get in the car and go but I was too scared to move. I froze. He walked up to her and tried to hold her back but she was too big and strong. She started yelling at me or at him, I couldn't understand what she was saying.

"So is this the woman you been sleeping around with, giving all my hard earned money to? Huh?" she demanded to know.

"No Lucille, baby. I was just giving her directions. She stopped in because she's lost. That's all."

"You lying fucker. I ought to cut ya right now! Betty done called me up here to see for myself. She said you was at the bar with her buying drinks now I want the truth, dammit!"

"I told you the truth."

"You probably bought her that car she in. Got me driving around in this beat up ole thang while she driving a nice car. A BMW at that! I got a good mind to take it since I'm the one done bought it."

Shit! I cant let her do anything to April's car but no one was trying to stop her. A crowd of people had formed around to see the action. I couldn't back down now. Where I'm from, people don't disrespect you and get away with it. She got next to the car and began scratching it with the knife. She was a lot of woman so my first lick would have to be powerful. Pow! Right in the nose. She didn't even feel it. She grabbed me by the neck and lifted me off the ground saying, "Ill show you little hussy's not to mess with my man!" She raised her fist back to punch me, then I heard the gun shot. I thought I was dead when she dropped me to the ground. It was the woman from the card game. She had raised her gun in the air and shot to get Lucille's attention.

"Go on home, Lucille. This gal don't want John's little shriveled up dick and the reason he aint got no money is because he don't know how to play cards! You need to whip his ass for those sorry games he plays."

"You think your gun takes care of everything. Well not here, sister. You can get in line behind this slut for your beating!" Lucille was going to kill me. If the card lady couldn't stop her, nobody could.

"Look here, I run a straight house and you or anybody else is not gonna ruin my reputation. Now if you don't leave I'll be forced to put the law on you."

"Well put the law on me then cause' I ain't leaving till' I'm good and ready and I won't be ready till' I kick her ass!"

'Card Lady' aimed the gun at Lucille and pulled the trigger, shooting her in the kneecap. She fell hard and fast grabbing her knee shouting, "You crazy bitch!" 'Card lady' lit her cigarette, walked over to her, held out the gun and said, "Lucille, meet the law!"

She took a puff on her cigarette and walked back in the house. I jumped in the car and 'put the pedal to the metal'. I was doing 95 mph trying to get home before Lucille got up. I hope she doesn't call the cops to come looking for me, how would I explain it to April and Olandis? I knew April was over to Rakeem's and I was a nervous wreck, too scared to go to my room, so I decided to go to Olandis's room. His policy is, my door is always open, literally. He believes that anyone can crash in his room as long as they clean it when they leave. It's never locked and no one would even think about stealing from him, they wouldn't want to risk the embarrassing drama. I walked in and climbed up the bed shaped like a hand. I felt like the hand was lifting me off the ground trying to keep my spirits up. In less than a year I had turned my life into one giant fiasco! I fell asleep hoping and praying that when I awake, things were gonna change, for the better.

Loud music was blaring from Olandis's surround sound system. The speakers had to have been the size they use for outdoor concerts. They were so loud the windows rattled. I jumped up banging my head on his ceiling, I forgot how high his bed is. I started shouting for him to turn the volume down but I don't think he could hear me. I was about to get up to do it myself until I heard the water in his bathroom stop. He appeared in the room like he was the Queen of Sheba or somebody. He had green gook all over his face and a plastic shower cap on his head. He started singing into a toothbrush like it was a microphone. "She wants to leave, the glamorous life, she doesn't need a man's touch, Woa, baby yeah, without love, it aint much, leeaave! Hmmm, Hmmm." He danced around the room with that toothbrush like he was a diva on stage. I thought he was finished when that song ended but Kiss began to play by Prince. I pulled the pillow over my face and screamed. I know he probably has this song recorded ten times on the tape. He was running around the room licking his fingers and rolling them across his chest singing in a very high pitched voice. He stopped in the middle of the floor and put two fingers over his eyes while he shook his butt. Now was the big finale. He climbed up to the side of the bed and shouted, "I just want your extra time and your KISS !" He puckered his lips up to my face like a monkey.

"You really got a lot of time on your hands," I said.

"Good morning to you too, love. I just gave you my best performance and that's all you can say!"

"You need to use that toothbrush for more than just singing."

"Well, who pissed in your cornflakes this beautiful morning? Maybe you need to go to the litter box Ms. Kitty, then you'll feel better."

"I'm just tripping with you Olandis but I do want to know what is that green stuff all over your face?

"Oh, I almost forgot. It's time for me to take it off. It's my mask and if I leave it on too long, uh child, you talk about burning." He rushed in the bathroom to get a towel. When he came back in the room, he was brushing a wet hairpiece. "I had to recycle this weave honey. I cant go out on that football field looking like trash. Weave seems to hold up better under pressure than wigs and they give a more natural look."

I hope he doesn't quiz me on the difference between fake hair and real hair, I will fail. He opened his closet and asked me to come and help him pull a large trunk out. I was too scared to ask what was in it. Knowing Olandis, he could have a body in there.

"I normally don't let anyone in on my secrets but in case you talk too much, I wrote a contract for you to sign." He handed me a piece of paper that read, I _____ hearby swear to never tell a soul about the Beauty Box. Sworn to me on this date. He was actually serious and I was curious so I signed the damn thing.

"Okay Ms. Kitty, here goes the greatest secrets to mankind." The trunk was full of deodorant, baby powder, perfume and lotion sets, shaving cream, shaving gel, weave, hair glue, fingernail polish, false nails, G- strings, videos, chocolate cream, hair spray, combs and brushes, batteries, curlers, blow dryers, shampoo, conditioner, makeup, false eyelashes, and the list goes on and on and on.

"Damn! Victoria's Secret aint got a thing on your secret's!" I replied.

"I pull out the box for special occasions, only."

"Oh yeah, I overheard Denise talking yesterday. She was saying something about you and a float."

"She must've been talking about the float for the parade but don't worry. I wasn't getting on that thing anyway. I like to step out in style and riding on some box with wheels is not for me. I get motion sickness in an old car. Look in there and hand me that lotion." I found it and gave it to him. He applied it then reapplied it. "What are you doing?" I asked.

"You know the technique. You have to layer yourself in case the stuff wears off and leaves you stinking. Honey, I was in class one time and somebody forgot the PTA."

"What's the PTA?"

"Pussy, tits and arm pits! That classroom smelled so bad that I thought we were having a hot dog and fish sale. I said Damn, who brought onions to class today? After that whoever it was started washing in the morning or rather did the PTA. I know her man didn't go downtown too often. If he did he should've came back with a douche!"

I laughed so hard I fell out the bed! He took the blow dryer out the trunk and began drying the hair extentions. He sprayed some hair spray on them and plugged in his curlers. I looked in his closet for something to wear. He had a sweater about the same color as the professor's so I decided to wear it, so we wouldn't clash. Olandis didn't mind. He said, "Me casa is you casa," whatever that means. I went to take my shower, he was not going to talk about me, when the phone rang. I picked it up but before I could say hello he grabbed it out my hands and put his hand over the receiver.

"What is wrong with you? When I said me casa is you casa you took it seriously now scoot and don't answer the phone here. You and that little white gal just alike." He cleared his throat and said," Speak to me," in the phone. I retreated to the bathroom and I could hear him say what are ya'll, the bopsy twins? He came in and told me that it was April and she said to leave the car parked here and she would meet me at the main gate for the game. I didn't ask if she was still with Rakeem, she may not want Olandis to know. I finished in the bathroom and opened the door letting fog expel into his room.

"What the hell are you trying to do? Close that door before my curls fall out." He had put the weaves in and curled it in no time. It was tight, too; an asymmetric bob with a long piece over his eye. I wonder what Denise looks like right about now? He pulled out some foundation and powder that perfectly matched his complexion and applied it to his face with a cotton ball. I asked him if he would curl my hair, give me some ringlets.

"All you got to do is wet your hair and you'll have curls. If I had hair like you I wouldn't need weave but the Lord didn't bless us all. In fact, he didn't bless black people at all with this type of hair. You must have some cross breeding in your family."

I thought about what he said. I really didn't know. I mean there was a whole half of me that knew nothing about that side. My mom never talked about my father or his family and when I asked she would say he's a sorry excuse for a man and I'm better off without him. I wondered if she meant me or her. I didn't miss him, how could you miss someone you never met. What would you miss about them? Why would I miss someone that never called to say hi, even if there was no face to the voice. I guess she is right after all, he was a sorry excuse for a man to hate someone he never laid eye's on. Olandis announced that he was finished and held a mirror up for me to see his masterpiece. It was beautiful. I looked like an angel, seriously. I told him to spray lots of holding spray on it because I didn't want it to fall. I wish Quintin was here to see me now.

"Okay now that youre done get out the way." He shoved me to the side and started back with his beauty regiment. He stood up when he finished and asked , "How do I look?" He really looked good, I was jealous. I would have some mean competition if he were a woman.

"Now before I go I must do one last important thing. The Breath Test. Where did I put that breath spray? Oh here it is. I wonder why April has it on her keys." At that instant I looked around to see what he was talking about but it was too late.

"No! That's mase!" My eyes were already starting to burn. Olandis rushed to the sink and stuck his mouth under it.

"Oh. Oh, Lawd Jesus, my mouth, shit, my mouth is blazing! Please have mercy on me. Oh, Kitty Oh, Got damnmit. Look at my lips, look at my lips are they big? Just please don't let me have big lips! Tell me Ms. Kitty are they purple or blue?"

"Olandis, be quiet and let the water run in your mouth!" I was standing by the sink with him, beating his back and praying that we don't have to make a trip to the hospital. Where is April? My eyes were stinging and I know they were red by now but he only had one sink and I couldn't flush them with water so I held the wet towel on them. Ahh, this feels good. I thought about the old fable, See no evil, Speak no evil. We were living it in living color right about now.

"How does it feel now, Olandis?" I asked. I couldn't see him with the towel over my eyes and when he didn't answer, I panicked. I immediately removed the towel thinking he had drowned or passed out. He was sitting on the toilet holding his false eyelashes in his hand. His hair was flat against his head, wet, and his makeup had run down his face on his shirt leaving mocha colored stains.

"Oh dear, what am I gonna do? The game starts in less than an hour," he said.

"You still have time. You don't have to be there until halftime and it doesn't take you long to do your hair."

"I guess you're right. Let me start on this hair again."

"Can I do anything to help?"

"Yes. You can leave, now go on and get to the game. I need somebody there to cheer for me. And take pictures when I get my crown!"

I felt bad leaving him but I knew he meant it. I gave him a good luck kiss on his cheek and left him sitting in front of his vanity mirror taking out the wet hair pieces. It could only happen to Olandis I thought as I walked to the football stadium. The place was so crowded that finding the professor would be like trying to find a needle in a hay stack. Oh well, I'll just stand at the main gate and maybe he will show up and find me. I could hear the drums beating from the marching band. The sound was getting closer and closeruntil I could see shiny instruments and uniforms. The dancers were in the front leading the band up the hill and every five steps, they would stop and do a two step. It will take them forever to get up that hill and in the stadium with all that stopping and dancing. Their costumes were beautiful, silver and royal blue midriffs with matching short skirts. They had sequins on the ends of the sheer sleeves and a sequined head band that held back a lot of long hair. I knew it was weeve after my cosmetology class with Olandis. I wanted to be one of those girls, dancing and shaking my stuff with barely anything on. They looked like they were having so much fun. I could see the bright flags flying in the air from the color guards. It was at least thirty of them. The band was gonna take up the entire stadium with their two hundred members and no one would be able to see around those big hats with the slinky tassel on top of them. Just then I saw a member out of uniform, no it was more like out of place. It was the professor. He was right in the middle of them, trying to march in time with them. He couldn't get out of their line because it would mess the whole formation up. He spotted me and waved with this goofy look on his face. I waved back to let him know that I see him. Then he tried to walk over to where I was standing but the band turned and marched a separate way. They were going onto the field! He ran up to where the dancers were and tried to scoot by them but it was time for them to do their five step break. I would have paid big money to have a picture of him trying to dance his way between the dancers. He had no rythym whatsoever. One of the girls stopped and rolled her eyes at him and he was finally able to escape. He ran back to where I was standing.

"I didn't know you were a band teacher also." I joked.

"Yeah, I have to do a little moonlighting." he replied. I spotted April standing by the concession stand looking around, I guess for me. I pulled the Professor with me to greet her. When she turned around she looked as though she was seeing a ghost. I introduced them and informed her that he would be sitting with us for the game. She was still in shock but she followed us to find a seat.

"Oh, Ms. Kitty, save a seat for Rakeem," she said as we walked down the steps to find our seats. Maybe she's coming around now. The shock of seeing the Professor must have scared everybody because the stadium got real quiet when we walked in. We sat down and the band started playing again. I didn't mean to sit this close to them especially after the dance episode but we would cause another scene if we moved now. Rakeem walked in with popcorn, drinks, a blanket, and a bucket of fried chicken. I don't know how he found his way down the steps carrying all that stuff. He sat down beside April and they snuggled under the covers, eating the chicken and popcorn. He offered me and the Professor a piece.

"Ooh, is that Mrs. Mable's fried chicken?" he asked to my surprise.

"Yep," Rakeem replied, "it's the only kind I eat. Mrs. Mable can burn, cant she?"

"Umm, hmm. Give me some of that chicken, son. I haven't had it in years."

Rakeem passed the bucket down to him. I couldn't believe he was at the football game eating chicken, and sitting with students, two of whom were black. We must've looked like the Adams Family. The band did the wave and everybody joined in. We waved so much that my arms got tired. I wanted to ask April about her sexual ordeal but Rakeem was sitting right where he could hear. I also needed to tell her about the little scratch on her car but I didn't know how. I would hate for her to get loud with me in front of all these people so I decided to wait until we were safely back in our room. The Professor and Rakeem jumped up hollering, TOUCHDOWN ! Our side of the stadium went wild. We were winning by 14 points.

"Would you like something to drink?" said Professor Phillips.

"No, I'm treating you, remember?" April looked over at me with a curious expression on her face.

"Well in that case, bring me a root beer," he replied. I told him I would and asked April to walk with me. She jumped up from under the blanket and made her way across everybody. I knew what she wanted, an explanation.

"Ms. Kitty, what is going on? You and him are not sleeping together, please tell me you aren't."

"We aren't. I invited him out of pity, he's never been to a game here before. He's a really sweet man, trust me." The guy behind the counter told me how much the drink cost and I handed him the 100 dollar bill. I saw April's eyes get as big as golf balls.

"Where did you get that much money from?"

"Workstudy, remember? Some of us do have to work, we don't have rich parents."

"For your information I did workstudy my first year and I never made a hundred dollars. You've only worked three days and you made that much, what kind of workstudy are you on?"

"I understand what you're saying but it's an advancement. He paid me more since this was homecoming. It won't always be this much."

We heard the announcer tell everyone to stay seated for the halftime show. I grabbed the drink and rushed back to our seats. The band was already on the field, playing and dancing. I could see the Homecoming Queen from last year and this years future hopefuls lining up with their escorts. Olandis was nowhere in site. I got nervous and started trying to explain to April what happened. She looked as though she was going to cry. Rakeem assured her that he would show up especially after all we went through to get him this far. The girls proceded to walk across the field and the crowd started cheering. Everyone kept looking around for Olandis, they even looked back at April to ask where was he. I saw Denise walking with an older man. She looked like she was crying and she had on a flannel hat. I saw pieces of red and blond hair underneath the hat. The man was trying to hold her up and make her walk but she could barely move. Then she ran off the field into one of the port-a-potties, leaving the man standing there wondering what to do. He eventually walked back up the steps into the stands. April and I gave each other a guilty look, then laughed. The two men looked at us like we were crazy. Dr. Kendal walked on the field when all the ladies finished lining up. They have to wait, give him more time. The announcer thanked everyone for supporting the college and coming out today. Come on Olandis, where are you. He continued telling the crowd of fans that the winner is chosen by their peers and faculty. Please Olandis, show up now. The announcer told who the second place winner is. She walked out to receive her roses and trophy. He announced the first runner up, Denise! She was still in the potty so the old man walked back out on the field to accept her awards. He began to announce the winner but he stopped and said, "What is that?"

We looked on the other end of the field and saw April's red B.M.W. pull up. Olandis drove the car as close to the band as he could then stepped out. His hair was braided into cornrows with a long ponytail hanging down the back. He had on dark sunglasses and, oh my God, a full length, black, Mink coat. He carried a black cane with a huge diamond at the tip. He modeled in front of the band and said, "Hit it!" They started the drum roll as he walked up to Dr. Kendall and said, "I think you have something that belongs to me." Dr. Kendall was outraged! They struggled back and forth with the crown until the announcer said, "And the winner is Olandis R. Johnson !" Dr. Kendall had a horrified look on his face, he refused to touch Olandis to crown him and he threw the trophy down. The band played 'Glamorous Life' and everyone screamed cheers of joy. The professor gave me a big hug before he realized it. The Queen from last year asked Olandis to bend down so she could crown him and kissed him on the cheek. He waved to the crowd and did a James Brown impersonation with his mink coat. The former queen laughed as she picked the coat back up and tried to wear it. He blew me and April kisses and we returned them. It was the happiest day of my life. I knew things were going to change for the better.

Seasons

"GOOD MORNING, ALL," Olandis said as he walked in our room carrying a basket of laundry and wearing a scarf over his hair. "Get up. We have things to do."

"Olandis, it's 7:00 a.m. What things do we have to do?" April drearily asked. She yawned and wiped the sleep out of her eyes.

"April, don't go there. You know this is exam season and we have to be prepared. Ms. Kitty, girl, this school goes into hibernation during exam season."

"What?" I didn't want to get up so early but I know Olandis knows his stuff and I want to be prepared too.

"Ladies, we have to buy groceries, hair and beauty supplies and wash enough clothes to last for six months. The cafeteria will close early because Mrs. Mable has to cook Thanksgiving dinner for all her grandbabies. I heard she got at least fifty now."

"He does have a point," April said, "Last year, all the stores and restaurants closed. It looked like ghost town around here." I thought about what I would do for the holidays. My Mom didn't want me back home, I could feel it. The way April and Olandis talked, they must not go home, either. I wish Quintin would invite me to his house for the holidays. If I met his mother, I know he must love me because only the special girls get to meet the parents. I wonder if his mother is nice. She can't be anything like mine, they broke the mold when they finished making her.

By the end of the day, our room was stocked full of potato chips, soda's, bread, cakes, and the famous college room meal, Oodles and Noodles! April informed us that her parents may stop by for Thanksgiving but she wasn't sure. I can't figure out why she would want to stay on campus with us when she probably has a mansion to go home to. Come to think of it, I've never heard her say much about her parents. She could have just as many problems in her life as me.

They probably bought her that car to reconcile their differences. They may not have wanted her to go to an all black college, they wanted her at some Ivy League school where she can meet a future doctor or lawyer, a white male. I wonder if they even know about Rakeem? They would freak out if they knew she dated a black man. I know my mom would think I had finally lost it if I started dating a white man. Then again, she may be excited, like I had just hit the lottery or something.

"So, Ms. Kitty, what are your plans?" April asked.

"Oh, I don't know. I was kind of hoping I could hang out with you guys," I said.

"No sweat my pet," Olandis said, "If April doesn't go with her parents then she can come too."

"Come where?"

"Ha, ha! Dewayne and I have a cabin for the weekend, the more the merrier!"

"I don't think Dewayne wants us to come," I replied, "That would kind of break the mood, don't you think?"

"Oh no. Dewayne loves company, especially during the holidays. He was a foster child and he never had a happy holiday so now he tries to make up for all those years he was alone."

"I didn't know that, Olandis. I will try to be there with you guys. Rakeem is flying back to Jamaica in the morning and he wont be back until January. I'm gonna miss him."

I couldn't help but wonder what he does or is over there. It's a different ballgame. He might have ten wives waiting on him hand and foot. I doubt his parents knew he was dating a white woman. They probably wouldn't let him in the country if they knew. April is my girl and everything but she is so gullible, she'll believe anything he says. The phone rang and Olandis ran to pick it up. I started to say something since he went off on me about his phone but then I realized that it was probably for him, we never get phone calls.

"May I ask whose calling?" he said. There was a brief moment of silence, then he started to smile. "Ton? Ooo, a ton of what if you don't mind me asking?"

Now Olandis was starting to piss me off! I wanted to know who was he joking with on our phone. He turned toward me and asked me if I knew a Ton.

"No, but give me the phone anyway." I struggled with him for the phone until he inally gave up and handed it over. "Hello," I said.

"Hello, is this Ms. Kitty?" a male voice asked.

"Yes, and who might this be?"

"This is Ton. I met you a couple of weeks ago, remember, the step show?"

"Oh yeah, I didn't get your name."

"Well, it's pronounced Ton but its spelled T. U. A. N. My mother is Vietnamese so she tried to keep a little of our culture in my name."

"Ohh, I like that. Tuan must mean strong and handsome."

"Oh really? Well I'd like to know what Ms. Kitty means."

I had laid down the flirt, now I'm going for the gold! "That's something you'll have to find out."

"Well, when can I see you?" Yes, he was fiendish for a taste of me.

"This weekend sounds nice, if you're not too busy." I waited for his reply hoping he wouldn't reject me.

"That's perfect. My roommates will be away so I'll have the whole place to myself. I'll pick you up Saturday around ten."

"Fine with me. I just hope I can wait that long to see you."

"You can see me in your dreams. Okay, tell me what dorm you're staying in."

I gave him all the vital info and we said our goodbyes like we were long lost lovers. When I hung up, April and Olandis were staring at me like I had lost my mind. Olandis started first. "Um, excuse me, Miss, what was that all about?"

"Oh that was Tuan, a good friend of mine. He invited me up to his place for the weekend."

"Well it sounds more like a booty call if you ask me."

"That's why I didn't ask you, Olandis."

"Look girl, you better be careful, running around here with God knows who! All I'm trying to.." April intervened saying, "Leave her alone, Olandis. She said he was a good friend of hers. We don't know all of Ms. Kitty's friends."

"Well, friend or foe, it sounds fishy to me!" he said. "I'm off, chow." He walked out leaving the door open. Why is he so worried about me? He sounds disappointed that I wont be spending Thanksgiving with him and his Dewayne. Sorry, Ms. Kitty has a life of her own and right now that is Tuan! I cant wait until Saturday morning. My two hour getaway has finally come. Bite my dust, Quintin!

No one showed up for the Professor's class the next day. I guess they knew they had failed the exam before they even took it. It wasn't too hard, just real tricky. When I finished, I walked to his office and turned it in. He graded it for me right then and believe it or not I passed with a C+.

"Congratulations," he said.

"Thanks. Now is there anything I can do for you today?"

"Yes, I need those books stocked on the shelves." I started right away because I needed to get back to my room and pack. I didn't want to leave anything out for my trip. I noticed the Professor was acting a little strange, quieter than usual. He looked as though he was about to cry.

"Is everything alright, Professor?" I yelled back in his office.

"Everything's fine." I could tell by the sound of his weak voice that everything was not fine but I decided to leave it alone. He may be homesick or something and I was not about to ruin my weekend with him, no way! He came out his office carrying a tiny present wrapped in gold paper. I wasn't prepared for this. What if he made me feel guilty about not spending Thanksgiving with him? I would have to think of a lie, quick.

"Ms. Richards, I got you a little something for being so patient and understanding with me. It has truly been a pleasure having you here, in my class." He said as he handed me the box. I opened it to find a white jewelry box with the little ballerina spinning to music as you open it. She was dancing to my favorite musical, Annie, and the tune playing was, 'Tomorrow'. I remembered back to when I was a little girl and wished I had a Daddy Warbucks who would take me away from my mom and adopt me. I knew the words so I started singing along, then I stopped. The Professor was about to cry so he asked me to leave and he would finish up. "Go on and enjoy your holiday. You deserve it and be ready for next semester." I grabbed the box and paper and left. I almost dropped a tear myself but once again, none would form.

As I walked up to my dorm I could see Denise putting Gucci bags in the trunk of a rented vehicle. She was finally leaving. Yes! The less I saw her face the better because I was ready to open another can of whoop ass on her. She spotted me and started grinning. I wonder what her little sneaky ass is up to? Then my question got answered because at that moment Quintin walked out the dorm with her last bag, threw it in the back seat and got in the driver's side of the car.

She climbed in beside him and gave him a big wet kiss on the cheek while looking at me the whole time. I was not going to let her get away with this so I walked closer to the car but Quintin pulled off like he didn't see me coming. I just stood there in the street watching them ride off together. She was the special girl, she had won. I opened my jewelry box and listened to the music play. That's okay, he'll come crying back to me and it will be too late. By then, Tuan and I will have hit it off and the sun will come out, tomorrow, betcha bottom dollar that tomorrow, they'll be sun!

April and Rakeem were on the bed when I walked in and they jumped up when they heard me.

"My bad, I'll just leave." I started shutting the door and walking out when April stopped me and told me that they were late to the airport. They both grabbed some luggage that was sitting by our door and ran out the room. "Come on Ms. Kitty!" she yelled. "You know I cant drive that well at the airport." She cant drive well anywhere, if you ask me, so I guess I do need to be a third wheel in this party. She let me drive or should I say chuffeur them to the airport. They sat in the back of the car and I could hear him saying something about locks. Oh, this is some heavy stuff, he cut a lock of his hair off and gave it to her to keep. He says he will always return safely to her as long as the hair is in her hands. Oh la la. So what. If they kiss one more time in that back seat I'm going to puke. We finally arrived at the airport thanks to signs and maps. If I had to depend on them to give me directions, I'd be lost by now. Rakeem checked his luggage in at the gate and walked with us the rest of the way. I was hoping we could go on and tell him goodbye right then but I knew April wasn't leaving until his plane left the ground. I hugged him and walked over to the snack bar, leaving them with time alone. I picked up a magazine and found a chair to relax in. I could see them in the middle of the airport kissing and hugging, her looking like Jan Brady and him looking like Bob Marley! People would walk by and stare, I guess thinking to themselves, what an odd couple.

"Hello," I looked from around my magazine to see who was distracting my thoughts. Damn! I didn't know that men this fine were still walking the earth. I was speechless. This brother had it going on and on and on. He continued to speak when he saw I couldn't move my lips.

"Um, I see you have the last Ebony magazine. Do you mind me reading it with you?"

I wouldn't mind him doing anything with me. I nodded my head and slid over so he could sit on the chair with me. He smelled so good that I could've licked him up right then and there. He had on a business suit and a tie. He started unloosening his tie and kicked his legs up on the coffee table making the chair wobble. I pretended to fall slightly on his chest and he grabbed me around my back.

"Whoa, don't fall off. I would hate to get sued for trying to read a magazine. So, what page are we on?" he asked. I had to talk. Get it together, now or else he was gonna think I'm mute.

"Page twenty um, Mr...?"

"Mr? I'm not that old am I ? You can call me Trent."

"Well Trent, what brings you to the airport. Do you dress up and come here to hit on pretty women?"

"No, not everyday. And yes, you are a pretty woman. Lovely I might add. But seriously, I'm flying from Dallas for my job." Alright, I like that; a man with a career. He must make lots of money because his suit is not cheap. I have to know what he does.

"So what do you do?"

"I'm a P.I. Private investegator. And you?"

"Oh, I'm a.." What should I say? I cant let him know I'm in college. "I'm a lab technician. You know, Chemistry, that sort of thing." It wasn't a lie. The lady on the loudspeaker announced that all gates leaving for Dallas were loading.

"Well, I guess that's my ride. Here, take my card and if you're ever in Texas look me up, but you don't have to wait until then." He picked up his suitcase and walked away, with the magazine. I felt it was an even exchange, his number for my magazine. Well their magazine, I didn't pay for it. April ran over to me and asked was I ready to leave. Apparently Rakeem had to fly to Dallas then change planes to fly to Jamaica. I wished I was him right about now on that plane. Trent and I would become real close friends on that ride.

April looked very depressed on the way home but I had no training in the cheering up field. She'll get over it, I always do. There was a big camper, no, more like a mobile home parked in front of our dorm when we pulled up. I could barely see around the huge thing so instead of trying to park in our usual space, I pulled up behind it.

"Mommy's here!" April shouted. Now you know by now I'm thinking, what kind of shit is this? She's hollering Mommy? Nobody over the age of five says, Mommy, and I can't believe they are riding around in a Winnebago. There's a lot I don't know about white people. She jumped out the car and ran up the steps into the dorm. I sat and meditated before getting out. I had to be prepared for this one. I took my time walking to my room and I could hear lots of chatter. April asked Olandis where did I go? I wished I could crawl under a rock or somewhere, anywhere, besides here. I pushed the door open and quietly walked in.

"Oh, look, X, isn't she beautiful? A pure angel." This had to be Aprils mother. She was pale, very much in need of some sun and she had long, stringy, blond hair. I couldn't tell if that was a net she had on or a wanna be black dress over some polyester looking cloth. And lets not forget about the black spike heel boots she was wearing and all those beads around her neck and wrists. She may have looked like a gypsy only she was too white and gypsy's were more olive toned. A white man started talking to me. He was dressed a little neater, more like Mr. Rogers with that tight cardigan sweater and polyester pants. I wanted to ask what is up with all the polyester but I just met them and, I don't know why but I wanted to make a good impression on them.

"You are heaven sent. I haven't seen my little girl this happy in years." He replied.

"Well, excuse me but you will get my counseling bill in the morning." Olandis stated.

Her father laughed and said, "Oh, Olandis, You are still number one. You're my second son but you know how women are, they still need their species to cry with."

"Okay men of a different species, you all are scaring her. We haven't been properly introduced yet."

"Mommy, Daddy, meet Ms. Kitty. Ms. Kitty, meet my parents, X and Summer." April had to be kidding me. Where is the camera? I know this is a set up but no one was laughing yet so I guess I'll play along.

"Nice to meet you." I said.

"Same here."

"You know you have such beautiful skin, like its glowing. Are you planning another life?" Okay now her mother really had me confused. How can you plan another life?

"Mommy! Ms. Kitty's not pregnant!" Oh, I get it. She thinks I'm pregnant. Well I've got news for her, I cant have kids. They would probably freak out if I told them about my abortions.

"Thanks for the compliment anyway." I know I have beautiful skin but it feels good to hear someone say it. Just then a tall white guy with jet black spiked hair walked in our room. Normally, he would scare me in a dark alley but after this day, nothing scares me anymore. Now his attire was out of this world. He wore a black tee shirt that said, Save the Rats in New York, and green army pants with matching combat boots. His arm was covered in tattoos that looked like snakes, no I think they were dragons, and metal bracelets around both his wrists. To top his assemble off, he wore a leather dog chain around his neck. He fell on the floor and did a shake/ spasm sort of dance. Olandis stood over him and said, "I think I saw that on Oprah. See I told you all to get the boy some help years ago."

"Olandis, he's telling us that he's hungry. We've gotten better at his self visual expressions this year." Mrs. Summer Showers stated.

"Well, if he had fell out in the floor like that with my Grandma, she would have sent him to the mental hospital after she beat his butt for messing up her shined floors, God rest her soul." Olandis said.

"So, he still has decided not to talk? How long has it been?" April asked.

"Almost two years. We are so proud of him, he has finally accomplished something he set out to do," said Mr. X.

I think I have just landed in the discovery channel. This cant be happening to me. I need to call Tuan quick and make my getaway tonight instead of in the morning! Damn, I don't have his number so I guess I'm stuck. April's brother, I guess that's what, I mean who he was, started flipping around the floor like a fish out of water. April's mother picked up her purse and stood up.

"Oh dear, he's really hungry. Why don't we go find someplace to eat. Come on you guys, the last time we waited too long, he actually passed out." she said.

"Hump, his ass probably knocked himself out with all that jumping around in the floor. Get up, we are leaving and you better not skip a bite!" Olandis said to him. He stood up like nothing had happened and walked out the door to the camper. I was afraid to go but afraid that I would miss something. I was the last one in so I had to shut the door, not an easy task. Their house on wheels was nice. It looked better in here than our dorm room. They had a t.v., and vcr., a telephone, bunk beds, a bathroom, and a little kitchen with a table. Olandis turned to me and said," I almost forgot. Some lady named Lucille called for you. She said it was very important that she reach you."

I froze. Lucille must have found my number on that napkin. I couldn't let her find out where I lived, she would kill me. But I just met her husband that night and he never called. Maybe I need to try to reach him before she reaches me. He can explain it better when she's not so drunk. "Ms. Kitty are you okay?" It was April. I nodded my head yes. "Don't worry about Jake, he wont bite, I think." Jake the snake was the last thing on my mind. I may need him around when Lucille comes after me, he will definitely scare her away. Mr. X. pulled the camper into an empty parking lot of a resteraunt. We didn't care if no one was eating there because everything else was closed. We all walked in and sat at a big booth. The waitress and some other men stared at us like they had seen a ghost. I guess we did look weird. She strolled over to us, wiped her hands on her sloppy apron and said, "We don't serve coloreds here."

"Nobody asked for collards. Did you ask for collards?" Olandis had already started.

"I think she means black people." April's mom replied.

"No dear, she said collards because we are long past segregation. They have to serve us, it's the law." April's dad stood firm on his assumption and began looking at a menu. The waitress was pissed.

"I said colored, and we also don't serve gays or freaks."

"Well, look around, Alice, you don't look like you serving anybody in here so can I please order or do I need to get Mel in the back of this here diner?" Olandis had pushed her button but before she had a chance to speak April's father stepped in.

"No way am I going to eat their food. If she cant serve you or my son or Ms. Kitty then she can.. she can.." April and I shouted, "Kiss My Grits!" We all fell out laughing, all of us except our waitress and Jake. I hated to think what he would do if he didn't eat because he was holding his arms and rocking back and forth like he was going to explode any second. Whoops, he did it, he exploded. He jumped on the table and ran from booth to booth, kicking over the napkin holders causing the napkins to fly out everywhere. Mr. and Mrs. Showers tried to calm him down and make him stop but he was not trying to hear them. He grabbed his hair and then the ketchup bottles and began pouring red ketchup all over himself. He ran to the stove behind the counter and crawled up on it. Luckily it wasn't on but that didn't matter, he was determined to eat something, himself! He began licking the sauce off his face and hands. He scared the waitress and other customers so bad that they ran out the restauraunt and never returned. April's mother cooked us a good home cooked meal and after we ate, we cleaned up the place, left money for the meal and tip and left. Truly a night I will never forget!

We were asleep when April's father brought us back to the dorm. Her mother woke me and said, "It was a pleasure meeting you but we have to move on."

"Mommy youre leaving so soon? Why?" April asked.

"Well, we don't want the cops looking for us do we? Besides, your father has to speak at a conference in Louisiana tomorrow afternoon. We were just stopping by to see you, dear, not to stay."

"But you never stay. I can't even write you guys because you don't have an address."

"Well, you're welcome to tag along and you know our address."

"Mom, your address is my dorm room, remember? All I'll be doing is sending a letter to myself and you know I'm not about to ride across the country with Jake." Jake shot her a birdie with his finger.

"I know dear, but one day we will settle down and find us a nice house again and have family outings. Maybe you and Rakeem will have joined your souls by then. Until then, keep up your spirit and listen to that tape I sent you. Peace."

I helped her out the camper because we were both sleepy and Olandis had already walked into the dorm. I hope he was not on my bed because I was too tired to roll him over. I felt sorry for April. First her man leaves, then her parents. Damn, her life is almost as messed up as mine.

I jumped up at 5:00 am to pack. I haven't heard from Tuan but I know he will come, he cant resist me and he hasn't even had a sample yet. Olandis jumped up also with his eye mask still on, "What the hell is with you? The sun aint even up yet and you running around with all the lights on!" He looked like Batman with that thing on, all that's missing is the cape. I never noticed the water and little seeds that float around in it. "Go back to sleep, Olandis," I said.

"Well duh, that's what I'm trying to do but apparently your new job is to wake the chickens so they'll be up for sunrise." He positioned his eye mask back in place and pulled the covers over his head. I pulled out every piece of lingerie I owned and tossed it in my overnight bag. Then I showered and threw all the personal hygiene materials in there too, you know, soap, deoderant, toothbrush, perfume. Speaking of which, I'm almost out. Maybe I can talk someone into buying me some more. Okay, now the only thing left is clothes. I know I have to take my leather pants, he loved those, and only the tightest fitting shirts and a pair of jeans. Done. Oh yeah, my bra and panties. Nah, skip that. I want him to know I'm kinky. Well, that didn't take long at all. Lets see it's only 7:30. I may have time for a nap before ten.

'Knock, knock, knock.' Please let Olandis get that or April. 'Knock, knock' "Yeah, hold on!" Olandis got up and put on my bathrobe. "Who da' hell is it? It's eight am!" he yelled threw the door. He opened the door and quickly shut it. He grabbed his wig off the bed rail and put it on backwards. Then he snatched off the eye mask and opened the door back up. "Well hello. And DAMN, who might you be?"

"Um, maybe this is the wrong room."

"Oh no, you got the right one baby, uh huh!"

"Well I'm looking for Kitty. Does she live here?"

"Hold on let me check." I jumped when I heard my name. Who could that be standing on the other side of my door? I didn't have a robe to throw on because Olandis was wearing it so I grabbed April's 1970 shirt and wrapped it, some kind of way, on my body. Olandis was about to tell the man no until he saw me heading to the door.

"Who is it?" I asked him.

"Well I was trying to find out until your nosy ass woke up." I opened the door wider to unvail Tuan standing there looking fine as ever. He looked somewhat relieved to see me. I didn't want him to see me though, looking like a hippy." Hi, Tuan. What are you doing here so early, I thought you said ten."

"I did but I had to drop a friend off at the airport so since I was so close I came on over. You must not have gotten my message." he said.

"Oops, that was you? My bad." Olandis said. I snarled my teeth at him and he growled back at me.

"I can wait if youre not ready." Tuan replied. I am so glad I got up earlier. I guess the early bird does get the worm.

"No, I'm ready. Just give me a minute." I walked in the bathroom to change into my clothes but Olandis stopped the door with his foot. "Look, here's my pager number. Hit me on the hip if he tries anything."

"That's the whole idea, Olandis." I was dressed and refreshed and out the door in seconds. I was halfway out the dorm when I realized I didn't say goodbye to April. Oh, she'll be alright. He turned off the alarm before we even reached the car, a little red corvette. Olandis would die if he saw this. He probably was watching me from the window anyway. I'll know by the morning news. We were zooming around curves and mountains so fast that my head started to spin.

"Am I driving too fast?" he asked.

"No, it's just that I get turned on by speed."

"Well, I got turned on when you came to the door. Who was your little friend or doorman?"

"Oh that's just Olandis. Don't pay him any mind."

"He almost got knocked out. Man, I hate fagots!" That last comment jarred my mind. He didn't even know Olandis and was already dogging him out. I mean, sure Olandis is a big jokester and can get on your nerves sometimes but he doesn't do anything to deserve to get knocked out. If it had been a woman saying the same things to him, he would have enjoyed the conversation. I never really cared for a man who likes violence. I always thought they looked stupid beating somebody's brain out, use that energy for sex is my motto. I was silent the rest of the trip. He wasn't too concerned because he played tape after tape of all his gangster rap. Don't get me wrong, I like rap, but he should've brought something else besides fuck this and that bitch. Listen to that on your time, not Ms. Kitty's time.

"Want something to eat?" Finally he speaks! I nodded my head, yes. He pulled up to some Burger Barn and rode through the drive through window. He ordered two breakfast meals and paid the lady at the window without asking me if that's what I wanted to eat. He placed the cups of orange juice in his car cup holders and handed me the bag of food. He must have noticed the way I snatched it away from him and rolled my eyes. "What's the matter?" he asked.

"Nothing." I replied.

"Sure? Don't get homesick on me, yet." He touched the side of my face and turned it with his finger. "We only have about 45 minutes to go." He leaned over and kissed me, passionately, on the lips. He ran his hand all through the back of my hair like he was checking to see if it was real or fake. When he sat back, he smiled at me. Yeah, it's all real, baby.

We arrived at State exactly 45 minutes later. He had this trip memorized, almost like he traveled it a million times. I, on the other hand, couldn't tell you where I was. The campus and buildings were old, like haunted houses and old slave plantations. Their campus looked like ours, bare. I saw a few people walking around and they stared at me in the car like I was an alien. I know they haven't seen anything this fine hit their streets in ages. Tuan pointed to some historical sites with really didn't amaze me. I was ready to see the inside of his room. We drove around a football dome and onto some brick roads. I thought the roads were neat, I had never seen a brick road. He pulled into some colonial style condos and parked in front of a rusty looking one. "Well, this is it." He grabbed my bag out the back and got out. As soon as we walked in, he ran around trying to pick up empty beer bottles and underwear. He told me to have a seat on the couch and he would be right back. He walked into another room and I could hear him cleaning up in there, also. He must have checked his answering machine because I could hear the little beep sound that they usually make. I couldn't stand it anymore, just waiting in that room all alone, so I got up to walk in there with him. I stopped when I heard a female voice come on his machine. "Tuan, it's me. I'm sorry I haven't been there lately for you but I've been bogged down with exams. Um, give me a call when you get this message. I'll be waiting." I stood in the doorway, his back still to me.

"Who was that?" I asked.

"Nobody."

"Nobody? Yes I believe there was somebody on your phone."

"I meant nobody important. We tried to hook up, she never had time, and that's that. But now, it's all about you." He walked over to me and put his arms around my waist. "I will devote all my time to you. I kept my promise so far, haven't I?" He gave me a peck on the lips first then kissed me longer and harder. We stood up kissing for what seemed like eternity until he picked me up and carried me to the bed. He began kissing me again, this time all over my neck and arms. He raised up to take off my shoes and socks and began kissing my feet, then each toe one by one. I think I reached my orgasm and I still had on my clothes, go figure? I couldn't stand the heat anymore so I unzipped his pants and softly said, "I'm ready." He reached under the pillow and pulled out a condom. I helped him put it on and he gave me what I wanted over and over again until three hours later we collapsed in a deep sleep. I awoke to the aroma of oriental food. I could hear him stirring around with pots and pans in the other room so I got up, put on my nightie out my bag and walked to the kitchen. He was wearing a red silk robe with a dragon on the back. His curls were tossed around on top of his head but he still looked sexy in the robe. I sat down in one of the bar stools and leaned on the counter, admiring his body. I never had a man cook for me, I could use to this. He sat a plate down in front of me and kissed me on the fore-head. Then he turned around and continued cooking over the stove. He threw something in the pan and a gush of flames went in the air. He picked up the pan and tossed the food in the air until all the flames were out and placed some on my plate. I would've dove right in it because it looked delicious but he picked up a fork and began feeding it to me. "So, how is it?" he asked.

"Tuan, this is delicious." I said with my mouth full of food. "Who taught you how to cook?"

"My mother. We own a Thai restaurant back in California." He took a bite of my food and walked over to one of the cabinets. "I almost forget the wine." He pulled out a bottle of wine and two glasses. After pouring the wine, he said he wanted a toast. "To always have you here with me, in mind, body, and spirit." We clinked our glasses together, took a sip, and kissed. I am really considering changing schools next semester. Quintin has and will never do this much for me. Woa. Stop. Why am I even thinking about him at a time like this? I miss him. Tuan can still be my weekend getaway but Quintin, for some strange reason, still has my heart. I couldn't eat anymore after thinking about him. Tuan finished up the plate of food and put the dishes in the sink. We sat on the couch and he gave me a back massage. I found the remote and began flipping the channels.

"Oo, right there. That feels good." I said. I lowered my head so he could get to my neck better.

"You know nothing is on tv. Why don't I go rent some movies," he said.

"Do I have to go? I'm still exuasted from that three hour workout you gave me."

"Naw' baby. You can stay here and get well rested because tonight will be longer!"

He went to his room and walked back in with his clothes on. He grabbed his wallet off the t.v. and stood by the couch holding up his hands like he was measuring something.

"What are you doing?" I curiously asked.

"Getting a good picture of you in my mind. I know how you look now so don't move and I want you sitting there in that exact spot with that gown on when I return."

"Okay, it's not like I can go anywhere." He blew me a kiss and left.

About five minutes later he was knocking on the door. He must have forgotten something so I jumped and ran to open it without looking through the peephole. Five guys walked in and stared at me like I was the catch of the day. I headed for the bedroom to put on my clothes but one of them stopped me. "Hey, pretty, where you going?"

"I'm going to change."

Another one interrupted, "Change? We done seen you in that now and I like it." The other guys said, Me too and started laughing.

"If you're looking for Tuan, he just left which is what I think yall should do."

"Yeah, we were looking for him but I like what I found better," the first guy said. He told one of the other guys to lock the door. I was scared to death but I was not about to show it. They were like wolves and could smell fear a mile away. He walked closer to me and the closer he came, the further I walked back until finally I was cornered. "Why you running from me? I wont hurt you. Now my boy, Tuan, he may. I see he been up here wining and dining you but he does the same routine with all the ladies." I started shaking my head because I didn't want to believe what I was hearing. "Oh, yeah, he made you feel real special. But I know how you can get him back." One of the guys said, "Tell her, I want to hear this." He continued, "Sleep with us."

"Okay, I don't know what kind of shit you smoking but I wouldn't sleep with none of your tired asses any day. Your Daddy, maybe, if you look like yo' Momma!"

"This bitch has lost her mind. I think we need to teach her respect," he said. He grabbed me by the arm and slapped me causing me to fall. Another guy walked over and picked me up and threw me on the couch. I felt one of them hold my arms above my head and the ring leader stood in front of me and dropped his pants. He pulled his penis out and held it in his hands and I felt like I was going to pass out. "I'll teach you to talk back to your elders," he said. He got ready to shove it inside me but I kicked him as hard as I could and struggled to break free. He went down in pain but another guy appeared in his place and dropped his pants too. This time someone held my ankles. He was about to rape me until Tuan rushed in from outside and ran and punched the guy in the face. They stood in the floor about to fight and I was able to get away and run in the bedroom, slamming the door and locking it. I could hear them arguing through the door. "Man what the fuck is wrong with you? I thought we was gonna do this."

"No. I was down but now I'm out!" I could hear Tuan saying. So this was a set up the whole time. "She aint like that, man. She's a good girl."

"See, this ole' punk done got his and now he pussy whooped!"

"Yeah, you old sorry nigga'. You is a sell out!"

"Well, fuck that, I'm still hitting it."

"Me too man. Tuan done got his so he don't care anymore." Tuan came in again for my defense, "You all need to just leave. We just got out this same criminal shit three weeks ago and you're gonna do it again. What if she talks?"

"Man, what can she say. She already slept with you and she came up here on her own free will. You said she was jocking you from the start."

"I know, I know, but nobody will believe us this time. My Pop's paid a lot of money to get me off last time and I cant do time."

From the looks of things, Tuan was not going to be able to talk them out of it, their minds were made up. Three weeks of masterminding for me would be used. I had to think of something, but what? I couldn't run away, there were no windows in here and I was not about to go back out there. I decided to put on layers and layers of clothes, if they wanted me they would have to work for it. When I reached the last pair of jeans, the ones I wore up here, Olandis's beeper number fell out the pocket. He was my last resort. If I could keep the wild dogs tame long enough for him or April to get here, I would be alright. I picked up the phone and dialed the number. I looked around for something with Tuan's number on it and luckily, I found a student directory. He was the only Tuan listed in the book, Tuan Jennings, so it had to be him. The phone rang seconds later and I picked it up on the first ring. Tuan must've answered it also because I could hear his voice saying hello on the other end. When no one said anything he hung his end up. I whispered into the phone, "Olandis, it's me."

"I know. I didn't want to talk to your little boyfriend. So whats up, girlfriend? You been working him over time?"

"Olandis, you got to come get me, hurry! They're gonna to rape me."

"Say what! Who? Where are you?" I started giving him the information from the directory and he said, "Slow down, I cant write that fast and my nails wet. Okay got it. Ms. Kitty hang in there, I'll get you out." I eased the phone back on the receiver and prayed that he would come through. I don't know how he will do it but he wont leave me hanging, he never does. Just then someone knock on the door. "Ms. Kitty please open the door." That bastard must think I'm crazy. "If you do this I promise I will take you home but I cant talk them out of it."

"Fuck you and them!" I hollered through the door. I was so mad at him I probably could have killed them all with my bare hands. The funny part about all this was I always fantasized about having two or three partners during sex but I wasn't about to be forced into it. It had to be on my terms and I get to choose the men. None of those ugly rats would've been in the lineup. I searched his room for a weapon because I knew he had to have a key to his room, he was just stalling. If he could talk me into it and I gave in, then it wouldn't necessarily be gang rape. He kept beating on the door and saying, "I really liked you, you know. You were too pretty to want me but you still acted like you cared. I would do anything for you now that I know you better. I thought you were like all the other girls around here, out for my money, but youre different." I could hear the other guys in the room mimicking him. One even said he sounded like a real fag. I knew he had pushed the wrong button then because I heard him tell Tuan to put him down. "Ms. Kitty, baby, I'm real sorry about this. Honest, I want us to work this out." I couldn't tell if he was lying to get me out there with them or really sincere and telling the truth. I better just wait on Olandis. I don't know if he is at home or at the cabin. It was dark so he had to be at the cabin by now. I could've been there with them having a good time right about now but instead I'm stuck in this smelly room fearing for my life. Lets see, most cabins are in the woods and I must be close by because we traveled through the mountains to get here. It shouldn't take them two hours to get here, maybe 30 minutes at the most. Please let them get here. I could hear a lot of movement in the other room. What are they doing in there? It sounded like more men had come over to join the party. I heard a glass break and a lot of cursing. I don't think they were party-ing, it sounded more like fighting. Just then, someone kicked the door in and I screamed, watching it hit the ground. A 7 ft. man with ski mask on walked over to me and picked me up. I started punching him with all my strength but he was far much stronger than me. I clawed and bit his hands but he was unmoved. He carried me out the bedroom and through the den. I saw three other men wear-ing the same mask's over their faces with machine guns in their hands. Tuan and his friends were lying face down on the floor. The man carried me out the front door and to an old, Buick, Deuce and a Quarter, with gold rims on the wheels and dark tinted windows. The rest of the ski masked men followed behind him and got in the car. I ended up in the back seat between two of them. The driver drove off leaving skid marks on the street and none of them said a word. When we were far enough away from the campus, they pulled off their hats. They were all black men whom I had never seen before. We rode to a log cabin, which must have taken about 40 minutes, in silence. I spotted April's car and another BMW parked in front. The driver got out and walked up to the front door. It was so dark and I couldn't see that well but I think he was talking to Dewayne. They walked over to the car and Dewayne peeked in. He patted the man on the back and handed him some money then the two guys beside me got out. One of them held out his hand to help me out of the car and as soon as I got out, they jumped back in and drove off.

"You alright?" Dewayne asked.

"Yeah, thanks for ge.." He held up his hand for me to hush.

"I don't expect payback but if you feel the need, here's my card." I read the words, Club Destiny, on the card and two mobile numbers at the bottom. Olandis rushed out the house and over to me. He grabbed me and hugged the life out of me saying, "They didn't do anything to you, did they? I didn't like his little smart alec mouth the first time I heard it. I hope your boys beat him good, Dewayne! Do you need to go to the hospital or the liquor store, Ms. Kitty? You just tell me, honey child, what you need. And don't worry about April, she been sleep the whole time. That girl's gonna sleep her life away, wake up one day and Damn, she's old. She better not ask me what happened because I wont know, I was out partying." He put his arm around me and walked me in the cabin. The inside of the cabin was beautiful. There was a bedroom with a king size bed off to the side of a huge living space and kitchen, which by the way had a nice aroma coming from it. It smelled like turkey baking and fresh hot, apple pie. I wonder who prepared all this food but knowing Dewayne, it was catered. I still would like to know who his mysterious men in black were. He is starting to remind me of Al Capone or somebody in the mafia. I mean, he has money, no let me rephrase that, he has a lot of mad money, but Olandis has never said what he does. He keeps Olandis happy and well dressed but how? I don't even think he's gay because he acts like he was going to hit on me outside before Olandis appeared. And what does he mean by if I want to repay him? Hell, I don't know what he did, yet. I better watch my back and lay low when I'm around him, I wouldn't want Olandis mad at me over some bullshit. But he doesn't have to worry about me, Dewayne is definitely not my type. I need a man with some meat on his bones, not skinny like him, and pretty hair, not fake, with pretty skin. I need Quintin. I can just picture those muscles, that emaculate body in my mind. I could see Tuan's beautiful eye's gleaming at me, wait a minute, Tuan? I still cant believe he tried to gang rape me. I would've given him the world and then some but he had to go and ruin things for himself. We would've had a good thing going, endless coochie supply, but he felt the need to share it with his friends. I guess I didn't need him anyway because my main man would have to have a strong mind of his own.

"Here Ms. Kitty, have a drink," Olandis was standing over me with a glass of champagne. Dewayne rushed across the room and snatched the glass out his hand. Olandis looked very surprised but he didn't say a word to him. Dewayne sat the glass down on the wooden dining room table rubbed Olandis's back.

"Olandis, sweetie, you have had enough to drink and I don't think your friend needs to join in with you," he said.

"I AM FINE!" Olandis slurred.

"Come on, let's go and lie down. You'll feel better," Dewayne said as he coaxed him back to the bedroom. Olandis stumbled and almost fell a couple of times on his way to the room. I heard April mumble something about his breath when he laid down beside her but he was to far gone to come back at her. I didn't notice how drunk he was at first but now that I think about it, he was babbling too much and his eyes were a little glossy once I saw him in the porch light. Dewayne walked back to the room were I was sitting, shutting the bedroom door behind him. Here we go, I thought. He walked over to the fireplace and shoved some logs around with a poker. Then he lit a match and threw it in the fireplace on top of the logs. At first, the flames were weak then they grew larger and larger. I wished that Quintin were here with me, the flames of fire were putting me in the mood for some male company and Dewayne was not the male I wanted. He must call himself trying to seduce me with all this but it's not going to work. He probably planned to get Olandis drunk so we could have some privacy and there's no telling what he did or gave to April. She is still asleep, why wont she wake up? Please let her wake up, please, I don't want to be trapped all alone with this man. He sat down on the floor in front of the fireplace and just stared at the fire. I didn't know what to do or say so I waited for him to make the first move. He must've stared at that fire for an hour like he was in a trance until I gave in and said something.

"Um, Dewayne, you okay?"

"Yeah. Have you ever just looked at fire? It's amazing to watch all the colors rise and then fall like a pattern. Trip' how fire does so many things and is used for so much. We almost couldn't live without it and its been around for years and years," he said.

This guy is crazy. I hope he isn't like one of those guys from the horror movies were they lure innocent people into the woods and then kill them and eat their flesh and bones, never to be seen or heard from again. I need to wake April and Olandis up and get the hell out of here but I think its to late. He got up off the floor and walked to the kitchen. Oh no, the knives were in there! I better think quick, stop him or do something before he does me. I walked to the bedroom and peeked in the door. They were in there snoring like puppies. They were know where near wake up time so that's out. I decided to walk to the kitchen, if he was going to have a weapon I was, too. I could grab a knife before him and cut him in self defense. I pushed the swinging wooden doors open to find him looking in the stove. He must be trying to see if we will all fit in there. He turned around and looked at me real funny, not saying a word. I may need to go on and shove him in there now, get it over with. He is real puny so I know I could take him. He closed the oven door and said, "Could you hand me a knife out that drawer." Well, he's a bold ass man. He really thinks that I'm just gonna hand over the murder weapon and let him slice my body up. Hump, think again. He turned back around and asked, "Did you find it?"

"No, um, what did you need it for?" I asked.

"I wanted to cut the turkey to see if it is almost done." So, he thinks I'm a turkey? "That's okay. I found one." Oh no, he's getting ready to kill me, what should I do? He put on a pair of mitts, clever, so not to leave fingerprints. Sweat was pouring down my face. He reached inside the oven and pulled out the biggest turkey I ever laid eyes on. It was so pretty and brown, thank God, it's not me. He cut into the turkey exposing juices flowing everywhere. I wanted a taste, just a taste, of that bird. I was still full from Tuan's dinner. What did he call it? Pho or Fo? Anyway, it was great. Why did he go through the trouble of making me dinner and everything if they were going to rape me? I just don't understand.

"Here, try some and be honest. Is it delicious?" Dewayne said.

"Oh yeah, umm, umm, it's good," I said. It was so moist, not dry like my mom use to make.

"Is it good like, makes me wanna slap my momma or is it just okay good?"

"Dewayne that's not fair. I always wanna slap my momma, literally."

"Yeah, me too, if I ever get the chance to meet her." I felt kind of bad for saying that about my mom. Here I was with a mother and he had no one. He is better off that way. He doesn't have to worry about trying to please someone or make them feel proud to be your parent. He wont have to get emotional when they act like they don't care or have to worry about what he did to make them hate him. I delt with that so much growing up that now I could care less about her feelings, but it still hurts. Dewayne must've had the same thoughts I did because I caught him staring out the window. Now I know why he seems so depressed and extremely quiet tonight, he was alone again on Thanksgiving. Why did Olandis have to go and get drunk? He wanted to spend time with loved ones and he barely knew me so I didn't count. I could make things right, turn around a messed up night.

"What else did you cook to go with this bird?" I asked. I was not hungry but I would have to stuff myself to make him feel better.

"Oh, I made yams, macaroni and cheese, green beans, and dressing and an apple pie for dessert."

"Damn! Hook me up with a plate. Where did you learn to cook all that? I cant even boil water without burning the pot."

"I cooked at the group home when I was little. We all had daily chores and I got appointed as one of the kitchen helpers. The older I got the more I had to do, so instead of having to clean the pots and pans, I chose to cook with them."

"Is that why you have so much food? Because you had to cook for so many people?" I asked.

"Yeah, I guess so. No wonder I'm always throwing food away, I thought it was because I didn't have an appetite but I must have too much food." He chuckled a little and I could see he was beginning to cheer up. Mission accomplished. We sat at the table and talked for hours as we ate until the turkey was all chopped up and almost gone. He told me everything about his growing up in a group home. He really has a lot of brothers and sisters when you think about it but all their records were kept confidential so he could never get in touch with the people he grew up with. He probably wouldn't recognize them on the streets because he was so young and that was so long ago. He ran away when he turned fifteen and has been on his own since then. He is twenty-six now. He met Olandis at a gas station a little over a year ago. Yes, I said gas station. Olandis was in there going off on the cashier about her over charging him for a soda and candy bar when he walked in to pay for his gas. He told the woman to put Olandis's snack on his bill. Olandis swore up and down that the woman overcharged him because he was gay and his hair looked better than hers and demanded that Dewayne not give her any money but he paid anyway and quietly walked out to his car. Now Olandis was pissed so he stormed out right behind him but when he saw Dewayne's car he changed his attitude. Dewayne asked him where he was headed and told him he could give him a lift and the rest is history.

He said he always knew he wanted to have money so he could buy all the things he ever dreamed of having, clothes being one. No one would hire a young, uneducated, runaway, so he had to resort to the streets. He hooked up with a drug dealer that he would see every night as he slept in an alley. The man showed him what to do and how to tell if its an undercover cop scheming on him. He sold drugs to the point were he wanted to try them, he wanted to see why everybody came back to him week after week and night after night to buy them. He was about to light one up when his dealer walked in and caught him. The dealer had warned him that he didn't deal with crackheads and that smoking the product was the same as stealing from him. He beat him so bad that he woke the next day in the hospital, all bruised and bandaged up. That's when he decided to invest his money, what little he had saved up. He went to beauty school and got his cosmetologist license and built his clientele up so much that he had to open his own beauty shop. Buisiness was booming at his shop. He serviced every one from the rich in deed to the rich in need then one day two girls walked in wearing these little skimpy, tight outfits. Everyone knew they were not his regular type of crowd but he serviced them anyway, why discriminate? When they pulled out the hundred dollar bills and paid for the two hundred dollar hairdo and facial he asked them where did they work. They told him that they use to work at Babydolls, a strip club down the street, but the owner was arrested for selling drugs and stolen credit cards that same day. Well, it turns out that the former owner was his old drug dealer so he went down to the jail and asked could he buy the club from him. He agreed since he knew he would be locked up awhile and sold the club to him for one dollar. Talk about luck. That's why he named it Club Destiny and it's been satisfying men for years.

Dewayne also feels the same as I do about kids and we are sort of in the same boat. I can't have kids and he cant, either. He went through the tedious adoption process but as soon as they found out he was gay and owned a strip club (which he does not work in) , they denied him. He said being gay has nothing to do with raising a child and if they can let women on drugs or welfare who have no intentions of supporting a child be a parent, then why wont they let a rich, caring, energetic, loving, black male adopt? Most black men run from their children and here he was, wanting one and couldn't have one. I know he would make a great father because he didn't have one and he knows how it feels to want one. He wishes that children didn't have to live in group homes. I use to watch Annie over and over and I remember how happy she was when Daddy Warbucks adopted her. Imagine where she would be if some court denied him the right to adopt her? I told him to try adopting outside of the country but he said he was not willing to fight anymore after that first put down. They must've been pretty rough on him. I now wish I had never killed my children. At the time, I didn't look at them as being people, being real. It was just so easy to go and do but it was still murder, just sugar coated with the name, abortion. Now I'll never be able to make things right, have someone to love me unconditionally and I give the same love in return. If only I could turn back the hands of time and give myself another chance, I would keep my baby, my babies. Please, God, take care of them, I didn't know how. I was so young and scarred back then and when one of my homegirls told me how easy it was to have it done, I came up with the money, lied about my age and did it. After the first time, it got easier and easier, like I was going to a picnic or something. The guys I thought I was in love with were too cheap to buy condoms and things would happen so fast that I wouldn't think about using one. I was a true freak back then, I could've won The Freak of the Year award. I would have sex in the park, or behind the school bleachers, movie theatres, back seats of cars and even behind a couch while his Great-Grandfather watched television. Now I feel older and moving on up to the college men, men with their own place. Who knows, by the time I'm out, where I'll be. I thought about Trent. He has to have a house since he has already started a career. I need to give his phone a ring as soon as I get back to my room. I bet he can work it and he's too mature to play games. He must work out faithfully everyday to keep that nice body in shape so he should be able to keep up with a young, chick like me. I may never get three hours again like I did with Tuan but it's got to be close enough.

Dewayne started clearing the table to wash the dishes. I remembered what he said about hating to wash dishes when he was growing up so I offered to do it. He hurriedly obliged. I glanced at the clock on the wall in the kitchen and noticed that it was 8: 15 am. And we haven't had any sleep. I hope he doesn't have to drive too far today because he may fall asleep before he gets there. I flung some dish water on him to wake him up and he jumped. There were some soap suds in his hair when he stood up and I asked him when did he get gray hair. He ran over to the kitchen sink and aimed the sprayer at me. I said," You wouldn't dare," and the next thing I know, a burst of water hit me in the face. I grabbed a cup off the counter and began scooping the dishwater out the sink and throwing it at him while he sprayed me with the sink hose. We were laughing and screaming, slipping and sliding around that kitchen like it was a water park that we didn't notice Olandis standing in the doorway. "Well, if it isn't Crissy and Jack from Three's Company! I guess I must be Janet since I'm being left out," he said. He tried to walk over to the refrigerator but slipped and fell flat on his butt. We all started laughing and Dewayne went to help him, unsuccessfully, sliding too. He grabbed the broom and used it for support. I didn't try to move because I knew I would fall, the floor was soaked and it was made out of linoleum. That stuff is slippery when it's not wet.

"Well don't just stand there, Ms. Kitty, get the mop!" Olandis yelled.

"Uhn, uhn. You all aren't laughing at me," I yelled back to him. I stood my ground over by the cabinets. My layers of clothes were drenched. It wasn't going to be an easy task trying to pull all this wet lingerie off me.

"Oh girl please, with all that ass you carrying, you'll bounce!" he said. April walked in the kitchen then not paying attention to us holding the walls and counters and moving in slow motion. She slid all the way across the floor, pass the fridge, and into the wall.

"Okay, what just happened?" she asked as she lay in the floor looking up to the ceiling.

"Welcome to Kitty's Fun Park," Olandis stated. She tried to move but stopped and let out a sigh of pain. I slowly walked over to her to try and help her get up. She put her arm around my neck and we somehow managed to make it to the den couch. When she plopped down, I could see her ankle starting to swell.

"Oh April, I'm so sorry. It's all my fault," I said.

"No it's not," Dewayne and Olandis appeared in the room with the broom as their guide. "I was throwing water, too," he said.

"No, it's my fault because I started it, I threw the first lick."

"Yeah but if I hadn't ..."

"Wait just a minute," Olandis started, "What is up with you two?" He turned his head around like he was trying to figure something out.

"What do you mean?" Dewayne asked. This is exactly what I didn't want Olandis to do, think that Dewayne and I were sleeping around.

"Well, I fall asleep with you all not knowing each other and I wake up with ya'll being the best of friends," he said.

"Well, while you were passed out, we did become good friends," Dewayne informed.

"Yeah, Dewayne is really sweet. You should be proud, Olandis." I said. I wanted him to know that I didn't want his man the same way he did.

"No Ms. Kitty, he should be proud to have me. Olandis doesn't share his time with just any ole' body," Olandis said as he pointed his finger and sat down on the sofa beside April. "Damn April! Your ankle looks like an elephant's ankle. You need to go get that checked out."

"It'll be alright. I have some sea salt that I can soak in if you'll go look in my bag for me," April said.

"Sea salt? What da' hell is Sea Salt? See salt pour, see salt not work! You need a doctor, girl," Olandis implied.

"Yeah, I think Olandis is right. We can stop by the hospital on the way home," Dewayne told her.

"Oh, now Dewayne, you know how I feel about hospitals. You go in with a hurt foot and come out with your arm cut off," Olandis said. "Count me out, I'm not going in there."

I started putting April's clothes in her bag. I didn't know what to say when she asked me how I got here. I made up a good lie and told her that Tuan had to go home for an emergency and he brought me here last night while she was asleep. She said she was sorry about my weekend but was glad I was here with her, she didn't think she could stand another minute of Olandis fussing at Dewayne. It appears that Olandis wanted to go southto the beach but Bewayne said it was too far to drive so he got the cabin instead. Olandis brought his bikini and every-thing thinking that he could entice him to change his mind. He should know by now that Dewayne is just as strong willed as he. I told her, I know and she looked at me real strange. I could barely zip up her bag with all the clothes in it and I had to sneak some of my stuff in there, too.

"That's funny," she said, "It closed before. Wheres your bag? Maybe I could put some things in it if that's okay with you."

"My bag? Oh, umm, shoot! I must've left it Tuan's car," I lied. I walked out the room with the clothes piling over the bag and yelled, "Ready!"

I didn't see Dewayne or Olandis. They must be outside in the car already. I needed one of them to help April walk to the car and Olandis was going to have to drive because I am too sleepy, thanks to Dewayne. I opened the front door and saw the two cars still parked outside in the same spot as the night before, noone was in them. I quickly shut the door because it was it was freezing out there. I guess they are in the kitchen so I walked back through the den and pushed the kitchen doors wide open. I was not prepared to find Olandis and Dewayne embraced in a passionate kiss. Olandis was sitting sitting on the counter with his legs wrapped around Dewayne's back and Dewayne had his arms around Olandis's back. They didn't notice me standing there because they continued. I ran back out the door and sat on the couch. I know he tried to prepare me for this but mentally, I was not ready. I was able to look at other gay men and women and it wouldn't affect me but this was different, he was my friend. I mean, I knew all along that he was a homosexual but I never really thought about it that way.

"Ms. Kitty," April yelled from the bedroom, "Can you bring me a glass of water?"

"Oh, Okay," I said. I didn't want to go back in that kitchen and find them at it again. I still had a good picture in my mind that would not, no matter how hard I try, go away. This time I decided to give them a signal, let them know that I was coming in.

"Did you say juice or water?" I yelled.

"Water!"

"Okay I'm going in the kitchen to get it now. Yep, the kitchen is where the water is. Water and a glass." I yelled, preparing them for my arrival. I stood in front of the wood, swinging, doors and took a deep breath but before I could push them open, Olandis's well manicured hand held out a glass. I was so embarrased. They knew I was there the whole time and I was acting like a true homophobic. I immediately took the glass out his hand and rushed to the bedroom. April took the water and said, "Well it's about time. Why are you sweating?"

I couldn't describe how I felt so I left it alone. She wouldn't understand why I was tripping out over it. Dewayne stuck his head in the door to see if we were ready. I wanted to take a shower before we left but I was ready to go. I walked pass him and on out to the car. Luckily for me, April's doors were unlocked. Dewayne came out carrying April with Olandis following behind with her bag and keys. He threw the bags in the back seat of her car and jumped in to drive. Dewayne put April in his car and I wished I could change cars, it's going to be a long ride. We pulled off to go to the hospital. It was closer to the college so it took about two hours to get there. I slept the whole time, mainly because I couldn't talk for fear of putting my foot in my mouth. He pulled in the emergency room entrance behind Dewayne. A nurse walked up to Dewayne's car and started putting April in a wheelchair. I got out to help assist her but she said that it was against hospital policies.

"See, I told you they are crazy. We should've never brought her to this hospital," Olandis shouted out the car window.

"Shut Up," I said back to him. He rolled his eyes and rolled the window back up. The nurse pushed April into the hospital and I followed. Dewayne told me he was going to park the car and would be right in. I found a seat in the lobby and waited for the results.

"Are you Ms. Richards?" I turned around to see a handsome black doctor wearing a green lab coat and matching pants standing in front of me.

"Yes," I answered in my sexiest voice.

"Hi, I'm Dr. Kennedy," he said. "Your friend is going to be just fine. She has a sprangled ankle and will need to be cared for a few days. She'll be right out as soon as they finish putting the cast on."

"Thankyou Doctor." I would love to play Dr. with him anytime. He must've noticed me staring at him with my powerful grey eyes because he stopped walking away and turned around. "Here's my card. Call me if you need anything. My pager number is on the back if you cant reach me with the first two numbers." He handed me the card slightly touching my hand.

"Ill page you, 911," I said. I just may get my chance to play doctor afterall. He smiled at me as if he knew what I was thinking and I started to blush. Someone called him and he walked away. The same nurse that brought April in, also brought her back out. Dewayne finally walked in the lobby only to be turned back around to get the car. April looked as high as a kite. She had a bandage up to her thigh but at least she didn't seem to be in anymore pain. The nurse handed me her new, ugly, crutches as I jumped in her car with Olandis.

"Well, what did they say?" he asked.

"She just has a sprang ankle," I replied.

"Well if that's all, why did they cut up her jeans and put that cast all the way up her thigh?"

Good question, I thought. Maybe Olandis is right about hospitals, you come in with a sprang and leave out in a body bag! We pulled in front of our dorm and when Dewayne got out and tried to open the front door, he realized it was locked. Olandis got out the car to see for himself and practically beat the door down. No doubt about it, it was locked. We drove to his dorm to find the same situation but at least there was an explanation note on the door. It seems they locked the doors to do repairs and no one was allowed back in until January 2.

"Well, I don't believe this. The schoolwill be hearing from me." Olandis said, "How am I supposed to get my clothes and beauty products? DEWAYNE, we need to go shopping!"

Dewayne said that we could stay at his apartment which is a one bedroom studio. I know I couldn't last one night with them, much less a whole month. I may see something worse than what I witnessed back at the cabin. Then I got a great idea, we could stay with the Professor. I know he has at least three extra bedrooms. I told Olandis my idea and he said no way, he was going with Dewayne. He handed me the keys to April's car and he and Dewayne drove off.

I was so happy to see the Professor's jeep in his driveway when we pulled up. April had fallen asleep so I eased out the car and rang his doorbell. He answered on the third ring and looked surprised but happy to see me.

"Ms. Richards, what are you doing here? I hope everything is alright."

"Yes. Well, no April and I went away for the weekend and when we came back our dorm was locked. We have no place to go so I was hoping..."

"Say no more. You guys can stay with me. I heard they were going to shut down the dormatories for repairs but they were supposed to make sure that everyone had someplace to go. I guess you all were gone when they asked around." He opened the door wider to let me walk in and I told him about April's ankle. He rushed back outside to help her out the car. I held the door open for them and followed him to the den with the big bear rug. A sophisticated white woman was sitting on the sofa with a wine glass in her hand. In all my enthusiasm, I never noticed the other car parked on the curb in front of his house. She stood up with a horrified look on her face. I think we may have ruined her plans.

"What is going on? Who are these kids?" she asked. The Professor laid April on the sofa and started trying to explain our sad story. She was not touched by it at all. She started arguing with him and he asked her if they could finish their discussion in another room.

"No. Make them leave," she demanded.

"I'm sorry but I cant do that. They have no place to go."

I was ready to pimp slap this woman in her face. There was plenty of room in this house to share and she had no right disrespecting us like that. She didn't even live here herself and she was telling him what to do. She grabbed her purse and keys and walked so close to him, you could smell their breath mixing together. I guess he thought she was going to kiss him because he puckered up and closed his eyes. She threw the wine in his face instead and stormed out the door. I felt kind of bad, busting up his groove like that but he didn't need her anyway. He was too sweet for her.

"Never mind Sherry. She was starting to get on my nerves. Let me show you to your room." he said. He took us to our room and went to get some towels from the hall closet. I stood in the middle of the bedroom floor and turned around admiring it's beauty. It was huge, all white with a pink border around the ceiling. To the corner was a shelf of beautiful china dolls, all wearing lacy and satin dresses. There was an octagonal, bay window with a sitting bench around it and pink curtains with ribbons holding them open for the sun to shine through. This is a room I always dreamed about while growing up.

"Here we are. The bathroom is the second door to your left down the hall. Are you hungry? I could fix you something to eat?" I thought about all the food Dewayne and I ate last night and I told him no, I wasn't hungry.

"Speak for yourself!" April yelled from downstairs. He laughed and went downstairs to cook her something to eat. I stayed in the bathroom for over an hour enjoying my bubble bath, something I havent had since I've been in college. April was pounding on the door for me to come out. "I gotta' go bad, Ms. Kitty. You're gonna turn into a prune if you don't get out that water!" She was right, my skin had already started wrinkling up. I grabbed the towel and opened the door. She was standing there with the crutches and pushed me out the way with one of them.

"Wait, I cant go out there. Where is the Professor?" I asked.

"He's not here. He went to buy groceries. He said we could wear his tee shirts until we find some clothes to put on, they're in his top dresser drawer."

I walked up the hall to his bedroom. It was a mess. It looked like a hurricane had run through and tossed all his clothes onto the floor. I looked in the drawer and found the tee shirts underneath a pile of old pictures. I recognized his sister on one of them. She was dressed like a man and the Professor was dressed like a woman. There was another picture of them on a boat with him holding a big fish. They laughing and looked like they were having so much fun, I bet he misses her a lot. I heard his car pull up outside so I slammed the drawer shut and ran out the room, almost knocking April over.

"Hey, Slow down and give me one of those tee shirts," she said. I threw one back to her and she caught it in mid air. "Good catch for a crippled person," I teased.

"Oh, screw you!" She turned and walked back in the bathroom. I could hear the Professor downstairs rattling with pots and pans. I changed into one of the shirts and rushed downstairs to see what he was making.

"Watcha' cooking?" I asked. He turned around, smiling and said, "You weren't hungry, remember?"

"I know but it smells good, my stomach is telling me I made a mistake."

"I'm cooking lasanga and there's plenty of it."

For some strange, unknown reason, I was excited about staying here with him. April walked in the kitchen hungry and ready to chow down. She searched all the cabinets until she found a plate and fork. When the pan came out the oven, she almost burned herself trying to be the first one to eat it. We laughed at her when she tried to sit at the dining table, her leg wouldn't fit under it with that big, ugly, cast. Professor Phillips suggested that we sit in the den, that way she could straighten her leg out on the couch. He grabbed a tv tray from behind the refridgerator and placed it in front of her. He sat her plate down and poured her some Kool- Aid in a glass. I sat on the floor with my plate and took a sip of my drink.

"Man, if I didn't know any better, I'd say you were black, Professor," I said.

"And why is that?" he asked.

"Because, this is what we call ghetto punch! You have to use a lot of sugar and water to try and stretch the taste," I remarked.

"It is kind of sweet," April implied with her lips twisted up. The Professor laughed at the face she made.

After dinner, he took our plates and walked toward the kitchen. I told him that I would wash the dishes but he informed me that Hilda, his housekeeper would be in tomorrow.

"Well ladies," he said while yawning and stretching, "I'm heading to my room. I'm real tired. There's a small t.v. in the other bedroom if you guys want to move it in your room and watch it. Goodnight."

April was about to fall asleep again after taking her medicine so I told her to get up and move to our new bedroom. She couldn't walk all that well with the crutches so about half way up the steps, she threw them down and hopped to the room. I tiptoed in the other guest room and spotted the small 13 inch t.v. sitting on the dresser. This room was a mess, too. It looked more like a junk room than a bedroom, I could barely find the bed. I walked back in the bedroom to find April fast asleep laying horizontal across the bed. I tried to push her over but after trying unsuccessfully, I snatched the covers from underneath her and sat on the floor. I must've fallen asleep somewhere between Jay Leno and an informercial because the telephone woke me up around nine the next morning. I let it rang until I couldn't stand it anymore.

"Hello," I shouted.

A male voice on the other end said, "Hello, may I speak to Marshal?"

"Um, who did you say, Marshal or Marshelle?" At first I thought it was some-one who knew me by my middle name but know one ever calls me by that name.

"Marshal, is he home?" the man said.

"Hold on a minute and let me check." I put the phone down on top of the night stand and went to his bedroom. It was empty. I heard him downstairs stir-ring around in the kitchen so I rushed down the steps.

The only problem was it wasn't him, it was a Spanish woman in her mid for-ties cooking some sort of tortilla omelet.

"Hi, is the Professor here?" I asked, "He has a phone call." She looked star-tled to see me and almost dropped an egg out her hand.

"No, not here," she said. Oh, I get it, she doesn't speak English to well. How was I supposed to find out where he was? I picked up the phone on the kitchen wall and told the person that he wasn't here. He said okay and hung up. She kept right on cooking, ignoring me like I wasn't there.

"Um, where did he go?" I asked in a loud, slow voice.

"Why you yell? I right here," she remarked.

I felt real stupid after that. If she couldn't understand English, then my yell-ing at her wasn't going to make it any clearer.

"He go run, evey day, he run."

Oh he must jog, something I use to do also everyday. I wish I had known, I would've got up and ran with him. The food was smelling so good. I watched her chop some onions and tomatoes to put in the omelet. She warmed some tortillas covered in cheese in the microwave. I wanted to try just a sample of that miraculous dish she was preparing but I didn't know how to tell her. I would hate to have to curse her out if she got smart with me. That would mean I ran two people away from his house in less than twenty-four hours. She saw me daydreaming about eating her Spanish omelet and she sighed and stared at me.

"You hungry?" she asked.

"Yes….mamm," I replied.

"Then I cook. You like toast?"

"Yes, but I was sort of wishing you would fix me one of those," I said while pointing to her plate.

"Oh, dis? You not like, you Afro-American," she said. I knew it. I knew she was going to get smart and I was ready to curse her out until I thought about my assumption of her.

"What is that supposed to mean?" I asked, "I can eat what I want."

"Okay but you not like. Make you real sick." She started preparing another omelet for me, now that's more like it. I did notice that she didn't use as many vegetables as she did with hers and when she finished she put it in a paper towel instead of a plate. She acted as though it was her food and dinnerware instead of the Professor's. Just then, the phone rang and she looked at me as if to say, aren't you going to answer it and I gave her a look back that said, youre the damn maid. She must've finally got the picture because she jumped up to answer it.

"Ola,…Si… no, no, you go slow. Who?….no, I not understand,"

She was started to upset me with that fake accent and I know whoever was on the other end of that phone was ready to slam it down in her face so I grabbed it out her hand.

"Hello," I said.

"Yeah, now who am I speaking to? I'm sorry but I didn't take Spanish, I'm fluent in French," Olandis said.

"Olandis, it's me, Ms. Kitty. That was Hilda, the housekeeper."

"Well you need to tell Hilda the housekeeper that she don't have to get no attitude cause' I will fly over there so fast and show her how I clean house! Any way what's up sista' girl? How are you the white girl holding out?"

"Oh, were cool, cant complain."

"Well, call me Mrs. Freeze, honey. Listen, Rakeem called and check this out, he wants April to come to Jamaica for Christmas. He says he misses her so much and he couldn't bear being away from her another day and child, when it told him about her leg, he practically jumped through the phone."

"That's great," I lied.

If April left me to go to Jamaica, then I would be alone here with the Professor. I guess I would have to go home then and face my mother. Moe, oh no, I cant face him. I'm better off here by myself, at least the Professor is good looking.

"Oh, wait a minute, let me finish telling you the best part. I complained so much to Dewayne about how good Rakeem was to April and he finally decided to take me out the country to the islands. Rakeem said we could stay with him, save money, and I know he's living large, his father and mother are doctors over there."

"For real, get outta' here."

I wanted to ask him if his parents knew April was white. I guess they will find out sooner or later. I was really sad, depressed is more like it. Since I came to this school, it's always been me, him, and April and now thanks to Mr. Rakeem, he was messing up our clique.

"Yeah girl, now you need to wake April up and get dressed. Dewayne gave me the charge card to go shopping for our trip and you know it's about to be on! I'll be by to scoop you all up in an hour. Chow."

I hurried and finished eating the rest of my omelet, which was now cold, and rushed up the steps to wake April. I was talking so fast that it took her a while to process all the information but when I said the name Rakeem, her face lit up and a smile expanded across her lips from ear to ear.

Olandis drove up right on time and blew the horn on Dewayne's car so long that the neighbors came outside to see who it was. I followed April out the door pas Hilda who was vacuuming the living room. I was sort of worried about the Professor because he wasn't back yet so I asked them to hold on while I write him a note. I found a tiny piece of paper and pen and left the note on the refridgerator. I felt a funny feeling erupt from my stomach and I barely made it to the sink in time to vomit. Hilda's Spanish omelet must not have mixed too well with Dewayne's turkey, the Professor's lasagna, and Tuan's Vietnamese food. I guess Hilda was right, I have an African- American stomach, not multicultural. I wet a paper towel and cleaned my face. Hilda had stopped vacuuming and was standing in the doorway when I took the towel off.

"Morning sickness?" she asked.

"No. Your sorry cooking."

I smarted off to her as I walked outside to the car. Olandis sped off leaving a loud screetching sound and waving to the neighbors as they stared in disbelief.

April asked, "Olandis, I thought you weren't allowed back in the mall"

"Honey, please. I have platinum plastic and nobody will turn that away!" he remarked.

He was right, money rules the world even if it is credit. We walked into one of the most expensive stores in the mall and he rushed around grabbing clothes without looking at the price tags. April picked one shirt and almost fainted.

"Do you that this one shirt cost $150? That's highway robbery. It's ridiculous how they mark up the retail price and they probally only paid $10 for it in the first place. Then they make poor little kids and women work in a sweat shop for a measley $5 a week or less."

"Well, that's they're stupid ass fault," Olandis said, "If they know how to sew, why dont they start their own clothing line? Now give me that shirt."

He carried an arm full of clothes to the cash register and sat them down on the counter.

"Oh Ms. Kitty, Dewayne said for you to pick out some things, too. You wont be able to get back in your room for a while so we got ya' covered. Get it? Gotcha' covered!" he laughed.

Perfect, I thought. I already had some things picked out that I would love to have so it didn't take me long to go find them and bring to the counter. The saleslady looked at us like we were bums off the street or something. She began ringing up the items without even speaking. I wondered if she was on commission because I was ready to take the clothes to another counter. Once everything was rung up, she stared at Olandis in disgust with her reading glasses hanging on the very tip of her nose.

"Um, will somebody buy this woman a camera so she can take my picture and then she wont have to stare so hard," Olandis said. April and I started to giggle. She obviously didn't know who she was messing with because Olandis would surely put her in her place.

"Will this be cash, check, or charge?" she asked April.

"Excuse, I'm over here. I'm paying by charge," Olandis said as he handed her the silver, translucent, card. She snatched it out his hands and asked to see his I.D. while she examined the card like a doctor examines his patients. She gently ran it through the machine.

"I'm sorry but the card has been denied," she eagerly said.

"Well it most be something wrong with your machine. Try it again and this time don't get your little dirty fingerprints all over it," Olandis said. She tried it again with the same result, denied. "Look Miss, I don't know what you did to my card but you need to fix it and quick!"

"Are you threatening me?" she asked in an I'll get you tone.

"No, I don't make threats, only promises!" Olandis said back to her. I could tell that this was about to get real nasty.

"I'm calling security!" She picked up the telephone and dialed a number but if this little stunt of hers was to intimidate him, it didn't work

"Well your gonna need security after I …" he started but April cut in and said, "That wont be necessary. Were leaving." She dragged him out the store by his arm. He had to have the last word so he yelled back at the lady calling her a mean old, coke bottle glasses wearing, blue hair bat! He was steaming mad when we got in the car.

"I don't believe this. Why would Dewayne give me a no good card and have me embarresed like that?I'm going to go to his shop and find out."

We drove straight to his shop and he pulled the car on the sidewalk in front of the door. He slammed it so hard when he stepped out that I thought the window was going to break April asked me to do the honor of going inside and calming him down, making sure that he didn't do anything drastic. I thought to myself that there's no stopping him now, he went beyond drastic back at the mall. Dewayne was putting the finishing touches on a woman's hair when we walked in. He saw the upset look on Olandis's face and started hurrying with the lady's hair. Olandis walked right up to him and said, "I need to see you now!"

"Okay, sweetie, just give me a minute. Have some new, complimentary, grape juice from up front." Dewayne said.

"I don't want no damn grape juice! Do I look constipated to you? Bonk, wrong answer, This is my pissed off look. If she don't look any better than this now, one more minute wont do any good." He bent down in the lady's face and said, "Do yourself a favor and buy a wig because this thin stuff you call hair is not working for you!"

The woman was so furious that she walked out the door without paying and still wearing the styling cape.

"Olandis, did you have to do that? Mrs. Lewis is one of my best customers," Dewayne said.

"Do what? I just told her the truth," he answered, "Now getting back to my problem, whats the deal with the credit card? You just don't realize how embarresed I was when that saleslady said it was denied."

Dewayne had a puzzled look on his face. "What do you mean it's been denied? There should be at least $800 on it. What all did you try to buy?"

"Don't play games with me, this is not wheel of fortune."

"I'm serious. I want to know just as bad as you what happened to all my money. Wait a minute. I remember sending Vixon to the supply warehouse to get some things for the club. I didn't have cash on me so I gave her the credit card but how much can toilet tissue cost?"

"VIXON! That little hussy! How could you give her the credit card? She probably bought herself a closet full of clothes and vibrators."

"Well, we ran out things, vital things, and I was in a bind so I sent her since she was the only who had a break. I didn't think she would go shopping, I give them anything they need."

"I hope this doesn't mean we cant go to Jamaica because Vixon is fixin' to get a beating personally delivered by moi'!"

"No, I bought the airline tickets with another card and please don't say anything to her, let me handle it, okay," he gave him a kiss on the back of his hand. Dewayne is one smooth talking brother to be able to calm Olandis down.

When we arrived back at the Professor's house, there were two Nike jogging suits laying on the bed, one blue and white and one purple and white. He left a note that read, *I bought these for you two. I thought they would be a little more comfortable and since I'm not up with the fads, I figure I cant go wrong with warm up suits.* He did go wrong, I wasn't into the twin thing. We tried them on, mine looked good but Aprils looked funny on her. I guess her body wasn't use to modern day clothing.

"I wish Rakeem could see me now," she said. He was better off seeing her in a negligee. "I wish I could talk to him, hear the sound of his voice."

"You will be able to see him in a week, and let me remind you, in one of the most romantic places in the world. Which brings me to another question, have you did it yet?" I said.

"No, but I'm working on it."

"How can you work on it? You either do it or you don't," I replied.

"I know but it's like I get scared that he's gonna leave me or I may pass gas while we're in the middle of it."

"Girl, if you are swinging it right, he wont even know that you passed gas and he wont be able to leave you because he'll be coming back for more!" I said while giving her a high five.

"What's so funny?" The Professor was standing in our door way sorting through a stack of mail. He was wringing wet with sweat. I know he couldn't have jogged all this time, where did he run to, China?

"I see the suits fit. They look nice on you guys so since you're all dressed up, lets go out for dinner."

"I hope you are going to do something about your self" I remarked. He sniffed up under his arms and said, "There's nothing wrong with me. Are you saying there's something wrong with me?" He walked over to us with his armpits exposed and grabbed me first putting me in a playful headlock. "Do you smell anything? Say mercy and I'll let you go!"

"MERCY," I screamed. "You don't smell too bad!"

April was standing by the bed laughing at us when the Professor yelled, "Get her," and we both shoved her on the bed while he put his arm pits up to her nose. "I cant lie, you smell!"

"Oh really, well do you know what I do to people who don't like to smell funk?" he asked, "I tickle them to death!" She was begging us to stop, knowing full well that she couldn't run with the cast on her leg. We let her up after she had convinced us that she had to use the restroom or she was going to pee all over herself.

We enjoyed our dinner but what I enjoyed most was driving the Professor's jeep. It sits so high, almost like you own the road. I could see over the tops of cars and he let me change the radio station from classical to hip hop soul. When we arrived back at the house, the Professor's light was blinking on his answering machine. When he checked it, we noticed the familiar, sweet, Jamaican accent begin to speak.

"Hello. I'm trying to reach April Showers. If possible, please have her call Rakeem collect at(303)976-0053. Tankyou."

"Oh my God, he called!" April tried to jump around the room, showing her excitement, but forgot she was injured and fell back against the sofa table, knocking over a glass vase. "I'm so sorry, Professor. I just got excited when I heard his voice."

"It's alright Miss Showers, but please let us know when you decide to call him back. I would hate to see what happens when you do get to talk to him."

"I think I'll go call him now, if that's okay with you."

"Sure it is. Here, let me help you up." He extended his hand to help her and she pushed the repeat button on the answering machine to hear the number again. I went upstairs to the bedroom and sat on the bed, upset that she was so happy to be leaving me. I turned the t.v. on when I heard her hobbling up the stairs. I didn't have anything to say to her and I didn't want to hear her praise Mr. Rakeem, her supreme God. She walked in the room all giddly with a big happy-go-lucky smile on her face. For her to be so in love and deeply missing him, she sure didn't talk to him long.

"We leave in two days," she said.

She acted like I really was concerned. I don't remember asking her for any information. Who do I look like, Delta? She continued jabbering, all the time I'm wishing she would just shut up about it.

"I told him about our dorm and he said not to worry, he would buy me some things once I got there. Less packing for me to have to do, I guess."

I turned the volume up on the T.V. with the remote and acted like I wasn't listening. I laughed at a commercial which really wasn't that funny but I made it seem like it was the funniest thing in the world. She stared at me, with her eyebrows raised, like I had lost my mind. She walked over to the T.V. set and turned it off.

"Hey, what did you do that for? I was watching that." I said.

"Why are you treating me like this? What did I do to make you so mad at me?" she asked.

"I'm not mad at you but I will be if you don't move so I can turn the T.V. back on," I replied.

"No, not until you communicate with me," she demanded. This girl was about to get it! Why do I have to communicate, as she calls it, with her? Did she communicate with me about her plans to run off to Jamaica? What was I to do about Christmas? That was a time to spend with loved ones and up to this point, I thought her and Olandis really cared about me. I see all they care about is the sun and sand. The way I figure, two days is too long to be with her, especially if she keeps rubbing it in my face about Rakeem and Jamaica.

"Are you upset that I'm leaving because you haven't said a word since we found out? If you feel that bad about it, maybe I should stay here."

Oh, I get it. Now she was going to try to run a guilt trip on me. Well it wont work. She would die if I told her to stay back with me, that I was afraid of being alone with the Professor.

"I just assumed that you had other plans for Christmas, like going home to be with your family. I've never had the traditional Christmas as other families. We were either on the road or I was left with the nanny. I finally get a chance at a real one and I feel bad about it. If I had the money right now, I would give it to you so you could go with us." She said with tears welling up in her eyes.

"April, stop lying. You have money if you really wanted me to go," I said.

"No, seriously, I don't. I gave my brother some money when they visited us and now I wish I hadn't done it. He probably used it to get high, but he seemed desperate at the time."

She won. She made me feel as guilty as a bank robber in a bank. It's hard to tell if she is telling the truth but it doesn't matter because I don't take charity anyway. I assured her that I would have more fun than them anyway and her smile slowly came back in place as I lay on the bed and fell asleep.

Two days later, Christmas Eve, I found myself to be the chuffeuer for our departing guests. We picked Olandis and Dewayane up from their apartment right on time. Olandis walked out the apartment wearing his favorite wig, the jet black one with a layered affect in the back. Dewayne struggled behind, carrying at least six Louis Vutton suitcases. I popped the trunk for him to pile them in but most of them wouldn't fit so he had to hold two bags in the car with him.

"Oh, I cant wait to lay out on the beach in my new two piece, showing off this gorgeous body!" Olandis said.

"Watch out. If I see anybody looking at that gorgeous body, it will be covered up the rest of the trip," Dewayne stated.

"Please, why do you think I work so hard on it if people cant stare in envy? Besides, I got to get a perfect tan before summer."

"Olandis, I didn't think black people needed a tan," I replied.

"What! We need tans the most. All these uneven skin tones walking around aint cute. Why do you think they have the fade cream in the black beauty supply section, because we are the ones who always use it."

He did have a point, as usual, even if it was something unimportant that no one would think about day to day. I pulled into the main terminal where they were leaving and Dewayne jumped out to get the bags. They were already boarding the plane when we arrived so I didn't have to do one of those long goodbyes. April asked me if I was going to be alright for the tenth time until Olandis pulled her away. Dewayne gave me the keys to his apartment and told me that I was welcome to stay there anytime while they were gone. I stayed to watch the plane take off, wishing that I would run into Trent again. I thought about giving him a call as soon as I found his card. It had to be in one of my pockets but which one? I hope it's not in one at the dorm because I would have to break in to get it. I drove back to the Professor's house in disbelief, disbelief that I was alone. No one was around me, just total silence. The Professor's car was there but he wasn't home. I found a note on the mirror in the bathroom from him that said he went out with Sherry and not to wait up (That's just great, I thought) Also, to call my mom. Was I reading that right? My mom had called or did it mean I need to call my mom since it was Christmas Eve. I guess it wouldn't hurt anything to give her a call. I hope she was drunk so she wouldn't remember anything, that's usually how she prepared herself for Christmas. Then after I opened all my presents and played with them, she would stand in lines all the next day to take them back and convince me that I had broke them and she would buy me something else. I never got the replacements but at least I got to open and play with something on

Christmas Day. I picked up the phone and went through all the channels to call her collect. She answered the phone but wouldn't accept the charges. I should've known better so I called her back, this time on the Professor's line. I was about to hang up on the fifth ring, I know she knew it was me, but she answered.

"Hello," she said.

"Hey, mama. It's me, Kitty."

"Yeah, yeah, I know. Why are you calling me now? Are you in some kind of trouble?"

"No. Why do I always have to be in trouble? Didn't you call me?" I asked before I realized that she couldn't call me, I was staying with someone she didn't know and I wanted to keep it that way.

"Well, anyway, how's school? You must be enjoying yourself since I haven't heard from you."

"Well Mama, you could call me once in a while, too. I'm the one who has to study and try to survive."

"Survive? You don't know the meaning of survival. All you're there to do is party and show every man your coochie while I'm here trying to pay the bill for it."

"I thought you said I got a scholarship. You were so happy that you didn't have to pay for my schooling, remember, Mama?" I thought the phone went dead for a minute until I heard her breathing. I wonder how many lies she has told over the past years?

"Look here, Ms Smarty pants, since you don't have a kind thing to say to me and called here to start a fight with me on Christmas Eve, I don't have to listen!" she screamed and slammed the phone down in my ear leaving a ringing sound. No matter how much she acted like one, I couldn't bring myself to call her a bitch. She was just being, Mama.

I ran upstairs to gather up my and April's laundry to wash and when I sorted through the clothes, separating the darks from the whites, I came across Trent's business card in my jeans pocket. I had to call him now while the Professor was out on his date. By the time he got the phone bill, I would be living back in my dorm room and he could take the money out my paycheck or I could say he was family. I slowly dialed the number, not knowing what to expect.

"Hello," he said.

"Hello, stranger."

"Um, who is this?" he asked.

"The person you've been waiting for all your life."

"And who might that be?"

"The magazine lady from the airport."

"Oh, I'm glad you called. What took you so long?"

"I was giving you time to get settle from your trip. Why, did you miss me?"

"Yes. I'm scheduled to fly back out for New Years and I thought I was going to have to track you down."

"Well now you don't have to. So are you going to call me when you get here?"

"I can do better than that, can you pick me up from our meeting place, the airport? My flight comes in at 6:00 pm on December, 31."

"Sure, I can come."

"Don't stand me up. I hate cabs." We hung up and I finally feel wonderful about being here. It was almost like a dream come true and talk about perfect timing.

I wished there was a way I could get in touch with Quintin but the more he is away from me, the more he will miss me when he gets back. I bet Denise and him have fallen out by now, wherever they are. They cant stand two seconds with each other without fighting. I wonder what he sees in her with her stuck-up, hateful self. And the Professor was out with another Devil's Advocate, Sherry! I cant believe he would leave me alone on Christmas Eve to be with her. I guess it's been a while since he's had some, but he's a good looking man, he could have anybody besides her. At that instance, I realized that I haven't bought him a gift. I hope he understands that I don't have any more money. I spent the hundred dollars he gave me on heaven knows what. The next time I get paid, I'm opening a checking account, cash money goes too quick through my hands. I know what I could do, I'll cook the Christmas dinner, then he wont have to. The kitchen already had the turkey, no hen, no maybe it was a chicken, anyway, it doesn't matter, it's a bird and it was sitting on the counter waiting to be cooked. I remember a little bit about cooking a bird by watching Dewayne so I unwrapped it and sat it in a big pan before putting it in the oven on 600 degrees. Now that the easy part was over, I had to decide what else we could eat with it. I opened the pantry and took out a can of vegetables. I couldn't find the can opener so I tried to cut them open with a knife. The sharp blade nipped my finger and blood began to pour uncontrollably. I grabbed a towel from the drawer and wrapped it around my finger while I danced around in pain, cursing the stupid knife. Since it seemed there was no way of getting the vegetables out the can, I decided to cook them in the microwave and let the Professor open them when he got home. After spending ten minutes trying to figure out how to program his state of the art microwave, I finally set the food to cook for twenty- five minutes since they say the microwave is faster than the stove. I heard a car pull up outside and people laughing. I hope Miss Sherry wasn't planning on staying; she would spoil our dinner. I rushed to the door, letting her know that I was still staying here in case he forgot to mention it. There was a big tree on top of the Professor's jeep. Sherry was carrying an armful of presents and almost slipped and fell on the steps. I walked out to help her bring them in; I didn't want her to sue this good- hearted man.

"Oh, thankyou, Ms. Kitty, um excuse me, I meant Katrina," she said.

"Nah, Ms. Kitty's cool, you can call me that," I said to her. I don't know if it was the Christmas spirit that had gotten into her, but she sure was being nice all of a sudden. I bet the Professor cursed her out real good for her to be this polite. I carried the gifts inside wishing one of them was for me. The Professor tried to carry the big Evergreen in the house but It was too big to fit through the door.

"I tried to tell him. That's what happens when you try to get the biggest tree," Sherry said to me.

"Well, we can sit it in the front yard and decorate it out here for everybody to see," I said. They laughed but I didn't think it was funny; I was serious. Why buy a tree for a day and only three people are gonna see it?

"Ms. Richards, I'm not going to let this tree beat me down. I'm going to cut it down and then it will fit through that door," he said while searching his trunk for the axe. Sherry followed me into the den and poured herself a drink while kicking off her high, heeled shoes.

"It's been so long since he's had company for Christmas," she began," that he's going haywire! Ive never seen him this excited; you've really made him happy these couple of weeks."

I was so shocked that she actually said that to me. She seems like the type to not praise any one for fear that they would think they were better than her. She continued," Look, I know I was very rude to you and your friend at our first meeting and I want to apologize. Friends?" She held out her hand for a hand-shake, more like a truce. I guess she finally realized that I wasn't going anywhere.

"What happened to your hand? Why is it wrapped up in that towel?" she asked.

"Oh, I cut my finger while doing something. It'll be alright."

"Well, here, let me take a look at it."

She tried to grab my hand but I snatched it back away from her. I wanted her to know that I still didn't trust her just because she made up that little apology. The Professor brought the tree in, now much smaller, and scurried around try-ing to find Christmas lights. After five minutes of searching, he appeared back in the room with a great, big, knot ball of lights.

"I hope these still work; I haven't used them since…." He started to say something but stopped.

"Um, Marshal, aren't they all different colors? That may look kind of tacky, don't you think?" asked Sherry.

"Oh, they'll be alright; It's Christmas. You better hope I don't have any left over after I cover the tree because I'll staple them all around the house!"

"No, please, not a Vegas style Christmas!" I yelled, "Those will do just fine for the tree."

I grabbed the big ball and began trying to untangle them when the fire alarm went off. We all jumped and grabbed our ears trying to drown out the loud, beeping sound and ran to where the smoke was floating out, the kitchen. My dinner! I totally forgot about my dinner. I waved the towel around in the air but the smoke would not disappear. The Professor grabbed it out my hands and wet it. I could barely see him or what he was doing but I think he was beating the microwave. Sherry rushed back out the room to call the fire department and I froze as I watched my world, fall apart. By the time I heard the sirens outside, he had gotten the fire under control and told me to go tell them that everything was fine now. Six men wearing masks and big rain looking coats greeted me at the door before I had a chance to open it.

"Wait, stop; Everythings fine. We got it under control!" I screamed but it was too late; they chopped a hole in the wall big enough for a person to walk through and began spraying their powerful, water hoses on everything, including the Professor.

"STOP…..STOP…..!" he yelled.

They cut their hoses off to listen. Sherry gasped when she saw the big hole in the wall and the water and smoke damage over everything. I couldn't believe they cut the wall instead of doing what a normal person would do, walk through the door. One of the men walked over to the microwave, opened its door, and pulled out the burnt can of vegetables. He held it up for everyone to see and said, "People, you can't put aluminum in microwaves." Just then I remembered the bird in the oven and took it out, black as tar, and turned off the oven.

"What in the world is that?" one of the firemen asked.

"I don't know. It looks like a cat," another said while laughing. I was so hurt. I mean all I wanted to do was cook him a nice meal and make this the best Christmas ever. He saw my disappointment and walked over to hug me.

"I know what you were trying to do and I appreciate it, really."

"But your kitchen. It's a mess, no it's more like a disaster zone!" I said.

"It'll be okay. I needed to remodel this outdated room anyway, but as a reminder, as long as you are here, please stay out the kitchen. Leave all the cooking up to Hilda."

"Don't worry about me coming in here. I was not meant to be a chef or a housewife."

The firemen grabbed up their hose and axe and left, this time through the door. Sherry invited us to her sister's house for dinner tomorrow and left also saying the smell was burning her eyes. "You need to start more fires around here," he whispered in my ear. I told him I was going to bed. After all this excitement today, it would take a long time for my body to wear down. I left him sitting on a wet barstool, staring in space.

I awoke the same way I have always done on Christmas since I was old enough to walk; running to the tree. I was halfway down the steps when I realized that I wasn't at home. I stopped and turned around to save myself any more embarrassment but the professor called me from downstairs. I slowly walked down the steps and to my surprise, the lights were brightly shining on the tree and a dozen presents were under it.

"I thought I was going to have to wake you up to ask you when did someone break in and leave all these presents for you?" he said.

"I already saw them last night and no, Santa is not real," I replied.

"Say's who? Who would say something so mean about Santa Claus?"

"I would because my Mom would take all the toys he 'made' and return them the next day at the stores." I didn't mean for that to slip out, it just did.

"You're trying to tell me that your mother would take back everything you got on Christmas?" I noticed a little anger in his voice. "Is that why you didn't go home for the holidays?"

"Well, no, not really. We just don't get along. And she has this boyfriend that I cant stand, either. I rather not see them and ruin my holidays." He looked sad but most of all upset. Did he care about me that much?

"Well, I'm ready to see what you got," he said with a smirk on his face.

"You already know, stop tripping. Aren't you the one that bought it?"

"No not all of it. April and Olandis left something for you and Sherry picked out some interesting things, too."

I tore into the boxes like my life depended on it, throwing wrapping paper all over the room as the Professor watched in joy. Sherry bought me two shirts and two pairs of pants to match. She has good taste, too. The Professor bought me a portable CD player with three CD's to listen to. But the best present I received came from April and Olandis. It was a broken piece of a silver heart charm. There was a cassette tape and a note inside the box that said, listen. I ran to the Professor's stereo system and put the tape in.

"Hey, Ms. Kitty. Hey Ms. Kitty, girl. I guess you got our little present, hunh? If you don't like it, it was all April's idea. Oh, shut-up Olandis and give me the microphone so I can talk. Excuse me, I said excuse me, April darling, but I am the future Oprah Winfrey and I know how to work a mic, okay so you need to sit down over there and be a good little audience. Ouch! Damn girl you didn't have to go ballistic, here take the mic. Hi again, Ms. Kitty. I hope you like your gift. We each have a piece of the heart to remember each other. Sorry we couldn't afford the necklace, too but you get the idea. I wish you could have gone to Jamaica with us but I know you'll have a good time there, you always do. Anyway, MERRY CHRISTMAS! Oh,

and don't do nothing I wouldn't do. Well that narrows a lot down; what is it that you don't do, Olandis? Oh girl, if you only knew. Ha, ha, ha."

I was cracking up after I heard them. They were truly a wild pair but now I was formally in their clique. We were a threesome and nobody was gonna tear us apart. The Professor told me to get ready; we were scheduled to be at Sherry's sister's house by noon. I really didn't feel like going but I knew I didn't want to stay by myself and starve on Christmas. What could possibly go wrong?

We were driving back to the Professor's house by two o'clock that afternoon. It turns out that Sherry's brother in law tried to make a pass at me after dinner and Sharon, her sister, caught him. She started screaming and yelling at him, saying how sick she was of his cheating and flirting and threw a knife across the room, barely missing his ear. Sherry kept apologizing to me while the Professor got our coats and stormed out the house. He told me he knew it was a bad idea to have dinner at their house. He couldn't stand Larry from the start. All he did was go to some strip club and spend all the mortgage money. I thought if those girls down at Dewayne's club had men giving up their mortgage and car payment money, just imagine how much they make a night.

I counted down the days, the hours, and the minutes until I would get to see that fine specimen of a man; Trent. I couldn't decide on what to wear for our second meeting but I knew it had to special. The Professor did the same routine everyday; wake up early to jog, shower, and then go to library and study all day or work at home on his computer. Hilda came on her regular days to clean the house and do our laundry. I overheard her complaining to the Professor about having to do extra work because of my being here and he doubled her salary until Febuary. She wasn't doing anything to being with and now she was making more money? I knew she was a con artist when I laid eyes on her. He hired some con-tractors to come out and take a look at the kitchen. They are scheduled to start working on the $4,000 project next week.. The Professor says he wishes it was a way he could sue the fire department and make them pay for it but he knew he wouldn't win. He and Sherry were going to a Masquerade Ball, New Years Eve. She hired a seamstress to design their costumes and would not tell him what or who they were going as, it was a surprise. I teased him so much about it that he demanded she tell him or he was not going. She called his bluff because he didn't find out that he was going as Adam and she was Eve until the afternoon of the party. They were real cute costumes although the Professor didn't like the idea of wearing nothing but a short, green, skirt designed to look like leaves. Sherry had the same skirt with a matching halter top and they both had grapevines for headpieces. She even had a fake, red, apple to carry around for the full effect. I took several pictures, which by the way would be used for blackmail later, and rushed them out the door. I was glad when he said not to wait up because the drive was an hour long and they would stay over for safety reasons. I was planning an all nighter myself and didn't want to have to give him any explanations. I hope Trent is not planning on staying here, it's too risky. I'll just pretend that I'm too tired to drive back to my place and make him get a room near the airport. I guess I should pack some clothes and clean underwear to take and keep in the trunk, just in case. As I gathered up some of my new jeans and shirts, I wondered if Hilda had deliberately shrunk them. They didn't fit the same as they did on Christmas. I walked in the Professor's room to look in his closet for a nice garment bag. A big, black, leather one was hanging behind some of his dress shirts. I pulled it out and realized he had something in it because it was extremely heavy. I unzipped it to discover 7 beautiful evening gowns and some designer pantsuits. I thought about Olandis and all his beauty secrets and wondered if the Professor was a cross dresser too. Nah, these are probably Sherry's clothes but they look too little for her, also. I tried on one of the dresses, a short red sequined, designer exclusive; custom made for a petite body. I looked like a supermodel. I had to let Trent see me in this, it would mess his mind up! In fact, I needed all these outfits if I was going to play the part of a successful, educated, career woman. I searched and searched for a nice pair of shoes to match and came up empty handed so my loafers would have to do. I took my shower, put on one of the pantsuits, experimented with the Professor's mouse and some water and finished with a beautiful, curly hairstyle. I wonder why I never tried this look before, anything was better than that tired, played out, ponytail I always sported. I grabbed the car keys and bag and headed out the door on my way to the airport.

My heart stopped beating for a minute and my panties went from dry to wet when I saw Trent walk through the airport terminal wearing a three piece suit. It lo0oked so nice on his emmaculate body that he could've been born in it.

"I wish I always had a fine woman picking me up," he said. He hugged me and I almost fainted when I felt his strong, muscular, arms around me and smelled the expensive cologne he was wearing.

"Well if you play your cards right, I could your very own personal chauffeur everyday," I flirted back.

I went to get the car while he waited for his bags to come around on the conveyor belt. He smiled a when he walked outside and saw me waiting in April's red BMW. He threw his two suitcases in the trunk and hopped in.

"So, were are we off to?" he asked.

"You tell me. Youre the one here for business, right?" I said.

"Well, actually this is personal. Remember last month when I met you?" I nodded my head; how could I forget? He continued," Well, I saved a gentleman from having to pay his now ex-wife a lot of alimony and half of his multi-million dollar corporation so he invited me to come to his annual New Years Eve Bash. They say it's the biggest throw down in this part of the country! I would love for you to be my escort tonight. I hope this isn't too late of a notice."

I couldn't believe I would be partying with the big shots tonight. I felt like Cinderella and he was my Prince Charming. I am so glad I brought that evening gown, but I hope it's not the same party the Professor is going to.

"Um, how are we supposed to dress for this occasion?" I asked.

"Strickly after five, black tie and evening gowns. Do you need to buy anything? Let me know because I forgot to tell you over the phone and I would be crushed If you couldn't attend."

"Well, I have a dress to wear but no shoes."

"Okay, take me to the mall and we'll pick out some pretty shoes for those pretty feet and those pretty calves and those pretty thighs," he said while sliding his hand up my leg until it was rubbing my inner thigh.

I could barely drive the five speed with his hands on my thigh. If he doesn't stop soon, we wont make it to the party.

He charged a pair of $200.00 shoes for me to his credit card. Impressive; I've never had a man spend that much on me. He already had reservations at this ritzy, hotel downtown, three blocks away from the mall. The valet took the car and the bellhop brought our bags to our room right as we were about to kiss.

I had been waiting for a sample of his lips once I saw him at the airport and now, this man ruined it while he waited for Trent to give him a tip. I got a tip for ya'; do not disturb! He finally left and we were alone again but Trent went to the bathroom to take his shower and get ready. He informed me that we were short on time and it's not proper ethics to show up late to something like this. I was so frustrated about not getting my kiss that I decided to do something about it, be bold and take charge. I walked in the bathroom and swung the shower curtains wide open exposing his outlandish, well proportioned (if you know what I mean) soapy, wet, body. I took off my clothes while he stared in desire and stepped in the shower with him.

"Oh, girl, what are you doing?" he asked;

"You said we didn't want to be late so I'm saving time by showering with you. You don't mind do you?"

I bent over to pick up the soap he had dropped while staring and felt his manhood harden against my buttocks. When I stood up, his fingers were massaging my pubic hair and I guided them all they way in with my hand. He gyrated his body against my back and kissed my neck until he brought me to that magical escapade. He turned the shower off and wrapped me in a towel. Then he carried me to the bed in the other room and poured lotion over my body. He massaged it in every spot he could find until I felt like I would slide off the bed. He unzipped my bag and pulled out the red evening gown and began putting it on my body. He stood me up to zip it and whispered in my ear, "I'm saving the best part for later." I sat at the foot of the bed and watched him dress. He knew exactly what he was doing to me and I was determined to hold out until after the party. He was so gorgeous in his tuxedo that I thought about raping him but decided to stick with my original plan.

"This is going to be hard with you in that red dress. Damn you look good!" he said while extending his hand to help me. "Ms. Kitty, may I have the honor of being your date tonight?"

"Yes you may," I replied.

I let him drive since he knew where the man's house is and boy, what a house. It had at least ten bedrooms, a gym, a game room complete with pool tables and pin ball machines, three or four living rooms, an office and a library, and a huge in ground pool. We were announced as we walked in the room where the party was held. There were only two black couples in the entire room, us and another couple and do you know the white people were friendlier than them. Trent walked around like I was his prize trophy. One time, I caught him staring at my every move when I went to get a drink so I put on a private show. I bent over the table to show him some cleavage and winked my eye at him. He rubbed his penis and winked back. We both laughed at our silliness. The owner of the house and past client of Trent walked up to him as I came back with my drink. He had two other rich white men with him.

"Come here, boys. I want you to meet the man that saved my life. Without him, I would owe that bitch a hell of a lot of money! He followed her around for months until he caught her in the bed with old Brewster. You remember Brewster, the one who tried to bribe Lawer for 15 million and the whole time was taking his money any way. I bet that stupid ex-wife of mine feels like shit to find out he was just using her to get to my money. He can have her, she wasn't that good in bed anyway!" The all laughed and grew real quiet after they noticed me standing beside Trent. "Well, Trent, who is this pretty lady you got here, your wife? If I had a woman as fine as her, I wouldn't care what she did as long as she came home to me," said the fat, old man.

"No sir, this is a close friend of mine, Ms. Kit…."

"Ms. Richards. You have a lovely home." I interrupted.

"Well thankyou. It cost me a fortune to get it like this, thanks to my ex, but now I can live in it peacefully," he said with a laugh. "It was good seeing you and you are welcomed to my house any time, Trent, anytime." He and his two little friends walked off.

"Well now that I've seen him, let's hit the trail," Trent said.

I knew he couldn't wait to get me back at the hotel and I couldn't wait another minute, either. We started kissing in the elevator of the hotel and ripped each other's clothes off while walking to the room. As soon as Trent opened the door, he picked me up and rushed to the bed, throwing me down on it. He snatched off my dress while I pulled down his pants and boxers. He thrust inside me hard and fast while still taking off the rest of his clothes. He still had on the bowtie so I used it like a harness on him when it was my turn to ride on top.

He really liked this game of cowgirl riding her horse and I wished I had a whip to make it even better. He started yelling, "Ride this horsey, baby, ride it, ride it!" until he pushed me off him and grabbed the condom. I leaned down and kissed him and told him goodnight. He was unable to move as he stared up at the ceiling.

I woke up around eight the next morning rushing to the bathroom. I guess the wine was the blame because I felt like I would never stop urinating. I took my shower and walked out wearing a towel. Trent was on the phone so I decided to tease him by nibbling on his ear. He kept changing the phone from ear to ear until he stood up where I couldn't reach them. I laid on the bed and took the towel off while he watched. His phone conversation sounded real strange to me. He was talking to a woman, had to be because he was talking in codes.

"Yeah… Tell them I miss them, too……Well we'll talk about it…. Um, yeah, I leave out today…" he said.

Today! No, he cant leave me today! He hung the phone up and walked to the bathroom. I followed right behind him.

"Why are you leaving so soon?" I asked.

"Business to take care. You do understand, don't you?" He began brushing his teeth like that excuse was suffice.

"No I don't understand. We just had a night of passionate love making and today youre gonna just up and leave? Who was that on the phone?" I demanded.

"You wouldn't know if I told you so just drop it, okay. Let's remember each other the way we were last night, not fussing at each other."

"Trent, who was that, your girlfriend back home? Be a man and tell me. It's not like we are commited to one another."

"You are so right. I'm glad you're so understanding. That was my wife and kids."

"Your Wife! You're married?"

"Yes, but we are having problems and I had to see you, take my mind off of it for a while."

"I guess you are having problems if you go around sleeping with innocent women. I cant believe you used me for a getaway from your problems."

"I didn't use you. I wanted your company. I thought that's what you wanted from me in return. You called me or did you forget?"

I couldn't hear a word he was saying, I was too busy putting on my clothes to leave. I took the car keys out his pant's pocket that were still lying on the floor and stormed out the room, leaving his half-naked self standing in the door shouting, "How am I supposed to get back to the airport?"

"CALL YOUR WIFE TO COME GET YA," I yelled back at him without turning around. I knew if I took one look at him, I would forget everything and stay. I got on the elevator and realized I would never see Mr. Trent, the Private Eye, again.

"Oh Ms. Kitty, it's so good to be home!" Olandis ran around his room, kissing his bed and the walls. "I've been away too long, thank you Jesus, I'm home! Where did that man go with my bags?"

"Right here. You could've helped me bring them up the steps. I thought they renovated this dorm?" Dewayne asked while carrying the suitcases in the room. "Why in the world is the elevator still broke?"

"You know how black people are, they cant be on time and don't know how to fix it. I wouldn't ride in the elevator if it was working, they probably used duck tape. We always use duck tape to fix stuff." Olandis replied. He began unpacking and putting things in his drawers.

"You right, baby, or super glue," Dewayne said.

"Child, that reminds me of the time Sis. Gregory used super glue on her dentures. She said she was sick and tired of her teeth falling out every time she got ready to do her solo so she soaked them suckers in super glue and put them in right before the choir got ready to sing. Well they got up there and started singing, 'Jesus will fix it', and when her part came, all she could do was hum. The organist played again, giving her cue and she hummed and clapped. Well by this time, everybody in the congregation started whispering and looking around until little Devlin, yes they named that bad child right, anyway little Devlin yelled, "The cat's really got her tongue!" and held up the empty denture box that was sitting in the seat beside him. One of the deacons walked over to him and took the box, smelling the loud odor and asked Sis. Gregory what kind of cream did she use. The usher, who was also a registered nurse said it smelled like super glue and asked if that was what she was actually smelling. Poor Sis. Gregory shook her head, yes, and the nurse went to call EMS. They arrived and some kind of way unsealed her mouth while the Preacher preached on the healing powers of God and the choir sang, 'Jesus will fix it'."

We were on the floor laughing our heads off when April and Rakeem walked in the room wearing matching straw hats." What happened? What did I miss?"

"Olandis was telling us another back home story," Dewayne said.

"Oh no, I don't think I could stand another one of those," she said.

"April, don't trip, darling. I know you got to have the best back home stories with your crazy, deranged, family. You just don't want us to know the real secrets of the Showers!"

"Okay you guys, I'm waiting to hear about the trip. Is Jamaica as beautiful as they say?" I eagerly asked.

"Well I wouldn't know," Olandis said.

"Why not? Werent you there?"

"He was there but the most he saw was the bathrooms. He drank the native water and had diarrhea the whole time!" Rakeem said while trying to keep a straight face.

"Do you know they left me to go sight seeing, Ms. Kitty? I was sick, practically on my death bed and they wanted to go look at a damn hut town."

"You were not going to die. Youre still living right?" April asked.

"Okay, see, um was anybody talking to her? No, I don't remember saying, Hey April, listen to me tell my side." Olandis was back. April was back. My whole crew was back and we were complete again. I was so happy even if I never got to find out about their trip and listen to April and Olandis argue all night.

Rakeem and Dewayne must've sneaked out during the night because when I woke up only April and Olandis were here. I jumped and ran to the bathroom. My bladder was full and I don't know how. In fact, it's been like that a lot lately, I hope I don't have a kidney infection. Maybe I'll go to the informatory later on today. I decided to get dressed and see if Quintin was back from his vacation. I looked in Olandis's closet and came up with a slamming shirt. I hesitated to wear it because it still had the price tag on it but his first time seeing me had to be just right. I was on my way out the door when Olandis stopped me, "Where are you going with that on?"

"Please, Olandis, let me wear it. I'm going to meet someone and they have to see me in it."

"I hope they don't see you in it. Look at yourself." He pointed to the mirror on his vanity. I was shocked to see the buttons about to pop right off and break the mirror.

"What size did you buy?" I asked.

"The same size I always get. You just need to push back from the eating table, girl! A diet will do you good. You must've ate that Professor out of house and home."

"I guess I did over eat. They say this is the time when everyone gains weight but I would've never thought it would happen to me. I don't know the first thing about dieting."

"Well youre in luck, Ms. Piggy. I took a nutrition course my first year here and I could help you get back to that petite size you once were. We'll get started ASAP. Deal?"

"Deal", I said and we shook on it.

He told me to go to my room and change into a sweat suit and grab some mitts and a warm hat. I was afraid to ask what he was planning on doing. I just wanted this extra weight off me and would do anything at this point. I couldn't let Quintin see me, he would definitely notice that I was a little chunky. As soon as I walked in my dorm, who should I run into? Denise of all people. Her and her little sorority sisters were laughing and hugging her but stopped when they saw me come in. I turned up my nose and walked on by like they were statues or something. Once inside the hall past the lounge doors, they continued with their silly chatter. I decided to eavesdrop on them since I had a funny feeling they were talking about her vacation and I wanted to know if Quintin was involved in it. I found out that he was more than involved in her vacation, they were engaged! How did she maneuver him into proposing to her? It didn't matter because there was not going to be a wedding, I'll make sure of that!

I met Olandis in the front of his dorm wearing a white wig, tight, spandex pants and a white Goosedown coat. He asked if I ever ran before and I answered, yes, plenty of times. He made me do stretching exercises and several jumping jacks before we started his workout routine. He pulled out a whistle and told me that over the next few weeks, whenever I heard this whistle, I was to stop and pay attention to him. He started doing a light jog around the campus which was nice, something I thought I could live with. Then he decided to take it to the streets since the campus roads seemed too easy for me. He picked up a little speed and we ventured into the outskirts of the campus. We were jogging on a little dirt road lined with trees when this big, beat up, Lincoln whipped around the curve in our direction causing us to dive off the road and into the woods. Olandis helped me up while cursing the driver out. The car slowed down and we saw it back up and turn around up ahead of us. I immediately got scared when I realized who the driver was, Lucille.

"Olandis, lets run for it!" I said.

"Wait till I give you the cue," he answered. As the car came closer and closer, I heard the passenger tell Lucille, "Yep, that's the one." She pressed down on the gas and charged right at us. Olandis blew his whistle and we took off, running full speed for our lives. She stayed right on our heels but couldn't catch us, her car was too ruin down to go faster than 40 mph. She called me all kinds of names through her window. I kept praying that her car would cut off.

"What ..did.. you.. do .. to.. this .. He woman!" Olandis asked while gasping for breath as he ran.

"I don't know," I said, "Maybe we should split up and bare off into the woods."

"Un, un, she aint killing me! Two hands are better than one."

I heard the car engine roar. The car mustve got some extra horse power from somewhere because it was gaining on us. Olandis wig fell off and he began slowing down and feeling his head. "Oh, hell no! I got to go back and get my do'!" he said.

"We cant, Olandis!" I yelled but apparently he didn't hear me pleading and begging because he turned around. I knew I couldn't leave him out here alone. It was me they were after in the first place. I slowed down to catch my breath and right as I was about to turn around, I heard the gun go off! POW! I screamed, "OLANDIS !" and stopped dead in my tracks. I was afraid to look back. I couldn't bear to see him lying there on the ground covered in blood. I listened for a second for some sort of sign then out of nowhere I was swept up in the air. It was him and he was alive, running like the wind. I heard Lucille yell, "I'll get you if it's the last thing I do!" My heart was racing as we turned the corner inside the campus gates. We didn't stop running until we were safely inside Olandis's room

"Hey, slow down, guys. You act like you've seen a ghost," April said as we rushed in the room.

"We have. A big fat one and oh, was she scarry!" Olandis said, "I aint fooling with you no more, Ms. Kitty. You too dangerous for me. Who was that by the way?"

"I don't know. Maybe she thought I was someone else." I couldn't let them know the truth about my adventurous night; they wouldn't understand.

"Well you need to change your identity cause that bitch is crazy!"

"Did someone try to hurt you two?" April asked.

"Try? She did hurt us. I paid 89 dollars for this wig, had it custom cut and shipped all the way from Malaysia and now look at it. It looks like a worn out poodle!" He held the destroyed hair piece up in the air and shook it trying to get it's shape back.

"At least youre not dead, Olandis. When I heard that gun go off, I was afraid to look ba…."

"Gun? What gun? That was her car tire. It's a good thing she was driving an old, raggedy car or we would both be hurt."

It was a good thing because Lucille wanted me dead or alive. She probably preferred alive so she could torture me to death. I had to let her know that John was not my man and I didn't want him to be but how. It was too late. She wasn't trying to hear any explanations. She lost her leg because of me and now she wanted revenge.

I walked around in a daze over the next couple of weeks. I was paranoid, thinking Lucille had maybe followed us back to the campus. I couldn't let her find out where I lived. Maybe I should talk to Dewayne and see if he can help me. As far as our work out routine, it was officially canceled. Olandis said he kept having flash backs and nightmares of him running until he ran out of streets and fell off the earth. He even went to his physic, Madame Crumeur, to try to figure his dreams out. She said that his time was running short and took all his money.

I saw Quintin every now and then around campus but never face to face, up close and personal. I wanted to know if the rumors were true. I still haven't seen a ring on Denise's finger, not that I was looking for one. He wouldn't return my phone calls or even look my way when we passed in the hall on our way to class. I tried to get my classes changed so we would have a class together but all his classes were full and you had to wait until next semester to get a spot in. He was a senior and had first priority since he needed those classes to graduate. I never gave up trying to win his love and attention back, until one day after weeks of chasing, he answered the phone.

"Hello," he said in that sexy voice that always turns me on.

"Hey, boo. How have you been?"

"Oh cool and you?"

"Cant complain. So why haven't you returned my calls?"

"You called? I thought you didn't want to talk to me since you never speak when you walk by," he said.

"I didn't think you noticed. It's all about Denise now."

"Nah. Don't believe the rumors. Were not together, she's just telling everybody that so no one will try to talk to me, especially you."

"Me? Why me?"

"Because she knows that you got me hooked, baby girl. I don't know why, but I couldn't get you off my mind these past months. I tried to get in touch with you but didn't know how."

"Is that so? Well once you got in touch with me, what were you planning on doing?"

"Satisfying you in every way possible."

"Hmmm, I like the sound of that. Can I get a little satisfaction now?"

"You name the place and I'm there."

"You know the room number." I hung up the phone, eagerly getting ready for my work out with Quintin. He mustve ran the entire way because he was knocking on my door in five minutes. I stripped out my clothes and opened the door.

"Damn, baby. This is what I've been missing." He kissed me and carried me to the bed and we began our magical escapade only to be interrupted.

"What in the name of Satan is going on in here?" Olandis screamed with his hands in the air. April covered her eyes like it really was a sin to see. Quintin covered his body up with the comforter and tried to hide his face.

"Is that that no good, Quitin, under there?" he asked.

"Olandis, this is my room and I'm sick and tired of you barging in unannounced," I said to him while pulling in my robe.

"Well excuse me, Mrs. Hot in the Pants, but it is the middle of the day and if you wanted a do not disturb sign for your door, you shouldve went to Motel Six! I'm out!" He said while slamming the door behind him. April gently opened it and hurried out, too with out looking back.

"I guess I should be leaving now," Quintin suggested.

"No, baby. You can stay, don't pay him any mind." He continued to get dressed and after putting on the last of his clothes, he left. Just like that with out a goodbye or a kiss. I was so mad that I thought about finding Olandis and cursing him out but he would make a big scene and I didn't want Quintin's and my business broadcast in the streets.

Olandis and I apologized and came up with a plan to keep embarrassing moments like that to a minimum. We devised a system where we used scarves. The yellow scarf meant I was busy but you could still enter and the purple scarf meant I had company, do not disturb. I used the purple scarf a few times over the weeks with Quintin but I noticed a dramatic change in his behavior or should I say his performance. After the third time of not getting satisfied, I decided that we needed to talk.

"Quintin, whats wrong? You seem ..um.. tired lately. Are you getting enough sleep or am I just that good in bed?" I asked hoping to see a smile on his face. None ever came.

"I'm going into the service," he said bluntly.

"What service. Who are you giving service to besides me?"

"Quit acting stupid, you know what I mean. I have to be able to provide for a family and I've tried to get interns and job offers in my field but no one wants a well, educated, black man, except Uncle Sam."

"No baby, you cant leave me. You don't have to take care of me yet. We have plenty of time to start a family, just enjoy us, our time together, now. Youll get a good job once you graduate. They just want to see your degree before they hire you."

"You just don't get it, do you? I have to take care of my family. Look Ms. Kitty, I love you and all but youre just too young. You have time to move on and find somebody else but Denise has been there for me through thick and thin and I wont find another girl as special as her. She moved the wedding date up to June, once we graduate, because I'll be shipped out for the Military the end of that month."

I couldn't believe what I was hearing. She knew exactly what she was doing, trying to ruin our romance, our relationship, our love for each other. She had him completely brainwashed him. He loved me, he said so. He never said he was in love with her. I may need to go to Madame Crudeme and put a spell on Denise's evil ass, her powers were stronger than mine and I need help.

Time passed on and all I could do was think about Quintin. I couldn't understand why I was so in love with him, I just was. He sent me flowers, or at least I thought it was him. He wouldn't look at me, I guess he knew he couldn't bear the pain. That or either the fact that I had gained twenty pounds. I couldn't understand how I gained so much when I wasn't eating. Quintin had my body so messed up, it was going through withdrawals. I was really depressed. Olandis and April told me that he was no good for me or any woman for that matter. They constantly drilled in my head that I was better off without him and Denise was going to suffer for the rest of her life if she married him. How could I explain that he was the only man I was ever in love with. He was the only person that ever told me that they loved me. I wanted him badly. I made the mistake of telling April that I wanted to die and she had a team to sit with me around the clock, day and night, Rakeem, Olandis, Dewayne, her, and even 'Head'. After convincing her that I was only kidding and Head's razor bumps were grossing me out, she took the team off watch. One day out of the blue and two months after our last rendezvous, Quintin called while I was half asleep listening to the radio.

"Hey baby. I miss you so much. I have to see you. What are your plans for Spring Break?" he asked.

"Is this some kind of joke?" I had let time go by so fast that I forgot all about Spring Break. I didn't even realize it was spring.

"No, this is for real. I want to get away, with you, alone. I'm leaving for the beach tomorrow and Denise doesn't know a thing. I want you to come with me."

"Okay," I weakly said. I wasn't sure about his little plans but it wouldn't hurt to take a vacation and especially with the man I love. After a week alone with him, he'll come home singing a new song. So long Denise, it was nice knowing you! I went through my closet trying to find something that fit. I needed beach wear, something I had no clue about. I didn't own a bikini and my shorts were too little. I couldn't button them at all. I don't have time to loose weight overnight so I'll have to go and buy some new things. I can't let Quintin see me looking like this, he might mistake me for the humpback whale! Where is April when you need her? I don't have any money and I know she'll lend it to me until I get my work study check; which by the way will be very short because I haven't reported to The Professor in weeks. He called a couple of times to check on me but April told him I wasn't here. I didn't want to see or talk to anybody but Quintin. I paged Olandis and he never returned the call. My time was running out, the mall would be closed in an hour. I put on my too tight jeans and one of Rakeem's shirts that April had worn. It was big on me but it's just right for what I had planned. I ran out the room to catch the last bus leaving the campus for the night and was on my way to the mall. The bus let me off right in front of the expensive department store that Olandis vowed never to go in again. I walked over to the bathing suits and grabbed a couple of the designer ones with out looking at the price. It was all or nothing with Quintin and I had to 'dress to impress' as Olandis would say. I picked up some cute sundresses with the backs out, I was determined he would not forget me when he saw me. I grabbed a couple of shorts, size sixteen, to fit my now voluptuous rump. The cashiers were shutting down some of their registers so no one noticed me slip in the dressing room. I took off my clothes and put three bikinis on. Then I put on a pair of the shorts and one of the sundresses. I put my jeans back on and Rakeem's shirt. I folded up the other dress several times so it would fit in the bikini bra making me look like I had some big breasts. I left the other shorts and dress in the fitting room and rushed through the store to get to the train since the bus had stopped running my way. Right as my foot hit the pavement, a man walked up and grabbed me by my arm saying, "Come back in the store with me."

"What for?" I asked as I tried to free myself of him. He never answered, he just took me to a back room in the store where a woman and two other men waited for my arrival.

"Mamm, we have reason to believe you were shoplifting. Detective Booker will search you now. Do you have any weapons or narcotics on you that you wish to tell us about?" I shook my head. If I had a weapon, I would blow all their brains out. The lady searched me and found all the merchandise I had tucked under my clothes while another Detective totaled up the 'damage' as they called it. It wasn't damaged, they could resale it. When they finished, the total bill came to $725. The man that brought me in explained what was going to happen next. "The police are on their way down here and from then on, its out of our hands."

"So I'm going to jail?" I asked. "Why did you call the police? You got all your merchandise back so I really didn't steal anything."

"No, you got caught and shoplifting is a crime. Is there any one I can call for you? They may want to meet you down at the station with your bail."

I couldn't think of anybody to call. April and Olandis had disappeared and they wouldn't have money anyway. Besides, I didn't want them to know about me shoplifting. Just then, it hit me.

"Yes, can you call one of my Professors?"

"So you're in college? You should've smart enough to know not to steal," he said. I gave him the number and he explained to the Professor what had happened. He hung up and turned to me and said, "He said he'll be waiting down at the penitentiary. Is he a white man?" I had just about had enough of this jack ass.

"Are you? Excuse my manners, you're red. A big red neck and so is this store. If I had been white, you probably would've let me go but no, you had to call the cops. You didn't even check to see if I was under age."

"You are a criminal and that's all that matters!" he screamed. There was a knock at the door and two police officers walked in.

"Is this the suspect?" they asked pointing to me. I thought he just told me I was a criminal and now I was a suspect. Somebody get it straight.

"Yes," said the rude undercover guy.

One of the officers told me to stand up and he locked the hand cuffs in back of me. One of them told me to follow him and the other walked behind me, as if I could run away with these tight handcuffs on. They led me to the police car and carried me to jail. I was placed in a holding cell for an hour with another female inmate until someone came in to talk to me.

"Ms. Richards?" she asked.

"Yes," I jumped up and ran to the bars. The guard unlocked them and asked me to follow them to another room, more like a small office. I noticed the nametag on the desk and realized she was a Judge. She began speaking, "I have set your bond for 1,000 dollars. A gentleman has posted your bail. You are to appear in court two weeks from this date. If you have any questions, call this number." She slid a card across the desk to me. "You may get off light if you don't get into anymore trouble between now and then." The officer took my mug shot and fingerprints, after that I was free to go. I walked in the waiting area to see the Professor standing there with a worried look on his face. He ran up and hugged me, not wanting to let me go. "Are you alright?" he asked. I didn't know what to say or think. The reality check had not registered to me that I'd been arrested, partly because I couldn't get my mind off Quintin. I had to get in touch with him before morning. The Professor drove me to his house not saying a word the entire time or asking me if I wanted to stay with him. I wanted to be alone, in my room, well not entirely alone ; I wanted Quintin there. He parked the jeep and disappeared into his room. I couldn't tell if he was upset or worried but why would he be? I'm the one who went through the dramatic experience of being behind bars, not him. I waited until I was sure he was asleep and sneaked downstairs. It was hard trying to find keys in the dark but I did it. I eased out the house, let the handbrakes down and rolled the jeep to the end of the driveway, then jumped in and started it up. I wish I had time to wash all the prison grime off me but I was on a serious time consuming mission. I had to find my man and leave tonight instead of in the morning. I rushed inside his dorm, thankful that no one was on duty at the front desk, and pounded on his door. I heard a lot of scuffling around inside until he finally opened the door with a very surprised expression on his face.

"Ms. Kitty, what are you doing here? I thought you weren't allowed in the males dorm," he said while stepping in the hall and closing the door behind him.

"I know but I had to see you. I want us to leave tonight, please. I'll explain it later, just get your bags and come with me," I pleaded.

"I cant, I mean I don't want to leave tonight. I stayed up half the night doing an essay and I haven't had any sleep."

"Well fine then. I'll just come in and sleep with you until youre ready to get up." I pushed the door and he grabbed my arm, stopping me.

"It's a little messy in there. My roommate is sleep in there too so why don't you go on to your room and I'll call you first thing in the morning," He said as he kissed my forehead and tried to shoo me along but just then a female voiced asked, "Quintin, baby, who are you talking to? Come back to bed!"

That damn Denise! How could he have her in there, sleeping in his bed? I pushe dhim out of the way and barged in the room, turning the lights on. I was ready to give Denise my last bit of beating that I had saved for so long until I realized it wasn't Denise in his bed. It was some other chick! She jumped up, gathering the covers around her naked body and screamed, "Who is this?"

"Who the hell are you?" I asked with an attitude. Quintin walked up to me and grabbed my arm, keeping me from being able to reach her. He shoved me to the door and pushed me out yelling, "Respect my room! And quit calling me all the time!" He slammed the door in my face. I was too hurt to cry and too mad to go back and fight. He was a dog and I knew, I knew the whole time. I drove around for hours trying to blow off steam until eventually, I parked the Professors jeep in a deserted alley. The morning sunrise shined right in my face, waking me up at the crack of dawn. No, wait a minute. This isn't sun, it's a police light shining in my face.

"Step out of the car, mam." he said. I did as I was told. I didn't want to go to jail two times in the same night.

"What's wrong? What did I do?" I asked.

"This car has been reported stolen. Do you have license and registration?"

"This car is not stolen. Call Professor Phillips and he'll tell you who I am. I borrowed the car from him. Please call him. He'll clear this mess up."

I guess the officer believed part of my story because he radioed in that he had found the car and was taking me back to the Professor's house. Another police car drove up and he drove the jeep back to the house. I sat in the den while the two officers talked to the Professor at the front door. I heard the door shut and his footsteps come closer to the den.

"Ms. Richards, you are to stay with me until your court date. During this time you are on probation. I want you in this house by seven o'clock each night, no telephone and no TV. And that little stunt you pulled tonight will never happen again or I'm signing my name off your bond and putting you in jail myself!"

I wondered if he could legally do that but I guess he knew more about the law than I did. My life had become a total fiasco. I lived day in and day out, depressed and mad at the world. I lied to Olandis and April about my living arrangements. I told them that I had gotten so spoiled over the holidays, that I didn't like living in the dorm room anymore. April was a little hurt and thought she was the reason I didn't want to stay there but I assured her that I would be back in a couple of weeks. Hilda didn't look so happy to see me but the Professor told her to be nice, it was only temporary.

The two weeks went by slow but finally, that glorious day came. I didn't know what my sentence would be as far as with the court but I knew my time was up with the Professor and that's all that mattered. He made me wear an ugly, church-girl, dress and told me to put my hair in a ponytail. I didn't protest because I wanted my freedom back. He explained all the do's and don'ts on the way to the court house. Do answer Yes mam or no sir and don't roll your eyes or suck your teeth; two bad habits I have. Do answer in complete sentences and don't tell them too much. By the time we arrived downtown and took our seat in court, I was a confused, nervous, wreck. People were in there for all type of charges, mine didn't seem all that bad compared to the others. The Judge called me to the stand after the sixth person had gotten their sentence and left the courtroom. I walked up to the front with the Professor.

"Plaintiff, what are the charges?" the judge asked.

"Shoplifting." He answered. I didn't notice the rude, red neck undercover guy from the store, standing at the other podium.

"Would you like to tell what happened?"

"Yes. At approximately 8:45 pm. The defendant walked in our store, grabbed a couple of items and went into a dressing room coming out with no items in her hand. One of the other detectives searched the dressing room and found nothing informing me that she was wearing the clothes. I apprehended the suspect at 9:03pm. as she walked out the door. Afterwards we stripped searched her and recovered 725 dollars worth of merchandise."

"Defendant, do you have anything you would like to say at this time?" the judge asked me.

"No.. mam.." I was speechless. How could I compete with his story?

"Okay, since this is your first offence, I'm entering you in a counseling and community work service program. Upon completion of this program, your record will be wiped clean of all criminal charges. You may see the clerk outside the courtroom, now. Case dismissed." She pounded her gravel on her desk. I really didn't understand what she was saying but it sounded good so far. We walked out the courtroom to talk to the clerk. She signed all my forms and told me there would be an orientation in about three weeks so look for my letter in the mail. The Professor made sure it came to his address. She said there was a two hundred fee for the sessions and twenty-five dollars for a drug test which will be given at that time. She handed me the papers and we were headed back to his house until I spoke up.

"I thought you said I didn't have to live with you anymore."

"So you don't like staying with me?" he asked, somewhat upset.

"No, it's not that. I just want to be able to do things, you know, like watch TV or go out with my friends at night."

"Fine. You are free to do those things. I think you have proven to me that you are somewhat responsible and I don't have to worry about you skipping town on me but I do want to take you to all your sessions." He turned the jeep around and took me back to my dorm. "I'll bring your clothes by later."

I was so excited to be back in my dorm, even if it did smell like a thousand different perfumes and all types of music was blaring from the rooms along with female screams and laughter. I put my key in and turned the doorknob. April had redecorated the place. Instead of pink on her side of the room, she now had midnight blue everywhere. I opened the blue blinds to try to get some sunlight in but it was still dark. I decided that this was a good time for a nap.

Four hours later, someone was jumping on my bed shouting, "She's back, She's back!" I awoke to see April standing over me. She started hitting me with a pillow and I grabbed the one from under my head and began hitting her back with it.

"So, children, are we finished so I can hit the café ?" Olandis said while standing in the floor filing a nail. April jumped down off the bed and said, "Come on, girl. You haven't had cafeteria food in a while. I bet your stomach cant wait to get some grease!"

I almost threw up when she said the word grease, making me think about the food they serve." You all go on. I'm not hungry."

"Well, if it isn't Miss Too Good for us!" Olandis said while rolling his eyes, "You need to come on down off that high horse the Professor done put you on, and ride with the little ponies again. Okay?"

"All I said was I'm not hungry but since you feel that way, I'm going with you. I'm going to watch you eat."

"I don't care about you watching me. People watch me all the time. They cant get enough of Olandis, honey, so knock yourself out." He walked out the room and April dragged me out behind him, covering my mouth with her hand.

April was right, it had been so long since I ate in the cafeteria, I had forgotten the scenery and the awful grease smell. I saw the girl that was in Quintin's room that dreadful night before Spring Break. She was so ugly and those clothes, oh God were they out of style! What in the world does he see in her? I walked across the cafeteria to get a plate and let her know that I was here if she wanted to set it off. I stared her down as I strutted back across the room and she did a quick laugh as she shook her head and continued eating.

"I thought you weren't hungry," April teased.

"I figured I might as well eat since I'm here." Someone had brought in a karaoke machine and set it up on the small stage. You know who had to be the first to test it out, Olandis. He grabbed the microphone and started singing, Proud Mary. It just so happens that he was unexpectedly wearing his 'Tina' wig. He shimmied and shook all over the place like he was loosing his mind. He knew every step to that song and when it ended, the crowd gave him a standing ova-tion. I was so busy laughing and cheering that I didn't notice Quinitn's love mate had moved to the seat beside me.

"Hey, Kitty, right? I wanted to talk to you," she said.

"Well, it's Ms. Kitty and I don't feel like talking right now."

"Good because you don't have to, I said I wanted to talk. Any way, I didn't know Quintin was supposed to be your man and all, but it doesn't matter because I don't want him like that. He's just somebody that I like to have sex with, no strings attached. I thought Denise was his one and only and I could care less about how she feels. That is if she knows, but we've been doing this for two years and I aint stopping now. I mean, you know for yourself that the boy has it going on in bed but that's about it. I just don't want you to be like I was my freshman year; all caught up with a no good dog. I was so depressed that I almost flunked out of school. He aint worth it, baby and if you think he's gonna change, think again. I'm not hating on you. I think you cute and I know you could have any guy on this campus because I've heard the fellas' talking about you but they didn't step to you because Quintin was playing you and they thought you were stupid or something. All I'm saying is you need to change what you're looking for because you definitely won't find it in him." She walked off without looking back and started talking to some girls that were leaving out the door.

"What was that all about?" asked April.

"Nothing. Just some good advice to live by," I said.

Two weeks exact, my letter from the Solicitor's office came. I was scheduled to appear for my orientation this Tuesday morning and take a drug test, which cost twenty-five dollars. The Professor picked me up in front of my dorm and drove me to the courthouse where I met my counselor who went over the rules with me. I signed a lot of papers and she gave directions to the lab where I was to take my drug test. On the way over, the Professor asked me if I ever did drugs.

"No. Do you think I would ruin my perfect body over some drugs?"

"I was just curious. You know drugs are real heavy at the school and I didn't know if anyone had approached you with them. I hope you know the effects of them and arent just talking to throw me off."

"I'm serious. I wouldn't touch a blunt. They smell too bad."

"Well I don't want you to have to go through what I…." He stopped and thought about what he was about to say.

"What were you gonna'say?" I asked. He hesitated for a minute and wiped the sweat off his face. "Um, you were saying? Come on now. You know everything about me but I don't know anything about you."

"Okay, you're right. Um, where do I begin? I was in college when I first experimented with drugs. I wanted to try them not thinking that I would get hooked on them but I did. I was on drugs for two and a half years until I met her. The woman that brought me back, gave me a new life. We fell in love immediately, she got pregnant, and I got worse. I couldn't take the pressure of bringing up a child so I started back taking drugs. I didn't even realize she had left until a couple of months later and when I found her again, she didn't want anything to do with me. I was hurt, devestated. I went back home to go to rehab and finish college while living with my parents and sister. She was the only one who knew about my dilemma and saved me from commiting suicide. I studied all the time to take my mind off it and before I knew it, I had a Ph.D. but I still thought about her."

"Did you ever see her again?"

"Yeah, but it hurt too bad. She hated me and I couldn't bear to see the sadness in her eyes, so stay drug free."

"Wow, that's some kind of speech," I said.

"I hope you don't think I'm making it up"

"No, I believe you." We pulled into the drug testing center and I could tell he was nervous as we strolled down the halls. He probably remembers the times he was in rehab. I saw room two twenty and walked up to the receptionist's desk and gave her my name. She gave me a form to fill out while I waited my turn and called me to the back fifteen minutes later. I peed in a cup labeled with my name, turned it in to the nurse and was free to leave.

"That was quick," said the Professor.

"Yeah, I'm glad, too, because I'm hungry," I replied.

He treated me to a deluxe chili, cheeseburger with cheese fries, a large milkshake, and an apple turnover for desert.

"Boy, you were hungry! If you don't watch out, your gonna look like the Goodyear Blimp!" He was right. I had acquired a huge taste bud, I ate all the time. I had gained at least twenty or thirty pounds in the last five months. Maybe that's the reason Quintin didn't want anything to do with me anymore. I was depressed, I had really let myself go, but I was determined to get back to my old self. My petite, beautiful, self. After eating, the Professor dropped me off at my dorm and since no one was in my room, I stuck my finger down my throat and made all the food come up. I was exhausted after throwing up and could feel my body still having convulsions. I felt real dreary, light headed, and then....

Life

"Ms. Kitty, Ms. Kitty.....Olandis, what is that?" I smelled a strange odor and saw April and Olandis standing over me when I opened my eyes.

"Girl, don't scare me like that again! What is that smell? It smell like something has crawled in here and died!" Olandis said.

"What happened?" I asked.

"You mustve passed out," April replied.

"I feel like I'm gonna pass out with this funk!" Olandis stated while spraying air freshener all around the room. He walked in the bathroom and yelled, "I found it! I found the rodent! Why did you leave vomit on the floor and in the toilet?"

"I don't know? I, I, I, thought I flushed it and I oh, God, I don't know why. I just felt bad. I'm so fat."

"Ms. Kitty, is that it? You made yourself throw up. Youre not that fat and youre still pretty but if you start making yourself sick, then you'll get ugly. Look, if you think you're so fat then we'll help you. We'll work out with you everyday and help you watch what you eat."

"I tried that already. It didn't work, remember?"

"We'll make it work, right Olandis?" April said.

"That's right. You know we got your back, sista' girl."

"Thanks you guys. I'll try harder this time but right now, I would like to take a nap." They agreed to give me some quiet time if I promised not to try that stunt again.

I slept all that day and night. When I tried to wake up, I couldn't. I felt like something was pushing me back down in the bed. I told myself I would never do this again. My body just could not handle the adjustment. I heard the phone ring early the next morning. I had to get up to answer it, I had to get out of bed and push myself to go to class anyway.

"Hello," I said.

"Hello, may I speak with Ms. Richards?" a lady asked.

"This is she."

"Ms. Richards, to verify your identity, could you give me your social security number."

"What? You called me. What kind of joke is this?"

I hung up the phone. I wasn't in the mood for games but whoever it was wanted to play some more because they called right back.

"Ms. Richards, this is the Center for Drug Testing," she said, "I need your cooperation in this matter, please." She said.

"Okay, damn, that's all you had to say the first time."

"Is your social 224- 78-1996?"

"Yes."

"Well Ms. Richards, when your test results came back, they noticed something in your urine and when we looked back at your papers, we noticed that you didn't write down that you were pregnant. We need you to bring a statement from your doctor showing how far along you are and if you are in good condition to do light community service. Your timely manner would be appreciated so we can process your paper work to send to the court."

"You must have the wrong person. I'm not pregnant. I cant get pregnant."

"Well ma'am, we have the results if you want to take a look at them but we do need you to bring us something from a doctor. Maybe you should get an appointment with an Obgyn if you feel our test isn't right." I hung up on her again. A thousand thoughts went through my mind. It had to be true, it would explain the weight gain, the depression, and the times I was sick and extremely tired. Now the next question was, who is the proud Papa? There was Trent, Tuan and Quintin. Lets see, Tuan used a condom and I remember being sick before I got with Trent so it had to be Quintin's. I threw on some clothes and called Olandis's room to tell them the news. Olandis answered on the first ring.

"Olandis, is April with you?" I asked.

"Yeah, what's up?"

"Meet me in front of the library in ten minutes with the car," I didn't give him time to ask for an explanation. They were waiting in front of the library as expected and I jumped in the car and told him to drive to the nearest clinic.

"Oh shit! What has that nigga' gave you. I told you if you lie with dogs, you'll get fleas!"

"Olandis, it's a little bit deeper than fleas. I think I'm pregnant!" He almost ran into a tree as they both shouted, "PREGNANT!"

"What are we gonna do?" asked April.

"I think that's up to Ms. Kitty. We don't have a decision in this." Olandis replied.

"I'm keeping it. I want this baby." They looked at me like I was retarded.

"How are you going to take care of it?" April said.

"It doesn't matter. We'll make do and he or she will have the best!" Olandis stated.

We waited in the waiting room for an hour until the nurse finally called me back to take my blood and urine samples. She lead me to a room and asked me to remove all my clothes. I didn't bother about asking Olandis to leave. He was nervous enough being in a hospital setting and I know he was not going to be left sitting alone. When I removed my too tight clothes, April shouted, "I can see it. Look in the mirror."

I turned around and looked in the mirror at myself. My stomach looked like a miniature beach ball.

"All this time you were hiding that belly from us. We need to start paying close attention to your sneaky ass!" Olandis teased.

"I didn't know myself. I just found out."

The Doctor walked in with his assistant and asked me to lie back and slide forward. He placed a cold instrument inside my vagina and gently slid it back out. Then he poured a jelly like substance all over my stomach and rubbed a funny device around in it. We heard a weird sounding noise come from the thing, almost like puppy breathing hard.

"What in the world is that?" Olandis asked, coming closer for a better look.

"That's the baby's heartbeat," said the doctor.

"That's the baby? It sound more like a dying whale out to sea!"

"Oh, that's so sweet. Ms. Kitty, you truly are blessed. Can you tell us what it is, Doctor?" April said.

"Sure, if Ms. Richards wants to know. I can squeeze you in for an ultrasound." The doctor replied.

"No, I don't want to know. I want it to be a surprise."

"Okay, but I still need to do an ultrasound to determine exactly how many months you are."

"Well, you can tell me. I can keep a secret," Olandis said, "Besides we have to buy clothes and other things for the baby." The doctor laughed and made Olandis and April sign a piece of paper stating that they will not tell me the sex of the child no matter what I tried to do. I knew Olandis would love knowing something I didn't. The doctor pulled out something that looked like a TV and had me turn my face.

"Wow, look at that!" "That sucker is big!" "Oh, it kicked something!" "It's waving at us." "It's going to be a star just like Uncle Olandis!"

I wanted to see what all the fuss was about but I was not going to look. It didn't matter what it was, I was going to love it. I got another chance and I'm not messing it up. The doctor turned the machine off and told me to come to his office once I got dressed. We sat in his office, admiring all his plaques and degrees when he walked in and took his seat behind the desk.

"Um, I'll make this brief. Ms. Richards, I estimate your pregnancy to be about 28 weeks. With you being this far along, I usually dont offer my services but I'm going to make an exception in this case. I know you're in college and probably don't have a lot of money so you may want to talk to the receptionist about Medicaid and I need to see you in two weeks."

We went to the receptionist and listened to her explain about Medicaid then filled out the necessary forms and was on our way out the door when, you wont believe this, Denise walked in. She was so shocked to see us that she almost passed out but the receptionist called her name and carried her straight to the back before she could sign in.

"Well, look what the wind blew in," Olandis said. April was terrified of what Olandis would do or say so she pushed him in his back all the way to the parking lot. "What's wrong with you, girl. I aint gonna do nothing. She is not worth my precious time!"

"I'm glad you see that now. Ms. Kitty, are you gonna be alright?" April asked.

"Yes, why wouldn't I be?"

"Well, I thought that after seeing Denise in there and all that you would be hurt. I wonder how many weeks she is?"

It never registered to me that Denise was pregnant also. She probably planned it that way. She might have known that I was pregnant with Quintin's baby and she didn't want to loose him to me so she got pregnant. She was so trifling but I wasn't going to let her get to me. He was gonna take care of this baby, too, and she couldn't do a thing about it. I cant wait to get back to the dorm so I can tell him the good news.

"Well Ms. Kitty, are you gonna tell him?" April asked interrupting my thoughts.

"Tell who what?" I said.

"Whoever the father is. Are you gonna talk to him?"

"April please, Ms. Kitty can do bad by herself! She don't need that sorry ass Quintin!" Olandis boldly stated.

"Quintin? You're having Quintin's baby?" she asked with a sad expression.

"Well who did you think it was, some angel just popped out the sky and said you're having the second coming of Christ?" Olandis said.

"I guess I knew but I didn't want it to be his. He's totally not father material."

"Wait just a dog-gone- minute. You all are talking about my baby's daddy! Quintin will make a good father." I shouted.

"Hmmp, if you think he is good at anything, you better think again, honey. Get ready because you in this thing by yourself. You cant depend on no man now a days. You got to get yours the best way you can. Now we are here to help you, we wont let you down but if you think Quinitin's gonna be there for you, get prepared for disappointment! April, hand me the cell phone. I'm calling my honey boo so we can go baby shopping. Lil Boo' will be here in less than two months and we got to get ready." He dialed Dewayne's number and told him the news. Dewayne must've been excited because he agreed to meet us at the

Babies, Babies, Babies store in twenty minutes. We pulled into the expectant mothers parking space at the huge department store. I never paid the place much attention up to now. We spotted Dewayne as he pulled up and April ran to get the last shopping cart while Olandis ran to get the last mommy and me wheelchair. I told him I didn't need it, I didn't look half as tired as the other pregnant women that werent able to run and get the chair. I walked around in a trance looking at all the baby gadgets that were in the store. Olandis threw everything he could get his hands on in the buggy and when we came to the clothing section, he made me go out to the car with April so I couldn't tell what I was having. I didn't like the idea of Olandis dressing my baby. It didn't matter if it was a boy or girl, he would still cross dress. They came out pushing three buggies full of baby furniture, clothes and toys. Most of it fit in Dewayne's car but the rest had to hang out the trunk of April's car. They looked funny trying to sneak all that heavy stuff up to my room. Dewayne put a blanket over the bassinet to try to disguise it but it made passerbyers more curious. A couple of residents asked Olandis if we bought a big screen TV and wanted to know if they could come to our room to watch it. He just laughed at them and called them noisy witches behind their backs. We spent the entire night hammering and putting pieces together. Dewayne and Olandis argued over everything from which end is up to which way is down. Around two that morning, I fell asleep and when I awoke the next day, the room didn't look the same. April had painted white clouds over the midnight blue walls giving it a sky scene. Then she painted a mural of a rainbow with the sun reaching out in bright hues of orange, yellow, and red. She painted a picture of a black Jesus (I guess that's who he was supposed to be) between the ceiling and wall, like he was looking down over the rainbow on us. The bassinet sat in front of the wall mural trimmed in layers of white lace and satin. She put her pink comforter back on her bed, this time with flower and heart shaped pillows. The room was so beautiful, I was speechless. I couldn't believe I was having a baby. I thought about calling my mom to tell her but what good would that do? She could care less. Then I thought about calling the Professor but I decided against it. He would probably tell the dean and get me kicked out of school or worse, get me kicked out the dorm. I definantly could not risk being homeless right about now. I know who I have to call and quick; Quintin. Right as I was about to dial his number, April woke up.

"Ms. Kitty, are you awake?" she asked.

"Nah," I said. I didn't feel like talking, I had to break the news to Quintin.

"How does the room look?"

"Bright," I remarked.

"Yep, I can tell youre pregnant. Your mood swings are flying in!"

"Go back to sleep. I like the room, yada, yada, yada, and all that but I have to find Quintin now so I'm not in the mood."

"I thought you said you weren't gonna tell him or have anything to do with him."

"No, you all said that. I didn't say anything. He has a right to know, he is the father, remember?"

"I know and you are right but I don't want you to get your feelings hurt, that's all. Look, we said we would help you so don't go begging him for shit. Just tell him and get out of there, okay."

"Yeah, I hear ya'."

I put on my shorts, which I now could not button at all, and an old tee shirt. When I tried on my shoes, my feet would not fit in them so I grabbed April's cheap, two dollar, shower shoes. I tried to brush my hair but it also had a mind of it's own, it would not stay flat. Oh well, I thought, here goes nothing. I walked across the campus to Quintin's dorm. I had made up in my mind that whoever was visiting him at the moment would have to wait. Besides, I'm the mother of his unborn child. Lucky for me, Quintin was sitting in the lounge playing Dominoes with some of his frat brothers. He saw me come in but acted like his game was so interesting, he could not stop. I walked over to him and whispered in his ear, "I need to talk to you." He still ignored me so I said it out loud, "Quintin, I need to talk to you now!" His friends stared at me and put down their chips. One of them spoke up and said, "Man, go handle that, we'll hold the game."

"Alright, player, this wont take long," Quintin said to the guy. he followed me to a small corner of the room and angrily asked, "What the hell is wrong with you. You come up here looking like a fat ass bum, interrupting my game, and demand that I speak to you. What kind of mess is that? You must not know English too well because I said I didn't want anything to do with you and for you to stop calling me. You need to take your ass to the mall and buy some shoes. Oh and while your at it, get a pedicure because those dogs are barking!"

I heard his friends snickering at that last comment but I was determined to tell him what I came down here for. He had already humiliated me in front of these guys so nothing else could hurt me. I see what April and Olandis tried to tell me from day one but I wouldn't listen. I was so mad at myself for being stupid but it's too late to go back. I had a chance that I thought I would never have. I was going to make it without him, me and my baby were gonna be just fine, I hope.

"For your information, I came to tell you that I was pregnant with your child!" I said.

"My child? Bitch please, yall hoes do this every year. You get mad because nobody wants you anymore so to get revenge, you make up these stories about being pregnant so I can give you some money to have an abortion. Well that shit doesn't work on me so go find those other guys you been screwing."

"What other guys? You were the only one."

"Yeah right. You think I don't know about you giving it up to about 6 of my other frat brothers from State. Hmmp, they said you was willing to do more if they would've let you. If you are pregnant, you wouldn't know who the father was. Seems like everybody has had a taste of Ms. Kitty!"

Maybe it was the way he said it or the hormones kicking in, but I had about all that I could take from him so I slapped him as hard as I could. He felt the side of his face and before I could walk off, he punched me, dead in the jaw. He didn't stop, either. He hit me several times in the face until one of his friends jumped up from the card table and stood in between us. He shouted, "You stank bitch! Don't play me, I'm the man around here and I'll put you in your place!" I stood there, unmoved by his act of violence, and stared him right in the face. I decided then and there that no man, no where, no time, was gonna hurt me again. The guy started trying to pull Quintin across the room but I stopped him and said calmly, "Let him go. If he feels that hitting me will make him more of a man then let him. He needs all the manhood he can get but remember this, you will have to go to sleep sometime. And I'll be in every night mare, hell, I'll probably be there in the room with you, watching you suffer. And by the way, tell Denise she didn't have to get pregnant to keep you; I don't want your tired, no good, stinking, no car, broke, pitiful, limp dick ass!" I turned around and walked out, throwing my butt in the air like I always had to do, never looking back. Even though I still carried a piece of him daily with me, he was out of my life.

I met with my counselor today, a middle age, white man that reminds me of Mr. Rodgers from Mr. Rodgers Neighborhood. I didn't think I needed counseling now that the main problem was gone. With me finally over Quintin, I felt different, more peaceful and happy. My pregnancy was going well and I had three and a half more weeks until the big day. My counselor vouched for me since I was pregnant and got me out of doing community service but I still had to come back and see him two months after the baby was born. He says that he could tell I was not going to be a repeat offender but a lot of women have post pardom depression after having a baby and he wanted to make sure I didn't relapse. I told him I had so much depression before hand that I couldn't get depressed afterwards if I tried. He said he had to make it look good on the papers for the Judge when I go to get my record cleared. I didn't care what I had to do as long as the charges were taken off my record. The Professor never said anything to me about my pregnancy although I know he had to see it. I wore big shirts and left my jeans unbuttoned to hide it from the noisy people on campus and to my surprise, it worked. No one questioned me about it. Olandis made me keep meat on my face and wear dark sunglasses until my bruises healed. He was ready to beat Quintin up and April begged me to press charges but what good would it do? He would get out of jail and probably come to finish the job. Besides, the baby didn't need two parents with criminal backgrounds. He got his pay back when he questioned Denise about what I had told him to tell her. It turned out that he didn't know Denise was pregnant, and that's not all. She was pregnant by somebody else, one of his fraternity brothers. Notice I said was. She was getting an abortion the day we saw her in the clinic. I guess Quintin couldn't handle the dish he was being served because he left school and enrolled in the Marines earlier than planned. He was only two weeks away from graduation. I guess he knows now that what goes around, comes around. When I entered my room,

April and Olandis were arguing over baby names. They act like they are the ones having the baby instead of me.

"Ms. Kitty, tell this girl that you are not naming the baby after some some sky! You can keep all that weird stuff in your family, April." Olandis said while rushing to the door to be the first one to get his opinion in.

"Well to be fair, I have to hear her side. You had some pretty rough names yourself, Olandis." I said.

"Olande' is a whole lot better than Skyy." he replied, rolling his eyes, "Little kids will pick on the child and when they see it coming, they'll start shouting, THE Skyy is FALLING!"

"April, you really wanted me to name my child Skyy?"

"Whats wrong with it? It has so much power and boldness to it. Listen; Skyy….. Skyy.." she said softly.

"I knew something was wrong with her. She sits in and looks at all this stuff on these walls and come up with crazy ass names. Next thing you know she'll be telling you to name it rainbow, or curtain or even, Jesus!"

"Oh well, well, now. Hold up. Did we forget those outrageous names you picked out? Lets see, what were they? Oh yeah, Prince for a boy and Princess for a girl. Talk about teasing, kids will make little crowns made out of paper and ask the child to save them from the mean, old, dragon." April teased.

"Get it straight before you bend it, my dear. I did not say Princess, I said Vanity!"

"What's the difference? Skyy is still better."

April was determined to win this argument and I knew if I did not intervene these two would never stop.

"OKAY….STOP! I'm not choosing either of those names so let it go. I'll decide on a name when the time comes," I shouted. They both stared at me in disbelief.

"I hope your baby doesn't inherit your attitude. We cant live with two cranky people!" Olandis had the nerve to say with his hands on his hips. I wonder if he realizes the two cranky people he's referring to are him and April. I plopped down on my bed and covered my face with a pillow. I laughed uncontrollably as I thought about the month ahead.

"What the hell is so funny?" Olandis asked.

"I was just thinking about how you two are gonna act when the baby gets here. You can't even agree on a name so just imagine what ya'll will be fighting about; the milks too hot, no it's too cold! Or how about the diaper is too tight?" I said still laughing at the vision in my head. My friends didn't find the humor.

"Whatever, Miss Kitty. We all know, April will try to put the baby on some organic shit anyway." April threw her pillow at him when he made that comment. "Speaking of diapers, I totally forgot to get some. We better dash to the store and stock up."

"Olandis, what did you and Dewayne buy the other week? I thought you would've remembered to get diapers; the most important thing." April was still trying to prove her point that she was the more responsible caregiver.

"Ah hell now! You act like I wear em' or something; well only when Im playing the bad girl and needs to be spanked; but that's beside the point. I have never had kids. I bought all the essentials that would make Lil BooBear and I look good when we step out. No child will ride around with me looking like something off the streets. And ooh, girl, you should see the leather car seat we bought. It matches perfect with your car, April. And I have a great invention too. Im starting a baby hair weave line. Can you believe they don't have hair pieces for babies and they're the ones that need it weave the most. They baldheaded until they are at least two or three years old!"

I knew he wasn't joking, either. "Olandis, please promise me that you will not put a weave on my baby's head!"

"Don't trip," he said, waving his finger at me, "You just need to get on your knees and pray that it has good hair like you or else the baby weave will live on! "He walked over to the bed, bent down and started talking to my stomach, "Don't worry baby, Auntie Olandis will take good care of you. Now I know I wasn't able to do anything with your Plain Jane mama but there is some hope for you." I pushed his head away from my big belly and told him to shut-up.

"Well, I think you guys need to get going to the store and buy those diapers. Also, what about milk and bottles?"

"Quit worrying, April, were going. And what you mean by you guys? Where are going that you cant ride with us?" Olandis never missed a beat.

"I'm meeting Rakeem at the library. We have our last final in the morning so were studying together. You two can handle it. Here, I made a list." Olandis turned up his lip as he snatched the piece of paper from her. A thought flashed across my mind; what if April and Olandis left me by myself with the baby to go off to Jamaica again. I would freak out. I got so caught up in this fantasy dream world that I never stopped to realize I didn't know a thing about taking care of a baby.

"Will you come on, Miss Kitty! Damn, you really need to stop taking those pills the doctor gave you. They are messing with the part of your brain that controls motion," Olandis yelled. I grabbed my bag and followed him out the door.

He pulled into a handicapped parking space when we arrived at the store. "Olandis, what are you doing? You can't park here, this is handicapped parking."

"I know, aren't you handicapped?"

"No, I'm pregnant! There's a big difference."

"Same difference, now hurry up and get out this car so we can get this over with. I'm hungry and I know you are too." He walked through the sliding glass doors and asked the girl at the checkout counter which isle carries the baby items. We should've known where it was because of the loud noise. There were mothers with three or four kids running around screaming, babies in buggies wailing, gum and candy wrappers everywhere. It looked like a disaster zone. A little kid bumped into Olandis, leaving his dirty, sticky handprint on his silk pants. He shouted, "Have mercy, somebody needs to tie these demons up and never set them free!" Just then, a short, out of shape, woman who looked as though she had been drug through a cat fight, came and scooped the little boy up in her arms. She gave Olandis an evil look. I hurried and redirected his attention because I know he would not give a damn about cursing her out in front of these kids.

"Olandis, I see the diapers down there." I squeezed my way through the maze of children, paying close attention not to step on anybody. Olandis on the other hand, stole someone's shopping cart and barged down the aisle hoping to run over the little rugrats. I just shook my head and tried to pretend I wasn't with him.

"I cant wait until your baby comes. We'll show these little fuckers how to act when out in public! Now, lets see, there are so many diapers to choose from. I wonder which one is best? Oh well, I guess it doesn't matter since they are all used for the same thing; pee pee." At that instant, I peed on myself. I was so embarrassed. I knew I had acquired a bladder problem since I was expecting but I never thought it would get this bad. Olandis didn't notice the water running down my leg and kept chattering about the diapers. "Who knew diapers were so expensive? I only have five dollars on me; how much you got?.....Kitty? Kitty, girl, hello, I'm over here." He said waving his hands in my face. I was still in a daze. All I could think about was trying to get out of here without anyone seeing the wet spot in the back of my pants. Olandis was getting madder by the minute. He snapped his fingers directly in front of my nose and then came the chaos....

"MOMMY, that lady go pee pee on the floor!" one of the little bad kids shouted.

"Olandis, we have to go now!" I yelled out.

A little, old, white lady walked over to us and whispered in my ear, "Sweety, I think you're in labor."

"I'm sorry but I don't think I'm in labor, I'm not due for another two weeks." I informed her.

"Well, you may not be due but the baby sure is," she commented, "It would be wise for you to get to a hospital real soon."

"HOSPITAL !" Olandis screamed, "See, you didn't say nothing about a hospital. I knew you would try this shit on me. Why ME? LAWD JESUS, why did you have to go in labor with me? You could've waited until we got back to the room with April or Dewayne or somebody, anybody, besides me! Somebody up there is trying my patience and it is about to run out!" He looked up to the ceiling, throwing his hands around in the air. Then he ran up the isle to the check out line, pushing everyone out the way and grabbed the cashier by the collar, shaking him violently.

"Call 911, hurry!" he said. The cashier looked at him like he was crazy so Olandis reached over the counter and took the microphone off the hook and announced, "Somebody better call 911 or else I'm gonna put my size 9 up this cashier's butt!"

The cashier was just as frightened as Olandis. He snatched the microphone out Olandis's hand and announced over the loud speaker , "Call 911! This woman is having a baby! Clean up on isle seven."

People in the store stopped shopping and ran to isle seven to see what the fuss was all about. I tried to hide behind the shopping cart and act nonchalant like it wasn't me they were talking about but Olandis rushed up the isle toward me yelling, "Ms. Kitty, don't worry. The ambulance is on its way."

I could've killed him. Unlike me, he loved drama and attention. He stood right beside me, fanning himself and wiping the sweat off his forehead. You would've thought it was him having the baby instead of me with the way he was acting. I decided to have a little fun with him since I was already the star of the show. I grabbed my stomach and bent over moaning like I was in pain.

"Oh shit. No, no, no don't let it come. Not here, not yet! You don't want to have a kid in the grocery store, we'll have to name it shop and go!" Olandis cried.

I continued to moan, this time getting louder.

"Oh god, don't just stand there, bring me some hot water! And somebody bring me a bottle of Scotch! I need a drink."

The mothers began yanking their children up and rushing out the door with them. He yelled back at them saying he was sending his cleaning bill in the mail. He turned to a man wearing a business suit, talking on his cell phone. He walked up to the man and snatched the phone away from saying, "You can call them back later. Don't you see we have an emergency? Now do your little daily Good Samaritan duty and step off."

The man just stared at Olandis in disbelief while he called our room to tell April to meet us at the hospital. Apparently, she wasn't there because he cursed out our answering machine and paged Dewayne. He turned to the man and asked what his cell number is and punched in the numbers as the man called them out. The phone rang back as soon as he hung up. Olandis answered it and said, "Who? Oh he can't talk right now, were having a baby! Bye now." The man looked frustrated but he still did not say a word to Olandis. This time when the phone rang, I prayed that it was Dewayne.

"Hey sweetie, Meet us at the hospital, Ms. Kitty's about to have…" he started telling Dewayne but as soon as he saw the EMS workers bust through the door, he passed out. They rushed up the isle with the stretcher and looked at me then at Olandis lying there in the middle of the floor and asked, "Which one are we supposed to take?" The manager of the grocery store came forward and explained to them that I was the one in labor so they took me to the ambulance first and went back in to get Olandis. We were halfway to the hospital when Olandis came to. He asked, "Where am I?"

The driver said, "Were in route to the County Hospital." Why in the world did he tell Olandis that? He jumped down off the stretcher and started screaming, "Oh hell no! Y'all aren't taking me to that death trap! Let me out. I command you to stop this hearse and let me out!" He started kicking the door, causing the medicine vials and stretchers to fall over. He was hysterical, a mad man who was out of control so they treated him like one and stuck a needle in his rear end to sedate him. He slid down the door onto the floor and began talking like a drunk. "They...got me..I'm...gonna...die...now...I'll... miss...you."

When the ambulance pulled up, the emergency room staff rushed out to get us. When they opened the door Olandis fell out onto their feet, surprising them. A big dude picked him up and carried him inside the hospital as the other nurses pulled my stretcher out the truck to rush me inside. They took me to a room with a tiny bed and large object hanging from the ceiling, almost like the room I would use for my other procedures. The room started spinning all around and so many Doctors and Nurses were talking in a whole different language that I couldn't understand.

"Dilation is at 8 and a half centimeters...Pressure 140 over 95 ... Request anestegeologist for epidural? ....Fetal Monitor..."

Why wont they tell me what is going on? Is my baby going to be all right? When will I finally give birth? Oh, Oh, God, the pain! It's so much pain! I feel like I'm dying! Why is there so much pain all of a sudden? I guess this baby is the one sent to kick my ass for all the others.

"I'm sorry! I'm so sorry," I cried, "I didn't know what else to do. Please forgive me, Please! I loved you... I loved each and every one of you...."

"Ms. Richards, are you okay?" one of the hospital nurses asked, "What are you sorry about? Did you do something to harm yourself or the baby? Is that why you are going into labor early?"

Just then my OBGYN doctor walked in the room. "No, she's going to be just fine. You are forgiven Ms. Richards. You got your second chance."

I looked in my doctor's eyes and at that instant, I knew that he knew about my past but how? All medical records were kept confidential and the surgeon from that horrible place would never tell a soul for fear of losing his license and his career.

"Would you like to have an epidural?" he asked, "It will ease the pain."

"No. No I. um..I want to bear the pain. I deserve it and I cant risk anything harming this child, my baby. Where's Olandis? Is he gonna be alright?" I said.

"Ahh, yes. He's just fine. He's in the other room sound asleep."

April, Dewayne and Rakeem rushed in the delivery room.

"Ms. Kitty! We made it. I got the message just in time!" April yelled, running over to my bedside. She hugged the life out of me almost to the point I thought I was suffocating. I was sort of embarrassed with Dewayne and Rakeem in the room with me while my legs were up in the air spread wide apart. Rakeem started speaking medical language to the doctor. The doctor teased him and asked him to be his assistant for the delivery since he knew more than him. I didn't find anything amusing. Rakeem stood directly in front of the bed and stared at my hot spot. I couldn't believe April was sitting here allowing him to do this. He was probably so happy to finally see a woman's vagina since April had starved him from seeing hers. I felt a sharp pain, harder than the ones before, shoot through my stomach, around to my back and down my rear-end out through my toes.

"JESUSCHRISTHALLELUJAH!" I screamed.

Rakeem called the doctor and nurse over who were standing in a corner looking at some charts.

"It's crowning," Rakeem told them as he pointed to me. They looked surprise and ran to get a better view. The doctor put on a rubber glove and stuck his entire hand inside of me.

"Yep, kiddo', you're right. It's showtime!" the doctor replied. The nurse handed Rakeem a green labjacket and rubber gloves to wear.

"Okay Ms. Richards, when I tell you to push, you push but wait until I tell you to, okay," the doctor instructed.

That little bit of information went in my left ear and out my right because as soon as the next sharp pain hit, I pushed like I had never pushed before.

"Wait, I didn't tell you to push," he said.

"I DON'T GIVE A RABBITS ASS WHAT YOU TELL ME, I WANT THIS BABY OUTTTTTT!" I screamed at him and clutched Dewayne's shirt.

"April, do the breathing exercises with Ms. Kitty that we watched on that TV show," Rakeem said. April began breathing in and out in little puffs like she was going to run out of air if she used too much of it. She motioned for Dewayne to do the same and he started breathing just like her only a little unsure if it was right. They bent down in my face assuming that I would catch on and breathe the same way. They looked like two wolves about to howl and their breath on my face was too much for me to handle.

"GET OUTTA MY DAMN FACE!" They both jumped back, quickly.

"Okay Ms. Richards, give me a big push, come on, come on, hold it, steady, 10, 9 ,8,7,6,5,4,3,2,1…….."

I felt a gush of relief come over me. The pain… the pain was gone. I heard a tiny, sweet cry, so pure and so gentle but yet strong. My sweet, innocent, baby? No wait, this isn't my baby; it's OLANDIS!

"OHHHHH, AHHHHHH, I've always wanted to be a Fairy Godmother!" he said.

"OLANDIS!" everyone shouted.

"Ms. Kitty, you have a beautiful, baby girl," Rakeem said.

"A girl? Can I see her?"

"Sure, just let me cut the umbilical cord and wrap her up. Wouldn't want her to catch a cold."

He placed the delicate 5lb. angel in my arms and I couldn't believe how perfect she was; perfect cream-colored skin, perfect body, all ten fingers and all ten toes, and a cute little dimple in her cheek.

"She's beautiful," I said.

"And thank you Jesus, she's got good hair!" Olandis shouted.

Work

"WHERE IS THAT Olandis?" April said for the one-hundreth time.

I was trying to rock little Karisma back to sleep before he arrived. She was fighting sleep because she knew her favorite person in the world was coming to baby-sit her and she didn't want to miss him. It has been two weeks since we left the hospital but it feels like an eternity. I guess it wouldn't be so hard if I didn't have to keep her a secret from everybody. If anyone got word that I am raising a baby in the school dorm, I would be kicked out and we would be homeless! All in all, she's a good baby. She doesn't cry much, she smiles a lot (mostly at Olandis) and she doesn't drink that much milk which is good for me since our income is running real low. With all the charm and wit she possesses, we had to name her Karisma. Then I took her two Godparents names, twisted them together and came up with Alanda for her middle name. Names mean a lot to me. I don't like those Ghetto' names some people give their kids. That makes them destined to act ghetto' all their lives and why do some people have four and five long, crazy sounding names that they cant learn how to spell until they're in the fourth grade? That's ridiculous. Poor child flunks out of first grade because she can't spell her name, which by the way, is a requirement now. I think Karisma's name suits her just fine and at least she'll be able to spell it by the time she's three. Olandis will make sure of that. April has been reading up on babies a how to take care of them but I told her that no book will give her the vital information she needs. I will be so glad when school is out and we are the only ones on campus. Dewayne has begged us to come live with him this summer but I know there will be too many fights if that happened. You see, Dewayne and Olandis actually think that this is their baby! They are a trip when they get in the same room with her. They fight over everything like which outfit she should wear to which brush she should use. Just yesterday, I came in the room from taking my final exam with the Professor and they were in here fighting over Karisma's hair bows. It turns out that Dewayne dressed her in a cute little pink outfit with a yellow pocket and decided to put a yellow bow in her hair. Well Olandis got so upset and said that she wasn't matching and he didn't like hairbows that had to be taped to your head, it would ruin her silky hair. He was about to change her outfit for the third time since they couldn't agree on anything when I walked in and told them she wasn't going anywhere, she's only two weeks old so it didn't matter what she wore. The doctor said that it's wise if the baby and me did not go anywhere until our immune system built back up, whatever that means. I took part of his advice and never take Karisma out for fear of her immune system being low. I don't know what I would do if she got sick or worse, if she died. She had finally fallen off to sleep when someone knocked on the door.

"Thank god you're finally here!" April said while running to open the door. She looked up the hall and back down again, seeing no one." That's strange, I could've sworn I heard a knock at this door. OLANDIS, I don't have time for your stupid games, I have an exam to take in ten minutes!" April screamed in the air while slamming the door.

"April, you go on. I'll be fine. As soon as he gets here, I'll leave and take mine. There's no sense in you being late too," I said. I waved Karisma's little toy rattle in her face to try to cool her back down. She wasn't fussing but she was kind of upset that April had waked her back up.

"No Ms. Kitty, you heard what the doctor said. I can't let you walk to class, what if something happened?"

"What could possibly happen? I walk around in here"

"You know what I mean. You might pass out or have a heat stroke or bleed to death. You never know about these things. Olandis is just gonna' have to do better with his time."

I felt kind of bad making him give up his time to baby-sit my baby. He didn't have her, I did, but hopefully it would be over tomorrow and everyone will be going home. We could live somewhat feely again.

"Hi-dy ho. There's my sweet, precious, baby girl," Olandis said while rushing through the door to grab Karisma out my arms," Come to your beautiful Auntie Olandis! That's right, I lovey, lovey, love, you."

"Olandis, where have you been? We are gonna be late because of you." April informed.

"Is she talking to me, my little Pooh Bear? Oh no, she cant be talking to me because she wouldn't have that tone of voice with me holding you and your fragile little ears!" Olandis said to Karisma ignoring April. He loves to use her as his scapegoat. April was too frustrated to argue so she grabbed the keys off the bed where he was sitting and walked out the door only to be stopped suddenly. She fell over the box that was sitting in front of our doorway.

"Olandis, why did you leave this right here for somebody to fall over it?" she asked. I went to help her up.

"For your information, I didn't leave it there, I thought you all did and don't blame your clumsiness on me, honey, you were born a klutz!"

"What's in it?" I asked. April went to get the scissors to cut it open and Olandis squeezed the baby pretending that April was going to cut him. We pushed the box inside the room to tear into it. There were diapers and milk and some bottles and bibs.

"Wow, girlfriend, you got it going on up in here. Who sent you all this?" Olandis asked the baby.

"It has to be from her Daddy," I replied with a smirk on my face.

"When did she get a new Daddy because I know Quintin didn't buy this," he said.

"How do you know? I told you that Quintin would make a good father."

"I know because first of all, Quintin is overseas and there are no return addresses or postage on this box and second, Quintin is too cheap. Have you ever seen how the boy dresses?"

"Whoever it is didn't leave a note or anything," April said.

"Well we'll figure it out later, right now we are late for class." April and I rushed out the room to the stairs. Some things never change around here; the elevator is one of them.

I couldn't keep from blushing in the car. I know it had to be Quintin that sent that box. He's the only other person one knows about our little bundle of joy. He probably thinks I still hate him since the big fight and he thinks I wont accept the gifts he sends if I know they are from him. It was sort of romantic when you think about it.

"Well here we are," April said as she pulled in front of the building where I was to take my exam, "I'll be back to get you in an hour. Don't leave this building until I come back. My exam won't take that long."

"Yes Mother," I teased while stepping out the car.

Her and Olandis are taking this caring thing a little too far. If they don't watch out, people are going to get real suspicious of us.

I could barely concentrate on my exam thinking about Karisma. I know she's in good hands with Olandis but I still have a fear of something or someone hurting her. Why do I feel like a runaway slave, so fearful of being caught? Maybe if I told the Professor about her, he could help us. He may let us live with him but for how long? And then again, what if he doesn't like small children and says no to my suggestion about living arraingements. He would then have to tell the Dean and President about the baby that lives in the dorm and we would surely be kicked out. Homeless. I know for a fact that my mom is not letting me bring myself, much less a baby, back to her house to live. I wouldn't give her the satisfaction of turning me down and saying NO in my face. I cant understand why she doesn't know the power of motherly love, I have it now with my baby and she's only been here for two weeks. I guess she is just a mean old woman, down to her bones. I know what I have to do now if we're going to make it. Get a job. Get some income flowing in. I cant depend on Dewayne or April or Olandis all my life and who knows when my little secret friend stops sending those care packages.

"Okay, exam over. Turn in your test papers and I hope I don't see any of you in summer school."

Oh no, the exam is over and I have 2 more pages to complete. Well, bump it. I don't care anymore. I'll have to go to summer school anyway if I want a place to live but I cant do this single parent thing and go to school at the same time and find a job. April was waiting outside for me in the same spot where she dropped me off. She blew the horn, as if I couldn't see her parked there, causing everyone to turn around.

"April, do you have to be so obvious?" I fussed as I got in the car.

"What? I didn't know if you saw me or not."

"Well, I did and so did everybody else."

"So how did you do? Mine was a piece of cake."

"I didn't do so well. I have a lot on my mind and now is not the time for me to be taking exams."

"Tell me, what's on your mind?"

"Oh, come on April, you know I just had a baby."

"I get it, you're having separation anxiety."

"Sepa what?"

"Separation anxiety. I read about it in one of my books you guys were teasing me about."

"April, that stuff doesn't work with single, black, mothers. If anything, we want a separation, from our jobs, men, the kids, you name it. We have what you call everyday being a black woman in America stress!" At that instant I thought about what I had said and realized that's the problem with my mom. She's just stressed. She's a single parent, black, no real education, and no decent job. What is her job? It doesn't matter, I promise to never take my problems out on Karisma. She didn't ask to be born, that's my part.

"You don't know the half of being stressed, Ms. Kitty. Since you came here, you have done nothing but party. You breeze through all your assignments and when was the last time you went to work for the Professor?"

I could've gotten mad and went totally ballistic on her but I couldn't. She was right. I was just making up excuses for someone to feel sorry for me. I'm a parent now and I've got to start acting responsible. I know what I gotta do so I'm gonna do it.

"April, can you run me by the mall?"

"Oh, now you want to go shopping. You are getting weirder by the day."

"I'm not shopping for clothes, I'm job shopping."

She looked at me like I had lost it. "What? You said I don't do anything but party so now it's time for me to work."

"Good. I'm glad you see my point and I'll baby-sit Karisma free of charge when you go to work."

"April, you're supposed to. You're her Godmother!"

When we pulled into the mall parking lot, chills went up my spine. What if someone saw me that night I got arrested and remembers my face? I should have known better than to come to the mall looking for a job. Maybe I should put in a couple of applications since were here already. I don't want April getting suspicious and asking me a bunch of questions. Wouldn't you know it? She parked the car right in front of that racist department store. I can't go in there; they'll probably arrest me on the spot.

"April, you know I don't like this store."

"Me either. After the way they treated Olandis that day, I vowed never to step foot in there again but now I realized that it's not the store, it's the people that work there. That's why I want you to get a job there and show them how customers should be treated. They'll have to hire you because I'll protest and show where there are no African Americans on staff."

"No. I cant. Why do I have to be the dummy for the project?"

"Because you're the only one. Don't you want to make a stand for equal rights? Plus you'll be paying them back for Olandis. If nobody stood up to make a change, then who knows how the world be."

"I'm not doing it, case closed. I don't want to be the next Rosa Parks. I just want a job that will help me take care of my daughter."

"Okay, it's your life. But I'm not finished with them." The look on her face let me know that she was not giving up without a fight. I should expect this from her. After all, her father was a civil rights lawyer and she probably grew up listening to strategies on how to legally harm racist people.

After placing applications in almost every store, I was exhausted and missed my baby Karisma. I couldn't wait to see her cute little grin when she first sees me and her tiny, little, hands that try so hard to reach out to me. I rushed up the steps to our room and banged on the door until I finally heard Olandis say, "Who is it?"

"It's us." We answered back.

"He turned the door knob slowly, testing my patience, and peeked his head out the door.

"Move, stupid!" I said as I pushed him out of my way.

"Oh, Karisma. Did you hear what your mama called me? Bad Mama, bad, bad, bad. We don't use words like that around here, Ms. Kitty."

Karisma was sitting propped up on my bed. She looked like she was frowning, almost like she understood Olandis and I had hurt her best friend. I decided to apologize to him. I wouldn't want my baby to have any hurt feelings toward me, her own mother.

As the weeks went by, Karisma Alanda and I bonded, as well as April, Olandis and the rest of our clique. School was officially over and a lot of people had gone home for the summer, everybody except Denise. She either flunked out or her parents didn't want her back home. What I thought would finally be our freedom turned into a fiasco. With everyone gone, you could hear Karisma even louder and we never knew when we would run into Denise while out with the baby. I wish she would just crawl back under the rock she came from rock and die. Quintin was still sending the care packages faithfully every two weeks. He still never gave us a return address. I would go over to the Professor's house about once a week to let him know I was all right and to keep him from popping up at my room. I wanted to tell him about Karisma and I felt that he had a right to know but I didn't feel safe. I had to make sure we had someplace to live first. My chances were slim on getting a job because of my record. The shoplifting charges kept showing up and it would be another year before they were dropped and my record was clean again. I couldn't even get a job at Danny's Doggs! It was always the same old line, "Ms. Richards, were real sorry but you have a criminal background and although you may have changed or made a mistake, our company policy wont let us hire you." After the last telephone call with an unfamiliar voice, I said, "I know what your gonna say so save your breath," and hung up the phone. One day, I was lying across the bed watching Karisma sleep so peacefully, when the thought hit me. Dewayne could hire me. Those girls down at his club make a killing every night. I know I could make more than them. I probably dance better and have a better body, too, since my breasts were still round, big, and juicy thanks to the milk. I have lost all my baby weight and back to my petite, gorgeous size. I grabbed Karisma's bag and strapped her to me in her little Snugly, carrier and rushed out the door to catch the bus. I hated to take her inside a club but I had no choice, I was desperate. We needed money and another place to live and Dewayne was my last hope. I asked the bus driver if he knew where the address was and he chuckled a little when he answered.

"Do I know. Baby, that place has taken all my hard earned money for years. After going there, I don't even want to see my wife naked!"

I guess I never gave much thought to the fact that I would have to undress in front of complete strangers. Oh well, no point in turning back. I have to do this. I have to do this for my baby. He let me off right in front of the club and said, "Here you go pretty lady. Good luck and don't make em' spend too much." I covered Karisma's ears and straddled her closer to my body as I stepped off the bus onto the pavement. I could hear loud music blaring from inside the place. I opened the heavy double doors and eased inside. It was dark and smelled like a cigarette factory. To my surprise, the place was empty. There were no customers, only a bartender cleaning some wine glasses behind a counter. I walked over to him and tried to talk but he couldn't hear me over the loud music. He whistled at somebody and they cut the music off. Karisma was still sleep through it all; I may need to get her ears checked.

"Hi, I'm looking for Dewayne."

"He's not here but Sweet Flossy is in the back. She may be able to help you," he said as he put the glasses in a tray above his head.

"Sweet Flossy?" I asked.

"Yeah, she runs the club. She's in charge of all the business affairs but nothing gets approved without Dewayne. Go on back through that door and take a left. You'll see her office to your right."

I did as I was told. The closer I came, I could hear talking. It sounded like two women arguing. "I'm sorry Vixen, but I've had just about all I can stand from you and Dewayne feels the same. We've already made up our minds and you will get your sick leave pay and your vacation pay."

"But I don't want that. I want my job. I got mouths to feed. I been working here for over three years and this is the thanks I get?"

"We said the same about you." This Sweet Flossy lady sounded mean.

"Please, I wont do it no more. I promise." The Vixon girl's voice cracked; she was hysterical.

"Too late. You had your warning and I don't believe in promises. Now, if you don't mind, I've got work to do before we open tonight."

A tall, blond, lady wearing a thong and see through robe came rushing out the room with tears in her eyes. I had to stop and get my courage together before I walked in the room. Why couldn't Dewayne be here? I took one last breath and prayed that Karisma didn't wake up and peeked my head in her door. I almost fainted when I saw who the woman was sitting behind the desk. It was the woman from the juke joint; the woman that saved my life that night. The Card Lady.

"Um, Ma'am, they said you could help me," I said in a weak very shy voice.

"Well that depends on what type of help you want. I don't eat girl scout cookies and I ain't got no money if I did."

"I'm a friend of Dewayne and I wanted a job here."

"Well why didn't you say so? How old are you?" she asked without looking up from her desk.

"I'm 18."

"Awfully young. You sure you can handle a job like this?"

"Yes ma'am."

"Speak up. You can't be shy around here. Those vultures will eat you alive, honey."

What's your measurements?"

"I um, I don't know. I think I'm a size 5/6"

She had to look up to see who was talking to her. She put on her reading glasses and scrunched up her nose. Then she scratched her head like she was trying to figure something out. "I've seen you before. Where do I know you from?"

"I don't know. People say I look like a lot of people. I just have a familiar face I guess."

"Well, I'll tell you the rules of the house and let you decide if you still want to work here. We do have a position open for one more girl since I let that tramp go. Rule number one. We make money off the door so don't expect a paycheck. You make your money off the men's tips. You will get a weeks paid vacation and 40 hours of sick leave a year. Rule number two. Don't give out your number to any of the customers and no sexual relationships with them, men or women. If I find that you are sleeping with a customer, you will be terminated. Rule number three. No drinking, smoking, or drugs on the job. We will send you home if you come to work intoxicated. Got it?"

"Yes."

"Good. Now I run a straight house. You break the rules and you're out. If you have any problems with the girls or the customers, let me know."

She buzzed for someone to come and measure me. After about three minutes, the bartender walked in with a measuring tape around his neck.

"Jacob, can you measure Ms…"

"Ms. Richards, but all my friends call me Ms. Kitty."

"Ms. Kitty, huh? Jake, my boy, I think we got a winner. With a name and a face like that, were sure to pack the house every night." Jake and her laughed as he got prepared to measure me. I don't see what the big deal is; it's just a name.

I was as jittery as a flea in a pet parlor all day. Sweet Flossy told me I should start tonight to get broken in before the weekend crowd came. She told me to shave all the hair of my body, especially the vagina area. Karisma must have felt the tension in the air because she whimpered and fussed a lot today. I guess she didn't want me to go to work there but I had to.

"April, can you watch Karisma for me tonight?"

"I was wondering when you were gonna ask. Why didn't you tell me you got a job?"

She caught me off guard with that one. So she knew the entire time. I bet Sweet Flossy told Dewayne and he told Olandis and Olandis told April. How dare they talk about me behind my back?

"Who said I got a job? I may have a hot date."

"Please girl, on a Thursday night? Besides, I said I would baby-sit free of charge while you work but I didn't say it would be free while you play. So where's your new job? Is it at the mall because I could use your twenty percent discount. Karisma, we're going shopping!"

"Hey slow down. It's not at the mall, it's at…at…this um,…restaurant."

"Oh well Karisma, we may not get deals on clothes but we will eat hardy! Where is this place?"

"Huh? Oh, the restaurant? It's across town. I'll probably be working late since they don't stop serving until around one in the morning."

"That's pretty late. Maybe I should drive so you wont have to catch the bus. That's too dangerous."

"No, I'll be fine. I don't want you taking Karisma out that late at night. I'll catch a cab instead of the bus and once I've made friends there, I can ride with one of them."

"Why did you go all the way across town to look for a job?"

"I didn't plan on it, I was just over there one day and decided to put in an application at this restaurant. I didn't actually think they were gonna hire me."

"Well, I'm happy for you. So what time are you leaving because I was going to Rakeem's but I can take Karisma on with me now if you need time to get ready."

"Please do, if you don't mind." She doesn't know how bad I need time to get prepared. I have never shaved my flower pot before and who knows what might happen. I would hate to cut myself up; it might scare the men off. I went into the bathroom to begin my task. First I rolled my hair on some of April's big rollers and then jumped in the shower. I grabbed the razor and began shaving everywhere I could see hair. I saved the bushiest part for last. When I stepped out to dry off, the image in the mirror scared me. It was bald! Completely naked, just sitting there like a bare chesscat. I don't think I was supposed to shave it this close, I look like a 4-year-old child.

"Ms. Kitty, we're gone. Good luck on your first day. Tell mommy bye, bye, Karisma."

She made this little squeaky sounding voice to imitate Karisma's. As soon as I heard the door shut I ran in the room to put on my bikini. I danced around in front of the mirror to practice which moves looked the best. From my eyes, none of them looked worth mentioning. I doubt if I'll be able to go through with this tonight. I was debating on whether or not I should show up when the telephone rang.

"Ms. Kitty, this is Jake. Listen, Sweets wants you to come in a little early so you can try on your costume and see if we need to make any adjustments. See you around 6:00? Thanks, peace."

He hung up before I could get a word in. I guess that was a sign that I should go on through with it. I took the curlers out my hair, sprayed some perfume on my body, threw on some shorts and tee shirt and headed out the door to catch the bus. It was already 5:15 and if I caught the bus now, I would make it just in time. The same chubby bus driver was driving today. When he spotted me, he began talking to me like we we're the best of friends. I hope he doesn't think he can get some freebies' because he just happens to drive the bus route I need to get to work.

"Hey baby, where you headed today?"

"Same place."

"So you got the job, huh?"

"That's none of your business."

"I know. I was just hoping you got the job. We all need to work. I don't see the sense in an able, young, body sitting at home collecting welfare. I don't care what your occupation is as long as you got one."

He made me feel a lot better after that. I wasn't doing anything wrong, I was just dancing. At least I got out and got a job to support my baby and myself. She would have the best, no hand me downs. He started humming to the tune, 'God Bless the Child', and it's soothing melody calmed me and almost put me to sleep.

"Here we are, pretty lady. Wake up now. Will you be needing my services this evening?"

"Um, I may catch a cab. I don't know how late I'll be here."

"A cab? Such insults. You'll spend every dime you make tonight trying to get back home. Those cabs are expensive. I'll come back and wait on ya up till two but after that, I'm going home." He opened the doors to let me off and smiled. I hope he isn't some perverted old man, like Moe. I wouldn't be surprised if Moe showed up in Club Destiny one night. I would puke!

I walked down the street and into the double doors of the loud club. Jake was standing in his usual spot behind the bar. He motioned for me to go to the back. Sweet Flossy was in her office talking to a well dressed, handsome man about his liquor prices. She motioned for me to come to her and pointed to white, velour, cat suit with white fur around the collar and sleeves and a long, stuffed white tail attached to the rear. I took the suit off the hanger for a better look. Its fabric was so soft. Sweets' told me to try it on and I immediately obeyed and headed to the bathroom.

"Where are you going?" she asked.

"I thought you wanted me to try it on," I said.

"Yeah, you can try it on right here."

I felt stupid, awkward, to change in front of her and this man but what was even more stupid is the fact that I would be taking my clothes off in front of hundreds of men in the next hour. The gentleman stared at me anxious to see a free peep show. Sweet Flossy continued talking to him like I wasn't even in the room but he knew I was there. He kept giving me eye contact while I took every inch of my clothes off. I stood there, naked for about five minutes trying to figure out how to get in the suit until I noticed the invisible zipper in the front. I squeezed into the suit and stood there waiting for her approval. She finally finished business with the man and stood up to shake his hand and send him on his way.

"Now, Ms. Kitty, that looks like a perfect fit. Turn around, child."

I turned slowly around. I didn't like the idea of a woman examining my body.

"Honey, you are going to have to get over this shyness. I hired you because you were a friend of Dewayne's but most of my girls have to go through the interview. I don't know if you can even dance but it doesn't matter now, all these men want to see is a young pretty face. These other worn out hoochies look so old and bad. Don't let yourself go. Sometimes beauty is the only thing you got." She lit a cigarette and blew puffs of smoke in the air. "Okay, we got your music lined up. It's a slow number, nothing fast and hoochie, but classy, sophisticated."

"How am I supposed to dance off slow music? I'm used to dancing to upbeat music. I don't even slow dance with a guy, much less by myself."

"You'll do just fine. Listen to the melody and tune into it, not the beat. Since your name fits so perfectly, we decided to keep it and make the cat suit. There's a dressing room down the hall with the rest of your items. They should be on your makeup counter but if you don't see them, just ask Charm. She's usually here since she's the first to go on stage."

I walked into the dressing room to find charm greasing up her legs with Vaseline. She was a brown-skinned woman who looked around thirty years old. She had a bad weave job. I know if Olandis could see this he would die. She had streaks of blond mixed in with black and her own hair was nappier than the silky straight weave. For Dewayne to be a cosmetologist, I wonder why he lets these girls walk around like that.

"Hi, are you Charm?" I asked.

"Yeah."

Her name certainly did not suit her. She was about as charming as the wicked witch in Oz'.

"I'm Ms. Kitty and Sweet's told me you could show me my things and my makeup counter."

She pointed to this little raggedy table with a broken mirror attached to it. I walked over to the table and pulled up a chair. There were some makeup and other personal items still left from the last girl, I guess, because they had been used.

"I wouldn't do that if I were you." Charm said.

"Do what?" I hadn't done anything but sit down and look in my mirror. Just then another stripper walked in the room. She was sort of cute but not as cute as me! She began talking to Charm like she didn't notice me. "Hey girl, what's up? You ready for tonight? Did you see that guy last night with the Versace shirt on? He was spending mad money on me. I must've made five hundred on him alone!"

She walked over to her booth and stopped, turned around, and looked at me. I acted like I was putting on my makeup. She couldn't speak before so why speak now. "Where is my chair?" she asked, "Whoever has my chair needs to put it back now and I wont have to kill them for it!"

Now I know this little skinny heifer is not trying to threaten me. I would whoop her ass with my hands tied behind my back. I ignored to see what she would do next. Let her find her own chair. She was bold enough to walk over to me and tap me on my shoulder, "Excuse me but that looks like my chair you're sitting in."

"I don't see any names on it."

"Oh, no she didn't! Who is this girl? You better tell her a thing or two before I tell it."

Charm laughed and shouted, "I tried to tell her but she so stupid, she wouldn't listen!"

"So you're telling me she's a retard? How is she gonna dance? Like this?" she started walking around the room with he hands bent and made a silly face like a retarded person. She was about to press that last button but I held out to see how far she would go and she went there. I was messing with a whole new breed of women, a kind I've never dealt with because she pulled my hair and held a knife to my throat.

"So retard, are you gonna give me my chair?"

Just then a Puerto Rican girl walked in carrying a duffel bag and immediately sat it down and rushed over to me. "Star what are you doing? Why are you messing with the virgin?"

"Because I'm the star and she needs to recognize that!"

"Leave em' alone Sandy. You know she ain't gonna cut her, she's just bluffing," said Charm.

"I'm not a virgin!" I protested.

"Have you ever stripped before?" Sandy asked.

"No."

"Well you're a virgin. After tonight, you'll be turned out." She snatched the blade out Star's hand and walked away like she wasn't even standing there frowning back at her. I wanted to laugh but was too scared to do so.

"So, what's your name?" Sandy asked me.

"Ms. Kitty."

"No, I meant what's your real name. You don't have to use stage names until we're out there among the wolves."

"That is my real name. Well sort of. I've been called Ms. Kitty all my life."

"Wow. I couldn't imagine having a name like that. I bet you got a lot of play growing up."

I thought about it. I did get a lot of guys but I thought they wanted me because of how pretty I am. Most of them didn't even know my name. Star was about to say something smart but hushed when Sweet Flossy appeared in the doorway.

"Okay girls, let's put on a good show tonight. Remember the rules. Stay safe and oh, has everyone met Ms. Kitty? She's going on last so she can watch some of your moves from behind the curtains. Alright, get a move on, it's five minutes till showtime!" She clapped her hands and turned around to walk out but Star stopped her.

"Excuse me Sweets, why is she last? I'm the star. I'm supposed to go on last."

"Not tonight, honey. I've already explained why," Sweets responded without looking back.

Star was pissed. She gave me an evil look that would kill Satan. At that instant, she reminded me of someone I hated with a passion; Denise. Sandy pulled her hair up in a French twist and told me to follow her. She walked up the long hall and positioned a bar stool behind the red velvet curtain where I could see the stage but no one could see me. She eased onto the stage as soon as her music began to play. She did explicit moves across the floor and occasionally opened her legs in front of a male so he could put money in her money clip. She ended her routine hanging upside down from the gold metal pole in the center of the stage, her legs wrapped around it and her breast sagging, trying to fight against gravity. She picked up her bra and silk robe and scooted off the stage with a look of disgust. Next Charm came out, dancing and shaking to a fast Caribbean tune. Her costume consisted of colorful feathers that hung around her waist and bra and in a matter of seconds, all the feathers were on the ground exposing her bright orange G-string. The men went wild, throwing money on the stage as she shook her entire body like she was having a seizure. Right before the music ended, she kicked the feathers off the stage and jumped from the stage right into a mans lap, giving him a private lap dance. Jake walked on the stage and sat a Coca Cola bottle, a banana, and a cigarette down in a semicircle. When Star appeared, the men jumped up from their tables and rushed to the stage, pushing and shoving for the best spot. She slid on her belly towards the end of the stage and blew kisses in their face. Then she turned around and slapped her rear end and told them to kiss it. They all crammed into each other, trying to be the special one to kiss it. After the lucky guy puckered up and gave it a big, juicy wet one, she did a headstand and spread her legs apart in mid air. She flipped her body over and landed over the top of the Coke bottle. She did a split and picked the bottle up with her vagina. Then she picked up the banana, peeled it and ate it seductively in front of the male crowd. She rubbed it around her breasts and mouth and pushed the last of it up inside of her with the bottle still in place. When I thought her act was all over and no more could possibly be done, she did the ultimate. She called one of the men on stage and asked him to insert the cigarette inside her. She lied on the floor and he did as he was told. Then she asked him to light it. He acted like a kid on Christmas as he lit the cigarette. Star made the cigarette puff in and out like it was smoking, turning the men on until they couldn't take anymore. They all bumrushed the stage and the bouncers had to pull a couple of them off her and carry them out the door. She stood up, took the items out of her, and ran off the stage stopping in front of me with this wide, devilish grin on her face. "Top that!" she said.

I knew in a million years I would never be able to top her act but I couldn't back out now. I was eager to go on that stage. I liked the idea of men lusting after me but not being able to touch me. 'Do Me Baby' began to play, I guess, giving me my cue. I swayed back and forth trying to feel the beat and work my nerves up. I was about to go on stage when Sandy ran up to me.

"Here, you forgot these. I found them behind a chair in the dressing room." She handed me a pair of white cat ears to wear on my head. "Go get em!"

I danced unto the stage, listening to the men approvals and cheers but it was dark and I couldn't see their faces. Artificial smoke filled the stage from the left and I rolled around in it. I slowly started unzipping my catsuit. "Yeah baby, take it off…..Boy she is Fine!…..Damn, baby got back!…… Hey Dewayne, where did you get this cutie?…"

I eased out of the catsuit until I was completely naked. I ignored the men and tuned them out. I danced around feeling sure and confidant with myself, my new sensual side and I enjoyed it. I never imagined that it would feel this good, like I was lost on a natural high. I was free from racism, free from motherhood, free from humans, free to be me, free..free…

"What the hell are you doing?"

The music stopped, interrupting my thoughts and I ran off the stage to the dressing room. I could hear the men chanting my name, begging for me to come back out but there was no way I could go back. Dewayne wasn't too happy with my little performance.

"I didn't know, Dewayne. She said she knew you and you sent her," Sweets said. She was right on Dewayne's heels as they bust through the dressing room door. He walked right up to my mirror, banged his fist down on the counter and said, "Get your clothes on, I'm taking you home!"

"Why? What did I do wrong? Don't you hear that, they want me. ME!"

"She does has a point, Dewayne. Ms. Kitty is what we need to bring this place back to life. Once word gets out about her, you'll have a packed house every night."

"Shut-up. Look Ms. Kitty, this is your life. I can't tell you what to do with it but so help me God, if Olandis finds out about this, you're fired! Got it?"

"Got it."

"And one more thing, wear your G-string until your hair grows back!"

I felt stupid after that and charm must've set me up. She was supposed to give me the rest of my things and she never did. Then I thought about my money still out there on the stage so I grabbed a towel off the floor to wrap around me and ran out the door to try and get what was left of my tips but Sandy caught me before I got halfway up the hall.

"Hey girlfriend, you were awesome! Not bad for a virgin. Here, I think this belongs to you." She dropped hundreds of tens and twenties in my hand. There were so many, they fell to the ground. "You probably would've made more than this if Dewayne hadn't rushed you off the stage.

I bent down to retrieve the rest of the money off the floor, effortlessly trying to keep count in my head but it was just too much. Never in my life had I saw that much money and it was mine, all mine. I told Sandy thanks for looking out.

"Oh, no problemo'. So are you coming back tomorrow night?"

"And you know it. It's Friday, payday! I'll be here before the doors even open!" I yelled back as I rushed to Sweets office to change back into my 'good girl' clothes. If I ran, I could still make it in time to catch the last bus. Just as my new friend, Chubbs', promised, he was waiting for me.

"You almost missed me Pretty Lady," he said. I smiled and sat in my special seat, directly behind him.

I was the last person to get off the bus and I was scared to death to walk the three blocks to the dorm. The sky was pitch black and I could hear every eerie sound in the night air. The first thing I plan to do with my money is buy a car. I jogged up the steps to the dorm and when I tried to open the main door, it wouldn't buldge, it was locked. I banged and kicked it until I finally heard someone on the other side with a pair of keys. Well wouldn't you know, it had to be Denise! She stared at me with her hair tossed all over her head and sleep encrusted around her eyes and had the nerve to ask me what did I want.

"What do you mean by what do I want? I want you to move your ugly face outta' my way!"

"Look, I didn't have to get out of bed to open this door and put up with this. You can sleep outside for all I care." She tried to slam the door in my face but I caught it with my right foot and pushed it back on her causing her to fall a little. We squared off, staring each other down, face to face. She eventually turned and walked off. I guess she wasn't in the mood to get beat up. I walked up the steps to my room with a feeling of defeat. I was still on my natural high and just thinking about all the money I soon will make and moving out of here kept me motivated. I eased in my room so I wouldn't wake Karisma or April. I wasn't ready for her fifty questions about my new job and I was too sleepy to be able to remember what lies I may tell. There was a note on the bathroom mirror informing me that another package came today for Karisma. It contained the usual, diapers, milk and clothes. I felt so sad. Why couldn't he leave an address just to let me know he's safe. I want to send him a picture of Karisma, let him see how beautiful she is. I miss him, God, do I miss him. Why couldn't we be a family?

⊷⊷⊙ ⊙⊷⊷

"She works hard for tha money. So hard for it honey. She works hard for tha money so you betta treat her right, toot, so right!" I was not in the mood for Olandis's sunrise singing but Karisma seemed to enjoy it. I could hear her spitting and ripping up paper.

"Get up, girlfriend. You need some new clothes and we are ready to go shopping."

"What? Olandis leave, please. I'm tired."

"You got that right. I was wondering when you were gonna figure out those clothes were tired. They don't do nothing for your figure."

"Since you have so many jokes this morning, let me ask you this. Are you treating me to some new clothes?"

"Unh, uhn, honey. You are Big Money' now! You need to be treating me. I would become a waitress but my feet are too delicate for that. I can't have bunions and crap all over my toes, then nobody will suck on em'. I know they say y'all make a killing' in tips but Damn, you must've knocked somebody off for real!"

When he said tips I realized what he was talking about. I jumped up and saw him and Karisma playing with the money I earned last night. She was having a ball trying to eat and tear up the dollar bills.

"Olandis!" I screamed, "What are you doing?"

"Oh girl, ever since I saw that movie, what is it, Decent or recent or something like that, anyway, since I saw that movie I always wondered what it would feel like to roll around in a bunch of money." He grabbed a handful of greens and tossed them in the air like they were snow or something.

"Olandis! Give me that!" I reached over them trying to grab the money and Karisma started crying.

"See what you did. That's alright, Boo. She won't take anymore."

"I'll take what I want. It's my money!"

"Well, what do you plan on doing with it?"

"First I plan on buying a car or finding an apartment, which ever comes first. I haven't even counted it to see how much it is."

"Exactly $764.00" he said matter of factly.

"Where is April?"

"She's been gone. She left with Rakeem. She said something about going to the beach, or was it a lake?"

"What! Who is gonna watch Karisma tonight while I go to work? I knew she would pull this stunt on me."

"Slow down Miss Thang. I assured her that I would watch the little one. We were just about to leave to go to Uncle Dewayne's but I thought I should wake you and tell you where your baby was. You don't seem to care, though."

"What do you mean I don't care. I do care and I don't appreciate you all changing the routine without my consent."

"We had no choice. You were sleeping so peacefully. You know I don't mind waking your ass up but April insisted I leave you alone, since you worked so hard last night. Any who, me and BooBear are gone. See you tonight."

"Wait. Why are you leaving now?"

"Excuse me but it is 5:00 in the afternoon."

"Well, could I at least get a kiss?"

"O, I didn't think you cared, darling." He puckered up his lips to kiss me.

"Not you. Give me my baby." I kissed Karisma goodbye and assured her that I would spend the entire day with her tomorrow. I stood at the door waving until they were safely up the hall and completely out of sight. I could not believe how late it was. I barely had enough time to get ready for tonight and make it to the bus. I definitely have to get a car. Maybe I can go look for one tomorrow. Who knows; with all the money I make tonight, I'll be able to afford two cars.

⊷▬◉ ◉▬⊷

"Hey girl. I see you made it." Sandy was already in the dressing room applying her false eye lashes. I hope she plans on trimming them down before she goes out on stage. They look like two caterpillars crawling on her eyes. I sat my bag down and began oiling my skin with lotion when Charm and Star walked in. They didn't bother to speak to me or Sandy.

"Charm, did you see how the rookie dances? What kind of shit was that? Are we on Fame or something?" Star asked. They both began laughing hysterically. Sandy gave them an evil look and they just rolled their eyes but I had to let them know that I was not the one to be played.

"So I guess you think men like the way you torture your body, huh? They could go to the circus and see the same damn act," I said. Sandy and Charm sneaked a laugh in behind Star's back.

"I bet you made a measly twenty dollars while my 'circus act' brought in a thousand."

"Well sista', put your money where your mouth is. That is if you aren't afraid of losing all of it." I held my hand out for a deal shake.

"Girl, please. After this crowd tonight, there won't be any money left for any of you," she said as she shook my hand. Sweet Flossy walked in the room and gave us her same speech, put on a good show and stay safe, but she didn't walk out right then.

"Girls, tonight is special. I heard through the grapevine that Mr. Santeno Carrington will be visiting us. I want you to put on an outstanding show."

"Um, Sweets, who is this Mr. Santeno Carrington?"

"Honey you don't know? He's one of the richest men around. He's a realtor. Word has it that he owns houses and land in Paris, Jamaica, Dubai; all over the world. He is worth more than man himself now get a move on." She clapped her hands together, lit a cigarette, and walked out the room.

"Well I guess I will win this bet after all. Once Mr. Carrington sees me he won't see anyone else" Star said looking directly at me.

We heard the DJ announcing Sandy's name and she panicked because she wasn't ready. She eventually made it out to the stage, late and one leg still ashy. I grabbed a bottle of water from the mini fridge and went out to watch her. The club was packed tonight. I guess everyone wanted to see Mr. Carrington because they were dressed in their Sunday's best. Now I wouldn't be able to distinguish him from the rest of these leeches. Charm went out to do her thing and Sandy came up to me and informed me of the change in plans. It seems that Star complained so much to Dewayne about going on last that he gave in and told her we would alternate. She knew all along and she let me bet against her. Charmed walked off and my music began to play. I strutted on stage and listened to the cat calls until they were erased from my mind. I felt the same spirit I had last night and let myself go. The song had ended before I realized it and I picked up the money I had earned, nothing like last night's earnings but still a lot. I went to the dressing room brushing past Star like I didn't see her. I started changing into my clothes when Sandy asked me what was I doing.

"Arent you staying? Jake said he thinks Mr. Carrington is in the house."

I heard a bunch of cheering from the crowd outside.

"That's why I'm leaving. I can't bear to see her face when she walks off that stage with all her money. Here, give this to her." I handed over half of my tips. "Don't tell her what I actually made."

"Your secret's safe with me." She giggled.

I grabbed my bag and headed out the door before Star's music ended. I was happy anyway because now I could get enough sleep and be up and ready for Karisma in the morning. I was sitting at the bus stop waiting on my friend, Chubbs, when a long black limo stopped in front of me. I tried to act cool but I think the fear showed across my face. The back tinted window rolled down and a handsome looking, older man stared at me.

"Why are you out here alone? That's not safe."

"What does it look like? I'm waiting on the bus."

"Well, where are you going? Maybe I could give you a ride."

"I don't get in cars with strangers." What am I saying? I wanted to get in that limo with him. He was handsome and I had never ridden in a limo before, well not since Big Ma's funeral and I was too little to remember that.

"Well, how about I get out and let you ride to wherever you need to go and then my driver can come back to get me."

I decided to call his bluff so I agreed to it. He opened the car door and got out then motioned for me to get in. I walked over to the car and stood at the door waiting on him to call the bluff off but he didn't.

"So lets get this straight. You are going to let me drive away in your limo while you sit out here in the dark, by yourself and pray that this car comes back to pick you up?"

"Yep," he answered.

"Okay," I said as I sucked my teeth. I climbed in the limo, enjoying the feel of the soft, luxurious, leather interior, and told the driver where I was headed. He looked a little confused as he stared at the man, his boss, waiting outside at the bus stop in his three piece Armani suit. He motioned for the driver to go on and he obeyed his orders by pulling off. I curiously nosed around the car and pushed a button which uncovered a hidden TV in the wall. Then the telephone rang, startling me, causing me to shake. After several rings, the driver slid his tinted window down where I could see his face in the rear view mirror and said, "Madam, I believe this call is for you."

I picked up the receiver and shyly said, "Hello?"

"Are you enjoying your ride?" the male voice asked. He sounded even better on the phone than he did in person.

"Yes. Are you enjoying your wait?"

"Well, no, um,..that's why I called."

"You didn't think I would leave, did you?"

"Oh, I knew you would leave but I didn't think you would leave without me."

"Aww, is the big, tough, gentleman scared?" I teased.

"No, I'm not scared, just lonely." He mad me feel sorry for him but I didn't know what to do. What if he tried to rape me or something. I didn't know anything about this man but how harmful could he be?

"Driver, please turn around and pick Mr. Um.. you know, the man who owns this limo."

He smiled as he turned the big car around to go back and retrieve Mr. What's his Name. I know I had missed the bus by now so he would have to take me home after all. He looked like a child that lost his puppy. We pulled up in front of him and the driver got out to open the door for him to get in.

"So, I see you felt sorry for me." I just smiled but didn't say a word, I was speechless as I gazed into his eyes. "So... why are you waiting on the bus? Don't you have a car?"

"If I had a car, would I be waiting on the bus?"

"Well, I thought with all the money you made that y...."

"What! You know me? You're out here trying to pick me up? I don't know who you think you are but you better check yourself and whatever you're thinking about me, it's not gonna happen! Let me out of this car, now!" I tried to open the door to jump out the car but he reached across me and grabbed the door handle.

"No, no, no, I didn't mean it like that. I'm sorry. Please, I'm not trying to do anything to you or with you. I just wanted you to make it safely home, that's all. I did see your performance tonight and I must admit, I didn't like it."

"What do you mean, you didn't like it?"

"Well, I like the way you dance but not the way those men treated you. It was degrading and I feel you are better than that. You are so beautiful, your body is so..so ..lovely, you have so much class about yourself, I watched the way you dance and there was something different about your style. Have you had training before?"

"Look, I appreciate the compliment but I'm leaving now! I don't know what line you are trying to run on me but it's not going to work. I am not some little whore needing to be picked up by you. If you are so in love with classy women and the way they act, what were you doing in a strip club?"

"Believe me Miss, I just wanted to make sure you were safe, that's all and I ended up in that club by accident or well, I guess you could say for business purposes. I'm sorry, I have been so rude. Let me start over, okay. Erase everything from your memory. Hello madam, my name is Santeno Carrington, and I would love to offer you a ride this evening, no strings attached."

I smiled at his creativeness until I realized he was 'The Mr. Santeno Carrington,' then I got nervous. "Um, ...nice to..meet ..you, sir."

"Sir? Sir? Oh no, do I look that old?" he teased.

"No, I didn't mean it like that. It's just that ... are you the big rich guy that everybody talks about?"

"Me? People are talking about me? Wow! I didn't know I was so popular. Now lets talk about you. What's your name, your real name?"

"Ms. Kitty is my real name, well sort of. It's the name I've had for 18 years. My real name is Katrina Richards."

"Well, may I call you Katrina."

"Yeah, sure, I guess."

"So Katrina, what do you do for fun everyday?"

"Nothing really, unless you call taking care of my daughter and going to school fun because that's what I do everyday."

"So you have a child ? How old is she?"

"She's 3 months."

"Got any pictures?"

"No. I haven't had any formal pictures made, yet, but I'm planning on it."

"I bet she's beautiful, just like her mother. So is the father in the picture?"

I had to laugh at that one. "He was out of the picture before she came in it."

"Oh I see, such a shame. Hey, I know this great coffee shop not far from here. Would you like to go? Please, I would love to talk to you more, you seem so interesting and I am loving the vibe you put in this car."

I didn't know what he meant by vibe but I agreed to go anyway, although I hated coffee. We drove to a cute little café, with brick walls on the inside and a brick oven that baked all kinds of goodies. I told Mr. Carrington that I didn't care too much for coffee so he ordered a latte' for me and practically made me try one of their specialties, a cinnamon, apple, honey bun. We had an interesting conversation for several hours but seemed like minutes. I didn't realize the time until we saw the sun come up for daybreak. I panicked then, knowing full well that Olandis was raising hell right about now. I kept hearing his annoying voice in the back of my mind saying, If you really care. I felt so guilty about not being there for Karisma that I grabbed my bag and shouted, "I got to go, I got to get out of here!"

"Why? What's wrong? Did I say something out the way?"

"No, this isn't about you. I have to go pick up my baby. I didn't realize it was this late…I mean early…I mean, you know what I'm trying to say."

"I understand. I'm sorry, I lost track of time, too." He left some money on the table for our tab and we dashed out of there and into his limo. When we arrived at my dorm, I jumped out immediately and told him thanks for the ride and the latte' and ran up the steps, disappearing into the hall. When I got to my room, Olandis and Karisma were gone and April, apparently, hadnt made it back from her weekend rendezvous. I paged Olandis to find out where he could be with my child and after showering, a two hour nap, and one hour of cartoons, he finally called back.

"Yes, Ms. Kitty, what do you want?"

"What do I want? I want my baby. I have a fun day planned for the two of us."

"Well, your baby has had an extremely fun day already. My agent called me this morning for a job opportunity to be in this commercial and when you never showed up, I had to take Lil'BooBear with me so I packed up her things, hooked her hair up and out the door we went. Well, when we got to the studio, all the agents and crew members fell in love with Ms. Karisma and decided to use her in the commercial instead of moi' and you know I wasn't having that. I mean, I am the drama major here and I have spent hundreds of Dewayne's money on acting classes so I said they don't get the baby with out me. Girl, I cant wait until you see us on TV, we look so good together. Two baby faces!"

"Hold on, slow down. You and Karisma are in a commercial like as in TV?"

"You got it. We are the baby soft toilet tissue twins!"

I burst out laughing. Leave it up to Olandis to do something wild like this.

"I hope you and your baby soft twin are on the way here because I had a lot of stuff planned that I wanted to do with her today."

"Like what? Maybe we could meet you somewhere."

"Okay bet. How about I meet you at the zoo."

"So what are you implying, Ms. Kitty?"

"Nothing you idiot! Just be there in the next hour."

We spent the entire day at the zoo, shopping and eating at Olandis's favorite restaurant. We also took Karisma to have professional pictures made and I can't wait until they come back. She is so photogenic, a true charmer. We caught a cab back to the dorm so I wouldn't be late to work. Denise was getting in a car with some ugly dude when we pulled up and we ran the meter up waiting on her and her pitiful date to drive off. Couldn't risk her seeing Karisma. Rakeem and April were sitting on the bed with these distraught looks on their faces when we walked in.

"Hey," Olandis said, "I see the Honeymooners made it back safe and sound." Everyone laughed except April.

"Ms. Kitty, why didn't you tell us?"

"Tell who, what?" I responded.

"Well, someone named Sandy called. She said Dewayne needed you to come in, he forgot to tell you the club opens early on Saturdays."

"Wait a minute. Wait just a doggy, doggy, where's your bone gone minute! Are you talking about my Dewayne. The love of My life, the man who butters my bread and body, Dewayne?" Olandis asked rolling his head and eyes and finger, "I knew you had your eyes on him the whole time. Yall thought you had me fooled when I busted up your little Thanksgiving party. You have some nerve, Ms. KITTY!"

"Look, what I do is my business. I'm only trying to take care of my daughter. Me and Dewayne are not lovers and will never be. Olandis, if you really loved him you would know that and you would trust him," I stated.

"Oh, for your information, I do trust him. It's hussies like you and that, ..that, Vixon that I don't trust!" He stormed out the room in tears, slamming the door behind him.

"OLANDIS!" April screamed after him, "Olandis wait!" She turned and looked at me with tears in her eyes and said, "After all we've been through, all we've done for you, why? Why?"

"You guys are throwing this thing way out of proportion. Bump it, I'm late for work." I grabbed Karisma's diaper bag, slung her in the carrier and left to catch the bus.

⇒⊜ ⊜⇐

"Aww, she's so pretty. What's her name?" Sandy asked as I sat Karisma on the makeup counter.

"Sandy, meet Karisma. Karisma, this is Ms. Sandy."

"She is a doll baby. I didn't know you had kids. I got three myself, Jordan, Nicholas, and Sandra. They're all 9 months apart, the oldest is five."

"Wow, how do you do it?" I asked hoping she could give me some vital information.

"It's not something you think about, you just do it. Mothers have a natural instinct that guides them along the way."

"Do you think Sweets is gonna be mad that there's a baby in the club?"

"What she doesn't know wont hurt her, right? I'll watch precious while you dance but you better high tail it out of here as soon as you make that money tonight."

"I will, thanks. Um,..Sandy.. did you know Vixon?"

"Did I know Vixon? Hell, who didn't know Vixon! She was the supreme Goddess around here, almost like Star thinks she is but nowhere near."

"What made her the Goddess, as you put it?"

"She was Dewayne's woman or at least she thought she was. She would take all his money before he blinked his eyes. She turned him all the way out. She could do things with her body that had never been done before and he was infatuated by it. I don't think either one of them were in love, just in common. They both loved sex and money."

"But, I thought Dewayne was gay. I mean I heard somewhere that he has a boyfriend."

"He does, but he's not all the way gay. He's bi-sexual. In fact, I think his lover is the reason Vixon got fired, well that and she laundered too much money from Dewayne putting his account in the negative. Mucho negative! We're talking grands, baby!"

I was shocked by this piece of information but at least it explained Olandis's reaction this afternoon. Charm walked in with Star and hurriedly put on their costumes without saying a word. They scooted out the room, half dressed, never even noticing Karisma.

"Whoa, what was that all about?" I asked.

"They are money hungry leeches. See, on Saturdays, Dewayne brings in more girls to fill the place up. We usually have so many men trying to get in here that the fire marshal has to step in and send some of them out. He likes to get a peek, too. But anyway, just go with the flow tonight, don't let the other girls scare you. They can smell a new comer a mile away. Good luck and remember the rules, be safe," she joked, imitating Sweet Flossy. I heard her music playing and she dashed out the room. Karisma had fallen asleep in her little seat. I wished she was up so at least I could have someone to talk to. I needed to talk to Olandis and April and make things right. I would apologize, even though I felt I didn't do anything wrong, just to have them not mad at me. A girl dressed in a tight leather mini skirt and matching bra stood in the doorway holding what looked like two dozen red roses. "Hey, is your name Trina?" she asked.

"Yes, well it's Katrina," I answered.

"These are for you." She sat the flowers on the counter and walked back out the door before I had a chance to ask who sent them. I brushed my hair and started getting ready to go on stage.

"Okay honey, I'm back. Go on out there and strut your stuff. I got little Karisma here and she'll be just fine." Sandy was dripping wet with sweat as she walked in the dressing room. She grabbed a towel off the table and wiped her face with it. Then she went to pick up Karisma. I felt a little unsure about leaving my baby with a stranger but I had to go out there and make that money. I would leave as soon as I finished my performance on stage. I had to leave because I didn't want to get caught I turned around to see Santeno standing there, looking sharp as a tack.

"S.C. I should've guessed it was you who sent these. Nobody calls me Katrina."

"Nobody calls me S.C. I like it. It gives me a young, hip, look. I just wanted to send you the flowers as a thankyou for last night. I could've talked to you all night and day."

"Well you didn't have to get flowers for that, you already bought a latte' and a honey bun that I had to walk off my thighs today."

"Oh, is this Karisma?" he asked as he went to pick her up, "She's beautiful."

"Thankyou."

"Why did you bring her here?"

"I didn't have a babysitter so I had no choice. I got to work" I thought back to the incident that happened earlier. My stubbornness led me to bringing a baby in a strip club. How stupid can I be?

"What ever they are paying you to work here, I'll double it. It's your decision. I don't want you think I'm trying to tell you what to do, but I really hate to see you working here. Think it over before you decide."

I thought about the outstanding offer he just made. How could he pay me not to do anything? It seems too risky, too unsafe. What happens if I give up my job and he decides one day that he doesn't feel like giving me any more money, then what? He placed Karisma gently back in her seat and she woke up crying. He rocked her carrier and said, "Don't worry, little one, I'm still here. I wont leave you." He turned to me said, "Please, come with me."

He picked up the carrier and like a zombie, I followed right behind him, out the club. Sandy looked over at me and winked her eye with approval and continued giving some guy a lap dance. SC led me to an Infinity Q45 and hit the alarm button with his key ring. He put Karisma in the back and seat and handed me the keys.

"Please, drive safely. I wouldn't want anything to happen to my two sweet angels."

Now he had thrown me off because his limo pulled up and he got inside it. Older men are just senile, I guess. I started up the car and tried to follow the big black, limousine but his driver had skills and lost me at a red light, so I drove the Infiniti home. April nor Olandis was in the room when I got there. I changed into my night gown and started changing the baby's clothes when I noticed a piece of paper stuck down in her baby seat. That Santeno thinks he is so smooth.

Dear Katrina,

Thankyou once again for a lovely evening. I haven't been able to get you off my mind all day. I don't like the fact that you work so late at night and have to ride the bus home. I couldn't live with myself if something was to happen to you so I went out today and bought you a car. I hope you like it. I'm not good with colors and all so I choose black but if there's anything you want to change or have added, take it to the dealer, he knows me, and tell them what to do. I hope to see you again. Enclosed is my number if you feel like talking but if not, I truly understand. The car is yours to keep, no matter what."

I don't believe it, first he offers me money but no job and now he has bought me a car. I don't know what to think or do or say. I need April. I need Olandis. I want my two best friends back.

Karisma awoke early the next morning and whined and whimpered for an hour before she fell back off to sleep. I know what she wanted or rather who she wanted, Olandis and April. I missed them, too and it had only been a couple of hours but it seemed like forever. I called Rakeem's room but after not getting an answer, I hung up and paged Olandis. I couldn't take the pressure of waiting on the phone to ring so I found SC's number and called him.

"Hello,"

"Hello,..SC?"

"Yes. Oh, this must be the lovely, talented, Katrina. I see you decided to call, I'm glad. I thought I may never hear from you again. So, what's up? Did you like the car?"

"Yeah, yeah it's nice but…." I couldn't believe what I was about to say. "I cant keep it."

"Why not? Was something wrong with it. I'll take care of it."

"No, there's nothing wrong with it. I just don't, I don't know. It's so expensive. I've never received a gift that cost so much."

"Don't worry about it. Look, I had to learn a long time ago that money doesn't mean a thing with out happiness and I just want you to be happy. I'm happy when your happy but if you still feel that my gift is wrong, then I didn't buy it for you, I bought it for Karisma."

"Karisma cant even drive."

"And she cant walk either but at least she has something to ride in besides city transportation."

"Oh, I get your point. So what do you have planned to do today?"

"Spend time with you,… oh, and Karisma."

"Okay, so where do you want to go?"

"Um,… can you be ready in thirty minutes?"

I assured him that we would be. I ran around the room, picking out the perfect outfit. I don't know why I was so nervous, it wasn't like a date or anything. He wasn't even my type, he's got to be at least fifty, so what could we possibly have in common? His limo pulled up in front of the dorm and I watched the driver get out to open his door. I looked around the tiny room at the mess I had made and rushed out the door with Karisma. I didn't want him to see how untidy I was. I met Denise coming up the hall as I was going out. She stopped dead in her tracks and stared at Karisma before speaking.

"Well, well, well, what do we have here?" she said.

"None of your business."

"I knew the rumors were true and once the dean finds this out, oh boy, wont we have a glorious time."

"Bitch please, what are you talking about. I'm babysitting for somebody."

"Mighty strange she looks just like Quintin. Same big ass head and lips."

Now I play a lot of things but when it comes down to my child, I don't play. I sat Karisma's seat and diaper bag down on the floor and slung my fist in Denise's mouth. She tried to get in a couple of licks but I was too quick for her. I was pounding her with all my might. Karisma started to cry, hysterically, and I paused from the ass whooping to see if she was alright. Denise jumped on my back and began pulling my hair out and bashing my head against the concrete wall until SC walked in and tried to break us up. I was still swinging at her as he carried me away and handed me over to his limo driver. He walked back to retrieve Karisma and she calmly cooed in his big, muscular arms.

"What was that all about?" Santeno asked as soon as he climbed in the car with me. I couldn't answer him because I don't even remember myself, all I know is my head hurts like hell.

"Ms. Kitty! I am pleading with you over here to tell me what is going on. I mean, I walk inside a building and youre trying to claw some females eye's out and I should think you would be courteous enough to give me an explanation.... Okay, I'll take that as a no but I think you should go down to the police station and file a report before she does."

Did he just say police station? "NO!" I quickly answered. Just the thought of that place gives the chills. What if they remembered me? How embarrassing that would be. Santeno was staring at me like I was crazy and deranged so I had to come up with something quick. "Let it ride, okay. She's just a girl I know from school. We used to be roommates and we still had some unsolved issues to iron out. Now if you don't mind, I would like to take some Tylenol and lie down." He didn't argue with me or beg for more information, he just laid my head down on his chest and told the driver to go by a pharmacy.

I awoke to an unfamiliar room. I didn't know where I was or how I got there, but I do know I have a severe headache. I climbed off the king size bed and opened what I thought to be a door leading out but It was a closet with my clothes neatly hung inside. I walked to the other door and could hear my daughter's laughter coming from downstairs. I followed the sound of her squeals and curgles down the long spiral staircase, over the beautiful marble floors, through three lavish living rooms until I found her playing a game of bouncy baby with Santeno.

"Hi," I said quietly not wanting to alarm either of them.

"Oh look, Princess, it's Mommy," he said, turning her around. He talked as though we were a family and I'm not used to this type of language. He put Karisma on his shoulder and stood walk to walk over to me. He kissed my forehead, a gesture that Quintin used to do all the time. I missed that, I didn't realize how much I missed that tiny little kiss until now. It always let me know that somewhere in the back of his hard core heart that he loved me but what does it mean now? Does Santeno love me?

"How does your head feel?" he asked.

"A little better but still painful."

"Maybe you should eat something. Carrie, could you fix Ms. Richards something to eat?"

I looked around to see who he was talking to. Carrie, a middle aged foreign woman, nodded her head and rushed off to the kitchen.

"I don't know what I would do with her. That little woman works miracles and Karisma loves her, already. She is such a good baby; hasn't cried not one time. I went back to your room to get some of your things while Carrie watched her. I picked up some diapers and more milk. I don't see how you do it, I have a Ph.D. in business and I didn't know what to buy. I called Carrie and she went to the store for me, then she came home and fixed the milk, another lesson I learned."

"I'm sorry, I didn't mean to sleep so long, leaving her off on you like that." I said.

"You don't have to be sorry, I loved it. I never have company over. We have had so much fun together."

"Well, I'm glad, so um…now, I guess we'll be leaving."

"Why so soon?" he asked, worriedly, "You don't have to go. I have plenty of room for you and Karisma."

"Can I ask you something?" He nodded his head, yes. "Why are you so good to me?"

"Because I think you're special. Why wouldn't anyone be good to you? What have you done that's so bad, people should mistreat you?"

I thought about it and the answer was, nothing. I have never done anything to anyone but someone's always out to get me. I guess that's just my place in life, my duty on this earth, to make people hate me. Carrie walked in the room with a tray and sat it down on the coffee table. I walked over to the couch and began eating the soup and sandwich while she asked Santeno if he needed any more of her services. He assured her no and she walked off to her bedroom. I wonder if they ever did any freaky stuff around here. Karisma had fallen asleep on his shoulders. I wished she was awake because I didn't want to be alone with him. I'm not in the mood for lovemaking. Why else would he want me to stay overnight?

"Do you want her to sleep with you?" he asked.

"Um, sure.. yeah." He carried her up the long staircase and was back down in twenty seconds.

"That was quick. What did you do, throw her in the door."

"Ha, Ha, very funny. I know a secret to those steps. So is your sandwich good?"

"Um, hm. It's not like a steak or anything but it's food."

He sat beside me on the couch and began massaging my shoulders. I know he was buttering me up but it wouldn't work. I was not giving in. I thought of him as a friend and I wanted to keep it that way. When I finished eating he pulled me toward him, my back to him, and he held me. He never tried to go in my pants or kiss me, he just held me. I thought about April and Olandis. I missed them.

"SC, when you went to my room, were my friends there?" I asked.

"No. Nobody was there."

"Well, how did you get in and how did you know which clothes were mine?"

"I have ways of getting in and I know your style. I couldn't imagine you wearing some of those clothes that were in there, so I picked out the things that looked like you. If you feel better in the morning, we'll go shopping."

"You don't have to do that."

"There you go again. You know you want to go shopping, don't you?"

"Yes, but it's kind of hard with Karisma. The older she gets, the more she demands attention so shopping with her makes it ten times harder."

"Well, let's make a deal. I'll watch her while you go do your thing. I'll have Albert bring your car over in the morning and you can use my credit card to buy what ever you want."

"Are you sure?"

"Sure I'm sure, as long as you don't go over a thousand and you have to share it with Karisma. You guys need some new clothes."

I thought about Olandis. He would die to have a man like Santeno and here I am finding excuses to turn him away. I felt so safe in his arms. Now I can see why Karisma is always at peace with him. I was so calm and relaxed, not feeling any more pain; I fell asleep on the couch as he held me the entire night. I don't remember hearing her crying, but when I woke up the next day, Santeno was in the kitchen giving Karisma her bottle. She didn't even blink when I kissed her and told her good morning. The little heifer actually thinks this man is her father, not that he wouldn't make a good father for her, but he's not. Quintin is and will always be. Nothing can change that.

"So are we ready for the big day?"

"I am but the question is, are you ready?"

"Yes Mamm. I have bottles prepared, toys laid out, diapers already opened so all I have to do is sit her in them."

I laughed, I could just picture him changing a diaper in his nice shirt and silk tie. I said a silent prayer and told them I was going to get ready, last chance to stop me or change his mind. He waved for me to go on and I dashed up the steps. I told them goodbye as I walked out the door and drove off in the Infiniti. I decided I didn't want to shop at the mall; I was high class now. I went to all the fancy boutiques that I used to pass on my way to work. I always wanted to go inside one and whip out my credit card, not caring how much the merchandise cost. The clerks turned their nose up at me when I first walked in but as soon as they saw the platinum Visa card, they turned into over friendly, money hungry, leeches. Every store was the same. I found a unique baby store that carried nothing but a clothing line from Paris. I fell in love with the little Madeline outfit, a yellow coat and cap and a matching blue dress. It cost four hundred dollars but I had to have it. The clerk gift wrapped it in pretty pink and yellow boxes and put a big pink ribbon on top, not that Karisma really cared. It was getting late and

I couldn't wait to get back and show Santeno what I bought. He would be glad to know I didn't go over six hundred dollars but I felt kind of stupid. I only bought three things, well four if you count the earrings. I guess that's the way rich people do things. They have so much money that they have to spend it on over priced items. The cycle never ends when you think about it. They make more to spend more. I was driving back to Santeno's mansion when I realized I was near the Professor's house. I decided to stop by and speak since I hadn't seen him in a couple of weeks. I could talk to him about my problems here lately, he always has a solution. I parked the car in front of his house and rang the doorbell. Hilda came to the door and looked happy to see me.

"Ola, Senorita. Richards," she said.

"Ola. Is the Professor home?" I asked, trying to look in the door.

"Oh, no. He go to visit sister."

"Who's sister? You don't mean his do you?"

"Se'. He visit every year dis time. I tell him you stop by, okay." She started closing the door but I stopped her. I needed answers. I thought his sister was dead so all this time she's alive? Why would he lie about something like that?

"Hilda, I have to know where he is. Can you tell me how to get there?"

"Okay, but my memory not de best. Go tree' blocks down dis street, ..um.. turn right... then left. After that, go to redlight and ...oh, yes I remember now, make right turn go through the stop sign and you're there. You tink you remember all that?"

I knew I would. He was not getting off that easy and if I found out Hilda was lying, sending me on a wild goose chase, she would be dealt with, too. I followed her directions exactly, not missing a turn, and they led me to a cemetery. I was pissed and was about to turn around when I spotted his jeep. I heard somewhere that it was wrong to drive across people's graves so I parked my car and walked over to where he was standing. He kneeled down and placed some flowers on a grave. When he stood up, I could see he was crying. I walked up to him and hugged him.

"I miss her so. Why did he take such a precious person. She was so young and energetic, full of life. She made everyone smile and the room would magically light up when she walked in it. She did so much for everyone, especially me but she never got her wish. She died right before I could grant her wish."

"You didn't do it. Death has no warnings. She's at peace now. Professor, ... what was her wish? Tell me."

He looked me in my eyes, his bloodshot red and his hair frazzled and began talking.

"Her wish..her wish was to meet you. She loved you. Your mother was the one woman I truly loved. When she got pregnant, she was so embarrassed. Not because she was pregnant but because I was white so she distant herself from me. She tried to say it was because I was on drugs and I would do more harm by having me in your life. She refused to give you my last name but she did give you my first name. I cried each night like a big baby on my sister's arms and she gave me the encouragement to keep going, keep fighting for my parental rights but your mother wouldn't give in. I watched you grow from a distance. I gave her money for you, I bought clothes and food and I'll never forget those concert tickets you had to have. I waited all night in line to buy those things, the only white guy. She didn't want you and I to meet. It was hard enough for a poor black girl growing up in the projects and she didn't want the other kids to pick on you. I was there at your awards ceremonies, trying to out clap the other fathers. I was sitting in the front row when you received your high school diploma. I arranged for you to come here. I paid your tuition in full. Your mother didn't want it that way but she had no choice. She wanted you to go off to school but without my money, it wouldn't have been possible. I wanted to tell you sooner but she said you wouldn't believe me; that's why I wanted to form a friendship with you first. I wanted to know you, not just sit back and watch you like I had done for 17 years. My sister died right before you came. She tried to hold on but the cancer spread so fast. You look just like her, same beautiful, flawless, skin, pretty, gray eyes and that cute, pointy, nose. I sneaked in your house one night just to steal a picture to show her how lovely you are. I know about the abortions and I know about Karisma. I guess I'm telling you all this because I don't want to continue living a lie. I don't want my granddaughter growing up the same way you did. I want her to know me, not my gifts or how much money she gets from me each month. I realized how wrong it was as I was packaging up those diapers and bottles to send you. Little girls need a daddy. I wasn't there for you physically but I'll be damned if I allow it to go on like this. Please understand, I love you; always have and always will. I love Karisma and nothing will change that, nothing at all. You can't do me the same way your mother did. Please don't keep her away from me….Please…."

I couldn't believe what I was hearing. It's just too much to process all at once. I ran to my car, never looking back. He called my name, begging me to listen, begging me to stop and listen, begging me to understand but how could I. All my life, I wanted a dad and he was there in my face the whole time. I never want to see him or my mother again. How could they both do this to me? How could they make a decision so important about my life? They acted like irresponsible teenagers and I'm the one who suffered from it. I drove 95 miles per hour back to Santeno's house. When I walked in a bunch of people shouted, "SURPRISE!" but I didn't stop, I ran up the steps to the bedroom and slammed the door. A few minutes later, Santeno knocked on the door and said, "Katrina, are you alright?"

"Leave me alone."

"But sweatheart, all your friends are here for your birthday party."

I had forgotten all about today being my birthday. I wonder if the Professor or my mom remembered. I realized his sister died on my birthday.

"Please let me in."

I didn't move. He must've walked away to get Olandis because he was next at the door.

"Ms. Kitty, girl, you need to come on out here and try some of this rum punch I made. It'll make you feel better. Oh, I think I need a refill now. Hold on. I'll be right back."

"Ms. Kitty, it's me April. Please come out. I know you are still mad about the argument we had but I'm over that and I'm sorry. DeWayne explained everything. Besides, it wasn't my place to judge you or tell you what to do. I'm glad you are so strong willed, not afraid of anything. You got out there and found a job to take care of your baby. I would never be able to do that. I wish I was more like you. I admire you. Please come out so you can see Karisma dancing. It's so funny how Olandis can make her look like she's doing the moonwalk. Please say something so I know you're okay."

"Something."

"Um, Ms. Kitty, I wanted to wish you a happy birthday and many more to come. I understand why you left the club the other night and I want you to know I'm here for you whenever you're ready to get a new job. I give good references but you might not need one. You got the richest man in the city going crazy over you. You deserve the best. I'm happy for you."

I could hear a lot of whispering and giggling outside the door. Then I heard this squeaky, sound come from the other side. "Mommy, it's me Karisma. Please come out so you can play with me. Please Mommy." I had to laugh myself, they were a bunch of clowns. When I opened the door, Karisma was sitting up in front of it and I caught them trying to run down the steps. I picked her up and said, "Un, Un. Come back here you guys. You got me out the room so now what?"

April came up the steps and gave me a big hug. "Don't ever be mad at me again, you got it."

"I wont." I said as I hugged her back.

"Oh, give me some love, too. Group hug everybody, the more the merrier," Olandis said while running up the steps toward us. He squeezed me and April like he was picking out fruit and he said, "Ditto." I was getting hot in this little group hug idea so I mingled out of it and caught my breath.

"How did you guys know? Who planned all this?"

"Santeno, who else. You know I aint got no money," Olandis informed me.

"Yeah, we talked a long time when he came by to pick up your clothes. We told him everything, about our little argument and he said we should talk. We are too close to not be speaking to each other."

I walked over to Santeno and stood in front of him with a big grin on my face. He knew what was coming to him. "So you lied to me? Is this why you wanted me to go shopping?"

"Hey, I didn't do it by myself. Karisma helped."

"Now you want to blame it on this sweet innocent child. You used her as an alibi. I don't believe ….."

He cut me off with a kiss, a long passionate one. I almost let Karisma fall out my arms. He made me weak. Never before had I felt this way about a kiss. It was magical, it was telling me something; I was in love. I didn't want it to end.

We stopped when Olandis brought the cake in the room and sang his extended, concert, version of Happy Birthday. He told me to make a wish before I blew out the candles and I did just that.

"Yo, Ms. Kitty, what did you wish for?" Rakeem asked.

"NO!" Olandis shouted, "She can't tell you that. If she tells you then her wish won't be granted."

"Sorry Olandis. My wish has already been granted."

April and Olandis helped me clean up after our guests left. Carrie had too much of Olandis's rum punch and had retired to her living quarters an hour after Karisma went to bed. I put the last dish in the dishwasher when Santeno asked if he could talk to me in the living room. I followed behind him unsure and afraid of what he was going to say.

"I hate to leave on short notice but I have to fly out to Paris tonight. I've been working on this property for two years now and I think they are finally ready to sell. You and your friends are welcome to stay here. Carrie will be here if you need her. I'll call you as soon as I'm settled in but don't wait up. I get kind of edgy when it comes to work and I don't want to talk you when I'm in a bad mood." He kissed me one last time and walked out the front door.

Reasons

It had been exactly thirteen days since I heard from Santeno. I was a nervous wreck. Carrie kept telling me the same thing he had said about his work but I don't care. He could at least call. April and Olandis kept me company, mainly so I wouldn't go insane. Even Karisma missed him. She knew something wasn't right; someone was still missing from our clique. Olandis walked in our bedroom and started rummaging through the closet.

"Olandis what are you doing? If you mess up that closet after I spent all day yesterday re-arranging it, I'm gonna kill you!" He pulled out Karisma's little Madeline coat and dress set and held it up.

"Has she ever worn this?" he asked.

"No, why?"

"Well, put it on her and you need to get dressed in your Sunday's best."

"Why?"

"Because today is the day the Lord has set aside. We're going to church!"

An hour later, April, Karisma and I were waiting on Olandis to make his grand walk down the steps. We were dressed and ready to go somewhere but where? Olandis was banned from his church and the other churches were pretty much the same, no gays allowed. He walked down the steps wearing a three piece, lavender suit with matching shoes. He had a hat to match, the kind those old ladies wear with the net hanging over their eyes. He put on his lavender gloves, inspected us, and nodded his head with approval before walking to the limo waiting outside for us. We drove for forty-five minutes before finally pulling into a church parking lot. I could hear the gospel music playing inside, the drums and the piano and tambourine and people shouting, Hallelujah, thank you Jesus. The driver got out and opened the door for us. When we bust through the double doors and walked in the tiny, crowded, church, the room shut down. It became so quiet, you could hear a pin drop. I could hear people whispering, "Is that Ida Mae's boy? …It sure looks like him….I heard he got AIDS… Naw, he don't like he got a disease……." I couldn't believe it. I had to turn around and make sure this was a church. I felt so sorry for Olandis. I see what he has to go through each and every day but he didn't care what they said anymore. He proudly walked up the isle, stopping by the front pew to show off his hat to the Amen corner (a group of little old ladies) and asked the Preacher for a microphone. The minister gave him a mic., dispite the old ladies complaints about him disturbing their services.

"Um, Excuse me but I do believe this service is for the Lord," he said while looking right at them. He got a couple of Amen's and Preach Brother from some of the members of the congregation.

"It's been a long time since I stepped foot in this church. I was so angry at some of the people and the world that I just gave up coming. But then I realized, this world is not my home. I have a better place waiting on me. Can't nobody turn me around. Can't nobody judge me but Jesus. He is my father and my mother. My parents brought me into this world and they rejected me but I know a man who has never left my side, never let me down, is always there to listen to me when I call on him and his name is Jesus. Now many of you may remember my Grandmother, Mrs. Ida Mae Johnson, God rest her soul. She believed in me. She told me that the world isn't perfect and everyday would not have sunshine. She carried my weight on her shoulders, disputing those who talked about me. See, she wasn't worried about my soul because she knew I hadn't done anything wrong but she prayed every night for you, for him to forgive you. My Grandmother was a faithful member of this church for over fifty years and the day of her funeral I wasn't even allowed to come through those doors. Her only grandchild, the one person she loved the most could not come to pay his last respects. Well I want you to know, I have done the same thing my Grandmother did every night and that is pray. Pray that God will change your souls and your heart. I'm not asking you to change for me but for yourself. It's never too late. Reverend, I brought someone who I would like baptized."

He motioned for me to bring Karisma up front and April followed behind speaking and saying excuse me to everyone. The preacher sprinkled water on Karisma's head and said a bible verse. Olandis sang his eye is on the sparrow and there wasn't a dry eye left in the church when he finished, except for me. The Minister gave the benediction and told everyone to come up and greet our newest member, Karisma Alanda Richards. We were swamped with hugs and kisses and we went downstairs in the church's Social Hall to eat. There was so much food, ham and chicken, green beans, macaroni and cheese, cornbread, and the list goes on and on, we had to take our plate home.

Karisma was being passed from arm to arm and she loved it. She was so worn out by the time we got home, she didn't wake up when I changed her. Everyone agreed that a nap would be good right about now so we crashed on my bedroom floor.

The phone rang around one in the morning. I was too tired to get up and go answer it but I realized it might be Santeno. I ran out the room to the phone that sat on the pedestal in the hallway. Please don't hang up; I'm coming.

"Hello," I answered out of breath.

"Come to me," he said, "I need you,..here with me. Albert has your passport and plane tickets."

I didn't hesitate, I wanted to be with him too. I rushed back to the room and changed and woke up April. I asked could she watch Karisma; I was on my way to Paris.

→═◑ ◐═←

The airplane landed in Paris at night by their time but morning by ours. I had what they call jet lag. I saw a man holding a sign with my name on it. I walked over to him and said, "I'm Ms. Richards."

He asked where my luggage was and I realized I hadn't brought any. I followed him to a black stretch limousine and he opened the door for me to get inside. There was a note pinned to a dozen roses that said, I hope you enjoyed your flight. The driver will take you to the places you need to go. I cant wait to see you. I miss you. I love you. S.C. I thought that was so sweet. I have never had this kind of treatment from a man before and he is right, I deserve it. I was falling for him. I didn't care what people thought. He was old enough to be my father but so what. He was good to me, better than my real father. We pulled up in front of a hair salon that reminded me of those Vidal Sassoon commercials. It was so upscale I wish I had worn my boutique clothes. What was I thinking by wearing jeans? I'm in a whole new ball game now; I have to play the part. The stylist and I guess, manager greeted me in French and wisked me away to the shampoo bowl. He massaged my head, washing it at least three or four times but who's counting? All I know is it felt good, almost as good as an orgasm. He rolled my hair on jumbo sized rollers and sat me under a dryer. Then he said something to a young girl and she walked over to the dryer and began giving me a manicure and pedicure. Once she finished, the stylist walked over to me, turned off the dryer and waved for me to follow him. He took out the rollers and teased my hair like he was fighting it. I was scared to look in the mirror when he finished and turned me around in the chair showing off his master piece. It was beautiful. Some of it was pinned up in a new aged French twist while the rest hung loosely in pin curls. Another man came over and arched my eyebrows and began giving me a makeover. It felt like he was putting tons of makeup on my face but when I looked in the mirror, once again, it was beautiful. The colors blended so well with my complexion. I wished I could look like this everyday. He handed me a card with a heart on the front. I hope you like your new look, not that anything was wrong with the old one. Now that your is done and your makeup is on, you need a new outfit to compliment the look. The driver walked in the salon to get me and he drove to a boutique in the heart of Paris. I couldn't believe I was actually shopping and getting my hair done in Paris. A lady greeted me as soon as I walked in. She informed that she had several outfits picked out for me. All of them were formal. I picked out the fitted, cream sequined gown with the back out and two sequined straps cris-crsossing in the back. The tail hung like a mermaid. I tried it on and you guessed it, it was a perfect fit. The sales lady brought me a pair of Cinderella slippers with a sequined strap across the toe to try on.

"Magnificent!" she said as she handed me another note from Santeno.

Are you enjoying yourself? I hope so. Now that you have the dress, you'll need jewelry to go with it.

The driver took me to an exquisite jeweler. The store had police on the outside, inside and security cameras watching your every move. They would zoom in and out as you walked. A man with two ladies behind him walked up to me and said in a French accent, "You are beautiful. I can ze why he spends ze' money." He held up a tiny ring box in front of me and opened it. It was out of this world. The diamond was so big, I wouldn't be able to hold my finger up.

"Ahh, do you like? It is ze' best ring here, six and one half carats." He took the ring out the box and slid it on my finger. It looked GOOD on my hand. He handed me a note saying, The party's not over. I cant wait to see you. If you're hungry, have dinner on me. I didn't want to eat alone but I guess I had no choice. I was so anxious to see him. The restaurant sat beside a Riviera so I decided to eat outside on the patio. I watched the boats sail by while I sipped on some wine. I was too excited about seeing Santeno that I couldn't eat what ever it was I ordered. He must be held up in a meeting with some clients but when did he find time to do all this? I was truly impressed with his romantic ways. A man walked up to my table and began playing the violin. Just then, my night in shining armor appeared wearing a black tuxedo. He was so fine, I wanted to take him to the hotel and make love to him all night, real love. He held out his hand and I stood up to embrace him.

"I missed you," I said.

"Will you marry me?" he responded.

"Yes, ...yes I will marry you." He grabbed my face and kissed me. We sailed on the Riviera to an outside Cathedral where a priest was waiting for our arrival. We got married under the moon and the stars, in Paris, France. It was the happiest day of my life. We drove back to the hotel room and made love all night. He was an unforgettable lover, paying attention to every detail. He massaged every part of my body with his hands and his tongue. He lasted for four hours before reaching a full orgasm, I on the other hand had about five or six. I was exhausted. I fell off to sleep in his arms as he stroked my hair.

"This is the way I want it, you right here in my arms, never leaving my side. I could hold you forever. I love you, Katrina."

"I love you, too." I said half dreary.

I woke up the next day and reached for Santeno but he wasn't in bed. I saw him resting outside on the patio in a lounge chair. I held my finger up to admire my ring. April's not going to believe this and Olandis is going to beg Dewayne for one now but he will never have one like this. I thought about calling them and checking on Karisma but I didn't know how to use all those international codes and stuff. I called Santeno to ask him what to do. I know he would know. When he didn't answer, I climbed out of bed and wrapped the sheet around my body to cover my nakedness. I slid the glass door open and walked over to him giving him a kiss on the forehead. He was sleeping so hard that he still didn't budge.

"Santeno, honey. I wanted to call back home and tell them the good news. How do I do it?"

He didn't open his eyes so I shook him, causing him to drop the magazine he had been reading before he fell asleep.

"Santeno," I shouted while shaking him. He wouldn't respond, he couldn't respond. I felt his wrist for a pulse.

"No, no Santeno, You're not dead!" I cried, "Please somebody, help me! NOOOOO! I love you, you can't leave me now! Wake up, God, give him back to me. We just started our life together, please!" I sobbed on his chest. I cried for all the pain I held inside of me for so long. I endured so much in my life that I had hardened my heart, not allowing myself to cry, ever, but I cried now. I realized that I was always looking for love but it was there the whole time. S.C. helped me see it. I was surrounded by people that cared about me, I just didn't know how to obtain that love and affection. I wouldn't let love come into my stone cold heart. Maybe this is the reason why. Every time I found love, it left me. I still had the memories, though. I kissed him and climbed in the chair with him, automatically falling into his arms and placed my head on his heart. I still felt safe, I still felt love, I still loved him.

The Happy Ever After

WELL I GUESS you're saying every story should have a happy ending and it does. It turns out that Santeno knew about his heart condition and the Doctors had given him less than a year to live. He did love me, not meaning to fall in love with me but sometimes things happen. He left everything he owned to Karisma and I. He wanted me to keep Carrie and Albert on staff so they would have someplace to live. Olandis and April moved in with us. You should see Olandis room now, WILD! He spent weeks in there, hammering and sawing, never letting us take a peak until the project was complete. He also did Karisma's nursery in pink and white with little white lambs painted on the wall and her name painted on the door. The neighbors probably didn't like our living arrangements but that made it more fun. We would do weird things to give them something to huff and puff about like the one time Olandis cut the grass in his robe and shower cap. And I'll never forget the time April pretended to kiss me (her mouth touching my cheek) and Olandis staged a fight and started kissing both of his like he was trying to decide which one of us to choose as his main girl. Dewayne drove up and he ran out to the car to kiss him. It's a wonder we didn't give them a heart attack but they can't charge us, they were the one being nosey.

Karisma was growing so fast. She already has two teeth and is trying to crawl. She can eat, too. I caught Carrie giving her table food one day. That explains her refusal to eat baby food when I try to feed it to her. She practically spit it in my face. Olandis laughed at her and now she thinks her new little game is fun. He and Dewayne take her shopping every other week on Monday, when Dewayne is off. She comes back with her nails polished and new hairbows to match all her new clothes. I asked them why they buy her all those clothes when she never goes any where. Olandis's response was, "A lady must always look her best. I'm starting her off young. She is a D.I.T., Diva in Training!" I didn't argue with him. I know they cherish that family outing and me stopping it would do too much harm.

Rakeem practically lives in April's room. I asked her if she was on the pill and she assured me that she was and he used protection. She loved Karisma but she wasn't ready for her own.

They started college this fall but I stayed out. I still needed time to morn over S.C's death and my mind would not be in the books. I promised them that I would pick back up next semester. Carrie said she would watch the baby while I took my classes. She said Santeno would've wanted it that way; he wanted me to finish school. After all, I had his business to run. His lawyer was handling all the affairs right now but he was ready to retire in about three more years.

The doorbell rang while I was giving Karisma a bath. I wondered who could it be since everyone was in school.

"Mrs. Carrington," Carrie called from downstairs, "You have a letter."

"Okay, I'll be right down." I wrapped Karisma in her baby bathrobe with her name monogrammed on the pocket, Olandis's idea, and rushed down the steps to read the letter. She had it sitting on the secretary's desk in the front room. Karisma was trying to help me tear it open.

Dear Ms. Kitty,

I know you probably hate me by now, but please forgive me. I was young and stupid. The Army has taught me that family is important. I went to the Commander in Chief and told them about my baby, our baby. I signed some papers allowing them to take money out my check each month for the baby. I know it's not much but I feel better knowing she has it. I'm sorry for all I may have put you through. I hope you can find it in your heart to forgive me. I thankyou for not bailing out like I did and taking care of my flesh and blood. I think about you every day and it kills me not knowing what my baby looks like. All my roommates have pictures of their kids and girlfriends and I feel so sad and left out. Please send me a picture. My address is at the bottom of this letter. Once again, thankyou for all you've done.

Love ,
Quintin

I looked at Karisma's eyes and hair and her nose and for the first time I saw Quintin in her. She smiled at me and started sucking her toes. I didn't want her to grow up like I did. I didn't want her to hate me therefore I would never keep Quintin away from her but first, I had to work on myself. I picked up the phone and dialed his number, praying that he was home.

"Hello," he said.

"Daddy,… it's me, Ms. Kitty."

www.ingramcontent.com/pod-product-compliance
Lightning Source LLC
Chambersburg PA
CBHW060805120626
46557CB00001B/100